LEGACY FOUND

A PSYCHIC COWBOYS WESTERN ROMANCE

COPPER RIVER COWBOYS
BOOK FOUR

JILLIAN DAVID

ePublishingWorks!

Book and cover design by eBook Prep
www.ebookprep.com

May, 2019
ISBN: 978-1-64457-007-4

ePublishing Works!
644 Shrewsbury Commons Ave
Ste 249
Shrewsbury PA 17361
United States of America

www.epublishingworks.com
Phone: 866-846-5123

CHAPTER 1

A thin, high whistle grew louder.

Kaboom.

Kerr Taggart's teeth clattered as his head smashed into the ground somewhere outside of Jalalabad. Concrete crashed all around him. His aching skull did a gong act, making his ears ring. Inside the house, hot smoke and dust mixed into a thick wave until he choked.

What the hell happened?

Damn, his torso felt like it had been bear-hugged by a Sasquatch, but at least he was still breathing. He wheezed as he lay on pulverized earth. His heart was still beating. Even with the haze, he could still see. Sort of. He blinked back tears that turned gummy from the concrete dust and from God knew what other toxic crap he inhaled.

The deafening buzz in his ears that overrode the sounds of gunfire? Not a great sign.

But his arms worked, so that was something.

Angling his arm to adjust the M4 still slung over his chest, he grimaced and lifted a shoulder off the ground. In an awkward lurch, he pulled the gun up to tuck against his body-armor vest. At least the damn weapon hadn't gone off when he fell. Fuck, his lower back hurt like hell.

Laying flat on the floor, he stared at where the ceiling should have been. Between puffs of smoke and dust, a few shadows flickered light and dark, hellish reminders of the building that had stood there moments ago. To his side, he spied another flicker and heard a heavy scuff just out of sight. Hopefully, it was his buddies, because the alternative would suck.

At the sound of muffled shouts, he shook cobwebs out of his foggy brain. Each individual idea crept along his neurons in sludge-filled slow motion.

Enough already.

Time to get the hell out of this tomb before another explosive went off. Or before what remained of that precarious, creaking ceiling came down on top of him. Or before the friendly folks who shot that RPG stopped by to visit their new neighbor. He planted his hands and pushed back. Didn't move. Frowning, he spied a concrete beam in front of him. Bracing his left foot flat on the beam, he straightened the leg and strained to move back. Nothing. He didn't budge.

But his right leg hurt like hell.

He tried again. Nothing. What the…?

Sitting up sucked bricks, with his helmeted head still doing the ring-a-ding thing and every inch of his body screaming at him to quit moving already. One spot in his spine particularly hated him right now. *So sorry, bod, but there's no time to whine.* He needed to get his express ticket out of this hell.

He strained harder, digging in with his elbows, trying to yank his body back again, but nothing shifted. Instead, he was rewarded with a bazooka bolt of agony going off in the middle of his lower back.

Holy fucking hell dropped in boiling oil.

Once he breathed away the flashing pain by deploying every curse word he knew, he grunted and leaned forward, reaching out through the dust until he encountered the thick concrete ceiling beam lying at an angle. His shaking hand slid down the beam until he reached his…

What the fuck?

Half of his lower leg disappeared beneath the beam.

Dusty air sawed in and out of his lungs.

Sweat beaded his forehead. Shit. Shit. Maybe the leg was just buried. That's possible, right?

The pounding in his chest rivaled the aching throb in his head. And competed well with the expanding balloon of agony in his leg.

He clawed at the earthen floor next to where leg met beam, but made no progress on the packed floor. There was no space below the metal. Absolutely none.

That meant…

Voices filtered through the virtual hornets buzzing in his ears. Were the people speaking English or Pashto? The answer would determine whether he would live or die.

Actually, no. He glanced up as ceiling rubble popped and creaked above him. How long the mousetrap remained suspended above him would determine whether he'd live or die.

He pulled again, harder. Agony shot through his knee as the ligaments stretched against the immobile lower leg. *Houston, we have a problem.*

His heartbeat speed rivaled an automatic rifle going nonstop.

He groped around on the floor, arms turned to manic puppet limbs pulled by strings of terror.

Out. He wanted out of this place. Now. He was going to make it back to Copper River. He had never gotten up the guts to ask out…

Later. He would sort through his piles of regrets later. Air clogged his nostrils. He couldn't breathe. Stuck, like a mountain lion in a steel snare, he waited for the hunter to return.

Smoke thickened. Shouts increased in volume. Hey, at least his hearing had improved. Win.

Fuck.

Was his friend, Eric, out there? Injured? Dead?

The dust matting his eyes generated goopy, sandy tears.

Frantic, he patted around him. He had to find any way to escape. To free himself from the trap.

How would a wild animal get free of a snare?

He froze and sucked in a breath. Sand coated his mouth.

Shit.

One way out.

At the shouts right outside the building, he shook his head. No way would he wait here to be shot like a fish in a barrel. No thanks.

Going into a terrible autopilot mode, he moved his aching right hand to his chest sheath and yanked down on the handle of his M9 bayonet fixed-blade knife. He could barely see the beautiful, shark-tooth serrated edge and lethal tip. He didn't need to lust after and then marry the goddamned weapon. Just needed it to work.

And for it not to hurt.

Fat chance on both fronts.

Under extreme protest of his wrecked back, he sat up and reached forward once again.

Touched the beam. Walked his hand down to the beam. Where his lower leg disappeared, he cinched a piece of paracord around the —the what?—the wafer? The pancake? The bone sandwich? Holy fuck.

Maybe he wouldn't be able to feel it.

Son of a fucking bitch.

Kerr began to cut.

A buzzing noise dragged Kerr back to consciousness. He jumped, his entire body on alert, expecting bullets to riddle his gut or a collapsing building to bury him alive.

His chest heaved, and sweat chilled his skin, bare except for the boxers he wore. Even in the dead of winter, he never wanted to wear more than the thin cotton at nighttime. Anything more, including blankets, was too restrictive.

Besides, he went exactly zero nights without sweating through everything.

He clicked on the bedside lamp and checked the room. Log wall on one side and drywall on the others.

He inhaled. Familiar scents of wood, horses, deodorant, and laundry detergent grounded him.

Not trapped. No sharp scent of ordnance. He wasn't back in that kill box. He sat in own bedroom inside the family ranch house.

Back in Wyoming. Not in some shitty concrete coffin on the outskirts of Jalalabad.

He moved his legs. The ghost limb that was his right lower leg and foot tried its best to respond to the bogus nerve signals. Even twinged and ached. Yippee. No leg existed, but the nothing that was there still hurt. Irony didn't even cover how messed up that fact was.

Back to reality.

The flashbacks hit him every night, sometimes twice if he was lucky. Traded off with the dreams of that bizarre lava and woman reaching through fire for him. At least those dreams he shared with his siblings. They had all experienced the same dream over the past month. Lava. Fire. Faceless woman. Night after night.

If insanity was better as a group experience, then somehow sharing it with family made it okay. Enter the Taggart siblings. Each one with a special ability. He sure could have used big brother Vaughn's gift to detect danger back when Kerr was in that exploding hellhole. Growing up, Kerr and his siblings had always kept their abilities secret.

Middle school was hard enough to avoid being called a freak without manifesting a weird power to bolster the claim. As much as Kerr wanted to disappear—literally—when he was in school, he never used that ability in public. Same with his supersensory way he never got lost. Invisibility and a human compass: pretty useless gifts when a person was pinned under a massive beam in an exploding house, come to think of it. And sure, it'd be nice to Google powers like theirs, but no surprise, the search engine was no help in the mess of the Taggart clan.

Scrubbing his face, he sat up and inserted his leg into the upright prosthetic that stood next to the bed as a constant reminder of the worst thing he ever had to do. That damned engineering feat always stood right there, ready for action. The possibility taunted him: if he could just link up, like a capsule docking with the fucking international space station, that piece of metal and fiberglass would magically make him a complete human.

Houston, we still have a problem.

He rolled the silicon cup up and onto his knee and lower thigh, the material clinging, suctioning fake to real. His tenuous grip on sanity was the place where the two met.

It was a process, just to pace. But those crutches leaning against the wall didn't satisfy when he needed to wear a track in the rug. Without the limb that permitted him to walk, he'd be trapped all over again.

The buzzing that had woken him up fired off again, and he turned over the phone. Blinking against the LED glow, he focused on the text box and his link to something—someone—real. Not nightmares, not confusion and fear, but a lifeline in the darkness. A regret. Unfinished business.

Not unfinished. Never started.

His heart jolted. He checked the time on the phone. Midnight. Way earlier than her usual 5 a.m. texts.

Five a.m. The time right before each day became real. The time when there was a chance that everything could be perfect. The time before he had to face the substance of his life. The time before he had to pretend that everything was A-Okay.

But tonight she texted at midnight.

Are you awake? the message read.

Izzy Brand.

How could she remain at her family's ranch house after all her bastard brothers Wyatt and Tommy had done to Vaughn's physician girlfriend, Mariah, a few days ago? Sure, the Brands denied everything, but Kerr had been part of the rescue team, using his disappearing trick to get into that cave and distract the assholes so she could escape.

They said "house call." Mariah said "kidnapping." Potato. Pot*ah*to.

In the meantime, Izzy had no idea about the people she lived with. Or maybe she did. Denial wasn't merely a river in Egypt. Kerr would know.

Too bad the wheels of justice moved slowly here in Copper River, Wyoming, mostly due to the fact that the local justice system was run by the Brand family.

And too bad the nasty, demonic creature stalking the Taggart family had paid Kerr and the rescuers an unpleasant visit in the middle of the forest as they helped Mariah escape. That same relentless monster wanted to kill all of the Taggarts, but only if they were all together. So his siblings adapted. But something told Kerr that the volcanic, sulfur-breathing bastard would eventually get tired of the Taggart siblings' shell game to avoid family gatherings.

Somehow, that…thing…and the Brands had to be connected. But how?

Maybe the creature had resurrected Wyatt. That slimy monkey-fucker had been tossed off a cliff after he was stupid enough to attack Vaughn. Word in town, Wyatt was back, and by all reports, completely uninjured. Maybe Kerr had misjudged the height of the fall.

Or maybe Kerr and his family were in way bigger trouble than they ever imagined.

So there was a vendetta with the Brand boys, an eerie cloud creature who wanted the Taggarts dead, and a woman who Kerr never got around to asking out…

Didn't matter.

Really, Poindexter? Did it matter that he finally had her cell number, after all these years? Got it a week ago in the hospital parking lot. He guarded that number like the combination to the Fort Knox vault. Shit, though, he was scared to confront her with the truth of her family, what with blood being thicker than water and how his information about her family could drive her away and dumb stuff like that.

During their late-night texting over the past week, she had deflected his queries with the finesse of a military bureaucrat. He should know. He was an expert. God knew Kerr had encountered plenty of non-answers from the Middle East to Walter Reed and all parts in-between.

But at least she wanted to talk with him. And like a drowning man clinging to a life preserver, he clung to that connection. Gripped it hard.

He walked around his bed, letting his stiff back loosen up. With a shake of his head to clear the last grip of the flashback, he typed back, *Sure.*

I woke you up?

Needed to be woken up. He raked a hand through his damp hair and wiped his palm on the bedding.

Another dream?

It's fine.

That wasn't the question.

He pictured her with a jutted jaw and blue eyes flashing, arms crossed under the swells of her breasts. Could almost smell the light citrus scent that was uniquely Izzy. He started salivating. Maybe he needed a sip of OJ.

Typing quickly, he said, *Are you doing okay with things?* "Things" being her nasty family members who fed her a line of bullshit about their involvement in a kidnapping. At least they stayed consistent jerks, lies or no lies. They sure took a lot of things out on Izzy, it seemed. Kerr ground his teeth.

Dots popped up; she was typing. He couldn't tear his eyes away from the screen. As long as he focused on the little dots—his life preserver—then the bad shit in his life couldn't get to him. Or so he needed to believe.

Same thing, different day.

They being assholes to you? He couldn't be depended on to remain civil if she got hurt.

Once, she might have been someone special to him, but that time was long gone. The time before his world literally crashed down on him. The time before her family went nuts and wanted to destroy his.

For now, Izzy was...someone to type to when the flashbacks took over. A friend. That was all.

No. He couldn't reduce her impact on his world as a therapeutic way to work through his demons. That gave so little credit to the person on the other end of this text stream who had become an anchor in the darkness.

A pause, then little dots. *Doesn't matter*, she typed back.

It matters to me.

That's why it doesn't matter. Wyatt and Tommy will go nuts if they find out we're talking. Linc, too.

Right. Because even if she didn't believe the town gossip about Mariah's kidnapping, Izzy still realized that her family members were a half-degree off plumb and that they were going to push that snow-ball of crazy until it grew and grew and finally rolled over the Taggarts.

Those Cro-Magnon Brand boys and their meathead cousin Linc didn't know she had this phone or Kerr's number. No telling what her unhinged family members would do to her if they discovered her early morning texting sessions. Talking to the enemy, no less.

How's your mom? he typed.

To say Mrs. Brand was a grumpy old cuss would be an understatement. However, the woman did have multiple sclerosis and had not recovered well from a recent bout of pneumonia. Of course, her care – and the brunt of her insults – fell on Izzy.

Having issues. Holding steady. How's your dad?

He knew a changed subject when he saw one. But he'd spot her this one. *A little better, but not great.* Recovering from the stroke hadn't been easy or quick for Pops, damn it.

More rolling dots. *Someone's coming.*

You okay?

No.

What's going on?

Virtual silence.

CHAPTER 2

*I*n the crazy world of the Taggart-Brand cross-valley rivalry, Kerr should have left well enough alone.

But the unanswered text, plus his imagination that created vivid scenarios of danger where Izzy and her sick brothers were concerned, had him on edge. Something was wrong.

In the military, his instincts got him out of more than one scrape.

He rubbed his thigh. Okay, not that one big scrape.

He tried one more text: *Everything okay?*

He waited ten minutes; cell phone reception sucked out there. Still no response. No bubble going from *delivered* to *read*. No dots while she typed.

The skin between his shoulder blades prickled. He paced.

Another few minutes passed. He checked his phone again. Nothing.

Peeking out his window, he flinched at the frosted landscape, his lungs burning in anticipation of the sub-zero temperatures. He pulled on insulated pants, a flannel shirt, and boots.

Didn't care about the cold. At minimum, Izzy was his friend, and she could be in danger on the Brand family ranch.

And more than minimum?

No comment.

Careful not to make too much noise, he hurried down the stairs, grabbed his hat, duster, and gloves, and headed to the barn. Wouldn't be a problem finding the Brand ranch in the dark, thanks to his super-sensory ability to never get lost.

He needed to know that she was okay.

Only because he needed to appease his instincts. No other reason.

Izzy knelt and scrambled to reach the floorboard under her bed.

Heavy footsteps reverberated through the hardwood floor and into her hands and knees. Louder.

Damn it. Someone stomped down the hall to her room. Again. A few hours ago, she had been having a perfectly nice text conversation with Kerr until her nosy brother Wyatt interrupted. She'd barely hidden the phone that time, and only a few minutes ago got up the courage to retrieve it.

Her fingers slipped as she fumbled with a loose piece of wood flooring. *Hurry*.

She wanted to ignore the weird week of town gossip about what happened with Mariah West and Izzy's brothers and cousin. Izzy was starting to believe the rumors about her family members and just how dangerous they might truly be.

Opening the secret space, she shoved the cell phone inside. She jumped up and dove under the covers, yanking the worn quilt up to her chin and froze in place, right as her door creaked open.

In the dim moonlight coming through the window, the square face of her creepy cousin, Linc, emerged from the shadows as a ghost in the darkness, the cruel angles of his face coming into black and white focus. He took one step into the bedroom.

Then another.

The air grew thick.

His grinding chuckle made her skin crawl as if worms squirmed all over her body.

A bead of sweat tormented her as it rolled down a temple, but she held still. She'd learned the hard way not to fight a jerk like Linc. Her bruised arms ached from when she had dared to ask for the real story about what had happened to Mariah West last week.

She clamped her teeth together to keep them from chattering. Damn it, this was her family's house. Their ranch. Her bedroom.

The one place she should feel safe.

Not with the heavyweight MMA fighter looming over her. She peeked under her lashes at him.

A red glow seeped from his beady eyes and bloodied the walls of her bedroom.

Each muscle tensed; every cell in her body wanted her to run. But if she bolted, Linc would pounce.

She could scream, but there was no guarantee Wyatt and Tommy would help. Normal brothers should protect their sister. Not Wyatt. Ever since she could remember, he had always been a little cold to Izzy. But Tommy? Her favorite brother, the guy who made sure she stayed safe around the ranch when they were growing up, had recently changed. He all but ignored her, unless it was to yell at her to mind her own business. Now Tommy and Wyatt were two surly peas in a pod, with their heads stuck up their...mining equipment in the garage out behind the house.

Mom couldn't get up and do anything to help. Obviously.

So that left...no one.

Izzy's only hope? Play dead and pray.

Linc's grin was a sick pearly gray in the moonlight.

A whiff of rotten eggs swirled around her as he bent down, his nose inches from her face.

Playing dead might be a self-fulfilling prophecy. How long he stood there, she had no idea.

Don't move. Don't breathe. Don't do anything that he can respond to.

Then what? Just wait for him to do something disgusting? Crappy plan. She rolled a hand into a fist. By God, the guy might be twice her size, but Izzy would make some memories if he touched her.

Her heart slammed against her ribs. No way he couldn't hear the pounding. Then, as if a string yanked at his head, his body ramrodded straight up.

Izzy held her breath.

Linc mumbled, "Yes, my Lord?"

Since when was the meathead religious?

"I will obey you, Great One." Linc spun on his heel and marched out like a mechanized puppet. If that was his religion, then Izzy supported it fully.

Pass the plate and everyone say amen.

Izzy waited a solid thirty seconds before exhaling. Slowly pushing to a sitting position, she unclenched her hands from their tight fists. Footsteps faded, and then she heard the *thunk* of the front door closing.

Swiping her damp brow, she sucked in a deep breath, trying anything to slow the rapid pulse racing through her veins.

In slow motion, pausing every few seconds to make sure no one else stirred in the house, she crept from the bed and to the bedroom door. She eased the door open by degrees, cringing at every tiny creak. As she peeked down the long hall, shadows played tricks, shifting like living creatures. That nasty smell of sulfur wafted past her. Before she could sneeze, she lurched back into her room, pinched her nose, and suppressed the impulse.

Be her luck she'd blow her eyeballs out of her head.

Almost as stupid as hanging around this horrible situation.

Nothing concrete had happened. No one had hurt her.

Yet.

But ever since Wyatt and Linc stumbled back into the house a few days ago, looking like they had wrestled a grizzly bear and lost, the mean-and-nasty levels had risen precipitously. Which was saying something about the ill-mannered people she had to call her brothers and cousin.

But even now, Izzy detected the faint, ever-present hiss of the oxygen concentrator that ran every night.

Mom. She might be a perpetual bossy grouch, but no way could Izzy leave her alone here at the ranch. Her brothers and cousin wouldn't care for Mom. She'd die of neglect.

But Izzy had a plan, and it didn't involve hanging around this town much longer. Given tonight's shenanigans and the increasingly weird behavior from the guys, she intended to put that plan into action tomorrow.

One step closer to freedom.

She eased the bedroom door with a soft click and faced the window.

Just in time to see a dark face filling the glass.

A scream bubbled up her throat.

CHAPTER 3

*N*othing said *Hey, just making sure you're okay* like trespassing and stalking in the middle of the night.

In retrospect, maybe Kerr's plan had a few weak spots.

He hung by his gloved fingers on a windowsill of the Brand ranch. Damned house looked like a series of afterthoughts and second-guesses. Nothing fit. Nothing felt right either, but the sensation had nothing to do with architectural design, or lack thereof. No, when he had gotten close to the main compound, it felt like his body weighed fifty pounds more, which made this crime even more challenging as he was literally hung out to dry. His toes cramped as he balanced on the upended ten-gallon bucket.

Praying that he had the right room, he propped his chin on the sill between his hands and didn't move a muscle. Izzy's pale face filled the glass. A hand covered her mouth, her eyes opened wide.

Now what?

Okay, yes, definitely his plan had a few weak spots.

Like how she blinded him with a flashlight beam. Ouch. He squinted and grinned for all he was worth. Even tried to wave without falling on his ass. See? Nothing wrong. Just another day, lurking in people's windows.

If she didn't shut that mag light off, not only would his retinas burst into flames, but someone would see him. Like whoever slammed the front door and now stomped through snow nearby. Crap.

The second that person rounded the corner of the house, they would see Kerr, dangling like tasty bait. No time to run. Nowhere to go.

Trapped again, this time by his stupid choices.

The crunching squeaks of dry snow compressing under boots grew louder.

Kerr closed his eyes and prayed he could trust her. Clamping his teeth together, he braced against the inevitable headache. His vision went filmy, like several layers of plastic wrap covered his eyes. Blinking against the stab in his temple, he clung to the windowsill. One foot still tiptoed on the bucket. With effort, he held the fade effect until he was completely invisible.

She pressed a hand against the pane, head whipping from side to side. She turned the flashlight off and shook it.

As much as he wanted to reveal himself to her and stop the pounding headache, he had to maintain the disappearing act for a little longer.

God, the heaviness in the air here—how did she stand it? Like breathing underwater. Even the typical ranch sounds of cattle and horses reached his ears in a muted way, like the animals didn't dare to make any noise. Just like at the Taggart ranch, no more dogs ran around here, either. A tendril of sulfur irritated his sinuses and made him glance back over his shoulder, expecting to see that bastard evil creature that had been terrorizing his family.

No cloud monster tonight, only Linc. With a clomping stride, the big man emerged from the side of the house, no more than ten feet away from Kerr's precarious position. Kerr would recognize that jughead anywhere. Linc, the guy who tried to kill Vaughn in the octagon last week. If Linc got hold of Kerr, he'd become the fighter's personal hand puppet. Shit.

At least tonight Frankenjerk marched with a determined step to the large metal Quonset-style garage on the other side of the main compound. Dude didn't glance to either side. No pause in that stiff stride until the metal side door closed behind him. Long may the asshole stay away. Kerr wished terminal frostbite on the guy, but no way would he be that lucky in eliminating a nasty Brand family member.

Waiting a few more seconds, Kerr finally exhaled and let go of the fade, nearly losing his grip when the headache receded from ice pick to dull throb.

Izzy's wide eyes locked onto him.

That damned light blinded him again.

He flinched and waggled gloved fingers. His arms burned.

"Hi, Iz."

What the actual hell?

Had she lost her mind? Kerr had been here. Then…not here.

She blinked and swiped at her eyes. Sure as heck, that didn't help. No disembodied head floating in front of her window. Knocking the metal flashlight on her hand, she flicked it on and off. Worked fine.

Across the open yard, Linc entered the big equipment garage, the side door closing with a metallic slam. Good riddance.

And, good grief, there was Kerr again, complete with Stetson and a cheeky grin pasted on his face. Was she hallucinating?

Another sweep with the flashlight beam made him squint. Yup. Kerr. She shook her head and pushed the window open.

"Hi, Iz." Kerr's voice sounded strained.

"What are you doing here?" she hissed, keeping one eye on the garage. Linc or her brothers could return at any time.

"In the neighborhood."

"But…huh? It's almost two a.m."

"Yeah, it takes me a while to get here, what with it being the middle of the night, there was that ten mile trek, and then the deep snow and all. Um, and I'm getting pretty tired, hanging here. Do you think I could take a break?"

Of course he wanted to take a break. Because Izzy was living in the freaking Twilight Zone.

"Fine. But be quiet."

She wasn't worried for her own safety. This was Kerr. She'd known him for more years than she could count. Trusted his character. But Kerr against her three weird family members wouldn't be a fair fight. Even if he did have nice muscles from all those years of ranching and military service.

He easily pushed his torso up to the window casing and, with a swirl of leather duster, sat on the sill and then stepped into her room. Every single noise made her flinch.

He stopped less than a foot away from her.

The guy filled up a lot of space in her small bedroom. Buffered her from the world outside. Stole the air in the best possible way.

And something about a cowboy in a Stetson and duster really rang her dinner bell.

Beneath the shadow of his hat, the gleam of his wry smile was visible. A whiff of sage and cedar, mixed with cold snowy air, swirled around him, and she inhaled deeply, like somehow filling her lungs with his scent would displace all the bad humors in her world.

Didn't work. Another stomp of feet and the slam of the ranch house's front door prefaced Wyatt and Tommy striding over to the garage to join Linc.

Window. Crap.

"Get down. Don't move," she whispered, stepping around him. She ducked below the casing, reached out, grabbed the frigid metal window edge, and eased it back until it closed. Then she whipped around.

"What gives?"

"Why don't you tell me what's going on?" His low voice made her insides quiver. And bless him, he remained kneeling with one knee on the floor, as she had asked.

Sagging down until she sat on the floor with her back resting against the mattress, she rubbed her palms on her pajama pants and sighed. "You really shouldn't be here."

He moved to sit next to her, stretching his long legs out in front of him. Taking off his hat and putting it on the bed behind them, he ran a hand over his head. Even in the low light, the orange in his hair glinted.

Tugging his gloves off and stowing them next to the hat, he studied her for a long minute. "I was worried about you."

"So the next logical step was…" She waved her hand in the general vicinity of the window.

A flash of another grin. "Didn't say I thought it through. Only wanted to make sure you were okay."

First of all, wow. Kerr cared enough to check on her.

Second of all, if he'd showed up when Linc came into her room…A shiver worked through her bones and she crossed her arms over her chest, feeling underdressed in her flannel pants and short-sleeve pajama top next to Kerr.

With a shush of the thick coat, he turned and pulled the quilt off the bed, draping it over her shoulders and around her knees. That simple move made her eyes water. Had to be the dry winter air, right? Damn him. Life would be much simpler if he were a jerk, like everyone else. As things stood, she wanted to jump his bones in the exact same ratio that she wanted him out of this house for his own safety.

He pressed his shoulder against hers, warmth seeping into her even through the blanket. The angle of his strong jaw made her want to trace it with her tongue.

Okay, maybe the ratio tilted more in favor of "jumping his bones." Then again, she had always had a secret crush on Kerr.

"Something happen tonight?"

Back to business. Scraping hair back off her face, she leaned back. "Linc came in here."

"Like, in your room?"

"Yeah."

He whipped around so fast she couldn't follow the movement. His hand gripped her arm through the quilt. Right on the bruise. "Are you all right?"

She tried not to flinch. "Yes. I pretended to be asleep. He left. End of story."

"Nuh uh. Not even close to the end of the story. I can feel you shaking." A ragged rush of air ripped from his mouth. "Did he...try—do—anything?" The grip on her arm tightened. Strong. Sure. That strength that promised things she had no right to hope for from Kerr. Things like security. And closeness. And hope. Things she hadn't dared say out loud for many years now.

Things that didn't exist in this bizarre nook of the universe at Crazy World Ground Zero.

She eased away from his grip, because *ow*, and slid her free hand from under the quilt and reached for him. He entwined her fingers with his and squeezed; a sensation halfway between an itch and a tingle passed between them. She hadn't felt anything like it before. Then again, she had never held hands with Kerr.

His simple action triggered a painful lump in her throat. She swallowed hard so she could speak.

"He just stood over me for a while. It was weird."

"It bothered you more than 'it was weird.'" His shadowed mouth pressed into a line. "You shouldn't be here."

"Tell me something I don't already know."

"Well, why don't you leave? You're an adult. You're not a prisoner here."

"Feels like it." Even now, Izzy imagined the hiss of the oxygen and the tubing snaked under Mom's nose. "You know the deal. I can't leave Mom."

"Yeah, but your brothers and cousin. You know they tried to, uh, kill a bunch of us last week, right?" In the shadows, she couldn't completely read his expression, but, guaranteed, he wasn't happy about his family and friends getting entangled in the Brand family insanity.

"I've heard the rumors. I can't believe that it would have been that bad." Didn't she? "The guys say that nothing happened other than a house call." She lifted a hand at the angry slash of his mouth. "Yes, I get it. There had to be more than that. At first, I couldn't believe they would do anything so...crazy. But, over the past few days, I'm seeing more threats, more secrets. Less brotherly love, especially from Tommy. Normally he's the sweet one. And I just know they're cooking up something out there." She inclined her head toward the window. "If I weren't such a chicken, I'd try to snoop around and figure it out."

He rubbed the pad of his thumb over the back of her hand, creating tingles and that weird itchy sensation again. "No. Keep your head down. The way they're behaving, those guys would retaliate if they caught you. Besides, whatever's going on, I'm confident that you want nothing to do with it."

"Somehow it involves your family. It's like they want to destroy the Taggarts, and I don't know why."

"Me neither. I mean, there's the thirty-year-old feud between our fathers, but you'd think that would be over by now, especially since your dad passed away. Maybe your brothers have picked up the torch. Doesn't matter. The last thing I want is for you to get more involved."

"Um, I live here." She shrugged. "I am related to the insanity. Could not be more involved." She rubbed her free hand against the blanket. Why the hell were her hands itching? Allergies?

"I'm serious. You need to get far away from this place."

Almost like he had read her mind.

"Don't worry. I have a plan to blow out of here." She chewed the inside of her cheek. "On second thought, probably should've implemented the plan yesterday."

"If Linc or your brothers ever threaten you again, call me."

"Linc's huge."

He sucked a tooth. "Thanks for the vote of confidence." His grin cut off her apology. "Hey, I might not be fast, but I have skills."

A rush of warmth flooded her from nose to toes. Unfortunately, the timing of her interest couldn't be worse.

She scowled. "Like disappearing? Or did I hallucinate that?"

He pulled away. "Uh." The scratch of his palm over jaw stubble made her insides gallop. "Can you keep a secret?"

"Seriously? I'm a hermit. I don't share anything with anyone."

"That's sad."

"You're dodging the question."

"Yeah." Glancing at her, he nodded. "Okay." He took a deep breath, rolled his hands into fists and, with a wince…faded from sight.

She windmilled, her feet sliding on the wood floor as she skidded away. Air rasped between her lips. A shimmer of light, like a heat mirage, existed where he had sat. "Kerr?" Her voice came out shaky, freaked out. Because, well, of course.

Reappearing again, Kerr bent his head and rubbed his forehead, then looked up. His stark stare made her press a hand to her chest.

"So there's that," he muttered. "Look, I trust you and all, Iz, but please don't tell anyone I can do that trick."

Her mouth opened and closed twice before she could put words together. "How. When did you start disappearing?" Air puffed out. "And how totally cool is that?"

Pulling back, he tilted his head to one side. "You don't think I'm a freak or something?"

She scooted to sit next to him, patting him on the arm, to make sure he was solid. Cords tightened beneath her hand. Oh yes, solid. "Of course I think you're a freak, but look who I'm related to. Also, that's still an awesome trick. Hey, we all have our quirks."

He snorted. "That's one way to describe it."

"Now I know how you got here without being seen." A twist in her chest. "Man, I wish I had the power to disappear." She rubbed her palms on her pajamas.

"Izzy," he said, dropping a hand on her shoulder.

Trying to ignore how nice the contact felt, she managed to say, "How long have you been able to do that?"

"A long time." He sighed.

"So—" A clang of metal outside made her scramble to her feet to peek out the window. Her stomach went into a free-fall. "Crap. You need to get out of here. All three of them are headed back to the house. Please."

He stood, positioned between Izzy and the bedroom door, hands on his hips, like he dared someone to come through there and try to get to her. "We're not done," he said.

"Yes. We are." If she didn't get him out of here in time…"Hey, thanks for checking on me, but as you can see, I'm fine." She glanced out. The guys disappeared around the side of the house, heading toward the front door.

She pushed the window open and gestured.

Kerr didn't budge.

The rhythm of her heart went double time.

The front door opened. Then closed.

The sound of footsteps and low voices commanded her attention.

Until Kerr closed the space between them, cupped her face, and brushed his lips over hers. A mere ghost of a movement with his mouth, so light she had to concentrate to know if it was real or not. He pulled away with a heavy sigh. She rolled her tingling lips together. Breathed in sage and cedar. Felt the velvet over muscle of his mouth. Yes. Real.

His sheepish grin made her toes tingle.

The clomping steps grew louder.

Shaking off a sudden lightheadedness, she grabbed his hard arm. "Oh my gosh. Go." She danced from one foot to another.

Those shadowed eyes narrowed. "I'm not happy about this."

"Me neither. There'll be another time to deal with them."

"I meant…having to stop." His tongue darted over his lower lip as he ran a thumb over her cheek, leaving a heated, sensitive trail. "You have my number, okay?"

"Yes, yes. Get moving," she hissed. Sweat prickled her lower back.

With ease, he climbed through the window and dropped to the ground below with a muffled grunt. "Hat?" His voice drifted back up to her.

Crap. She tossed his Stetson and his gloves through the open space and pulled the window closed with a clunk.

The footsteps in the hallway stopped.

She yelped at a hard knock at the door and wrapped the quilt around her. "Yes?" she managed to respond despite a desert-dry mouth.

"Open up, sis." Wyatt. He didn't wait. The door swung inward with a bang against the wall. He flipped on the light.

Anyone heard of boundaries in this house? "Hello? Private space here," she snipped.

"What were you doing? Why is it so cold in here?" His eyes narrowed.

"I got hot and opened the window for a few minutes." Spying

frozen snow on the floor, she stepped on it with her socked feet, gasping at the chill as it melted against her skin.

He stalked past her. "Did you get it closed back up and locked all right?" He opened the window and peered out. Izzy lost a few years off her life.

"Are you done? I'd like to get a few Zs. Kind of hard with the racket you all are making. Don't you people sleep? And what were you doing out there anyway?"

"Not your business." His voice rumbled lower. Echoed in her head, making her wince. Then he paused and tipped his head, like he'd just tuned into a whole new and way more insane radio station. His eyes bulged. Not a good look. "If we can trust you, then perhaps the truth will be revealed."

She rolled fists onto her hips, trying not to shiver. "Okay. Fine, I'm trustworthy. Now tell me what you're doing out there."

"No. You must prove that you're with us. Before we destroy our neighbors across the valley."

The Taggarts. Whoa. She leaned back. There was a rivalry, true. But no one had talked about destroying anyone. The Taggart ranch was home to people like Kerr's nephew, Zach, who was in elementary school. And Mr. Taggart, who had a stroke a few weeks ago, lived there.

There would be no destroying anyone or anything over there, if she had something to say about it.

"Neighbors?"

"Once you prove your loyalty, I'll consider letting you in on our secret."

More secrets. Great. "When?"

His eyes bulged. "Depends on you. And you'll know when to prove that loyalty."

She bit her lip. Choices. Leave now or stay and help the Taggarts.

"Done."

CHAPTER 4

The Taggart kitchen bustled with a surprising amount of activity for 5:30 a.m. on a Thursday. Red and white floor tiles, bright and cheery, along with breakfast sizzling on the stove, warmed the comfortable space. Vaughn had drawn cooking duties today and frowned over the cast iron skillets, gripping the spatula in his massive paw like he was prepared to bludgeon the bacon into submission.

"Morning," Kerr said as he opened the cabinets to pull out plates and glasses. The glow of the lights pushed back the chilly late December darkness outside the ranch house. Created a sanctuary, if only for another hour more until the light of day exposed all the things wrong in the world outside.

Like the wrong things at the Brand ranch. Kerr had only returned an hour ago, and already he worried about Izzy again. *Shut up, instincts.*

Vaughn looked up, dark hair sticking up in multiple directions. A yellow bruise was still visible at the neckline of his thermal shirt and over his cheekbone. A scab remained over his eyebrow. Not all of the injuries were from his MMA bout last weekend. Some were from his fight with Wyatt when Vaughn went to rescue Mariah several days ago.

Kerr pulled out a wooden chair and sat. "How's Mariah doing?"

"Good. She was on call last night, so I asked her not to leave the hospital when she finished. It's safer for her to stay there when I'm not around to watch over her." He glared at the scrambled eggs.

Right, Vaughn's psychic ability to detect danger. Worked great in his MMA fights, but that ability backfired when it recently shifted away from Vaughn to protect Mariah instead. Thanks to his opponent, Linc, and how Vaughn's radar for danger short-circuited, big brother had been one upper cut away from getting pounded into oblivion during that last trip to the octagon. Nobody knew how or why his ability had changed.

Vaughn rolled his neck, hard cords bunching up. Shit, his brother was a scary dude.

Kerr looked up from setting the table. "You going to stay with her tonight?"

Vaughn stared at the skillet as he turned bacon. Another muscle popped in his big, square jaw. "Yeah. Have to. I need to be near her."

"Your power still hasn't calmed down, has it?"

"Nope. None of our powers have downshifted after ramping up," Vaughn said. "You're the only one who hasn't changed yet. Lucky bastard."

"Lucky." Kerr dropped a fist on the worn wood surface. "Although I wouldn't mind my power changing, if it meant that I could hurt those Brand bastards."

"No arguments here. I'm just hoping my power doesn't bump up any more. Who knows, I might go actual supernova." His grim smile held zero happiness.

Vaughn's hypersensitivity to danger had morphed from mere detection to protection and then to detonation. Not only did the power crave to protect Mariah from danger, but when that evil cloud creature had attacked her? Big brother had freakin' *become* the danger. As a vicious MMA fighter, Vaughn was intimidating to begin with, but with the addition of this new power?

All Kerr could say was, he was glad his eldest brother was on the Taggart side.

Garrison, his next oldest brother, strode into the kitchen, nose in the air and a sloppy smile on his unshaven face. His checked flannel shirt buttoned only about three-quarters of the way up. Red marks stippled his neck. Ah, right. Because his girlfriend, Sara, had stayed over. Slumber party.

His dark red eyebrows shot up. "I heard you plotting against the Brands. My favorite topic. What did I miss?"

"Not plotting against all of the Brands," Kerr mumbled.

Garrison's gold-flecked eyes narrowed. "Want to say more about that?"

Kerr blanked his thoughts. Had to be careful around human lie-detector Garrison. "Nope." No one needed to know about his night-time escapades.

A flannel-clad shoulder rose. "Suit yourself. Hey, any more on how Wyatt Brand magically reappeared? Word in town was that he's working at the hardware store again, as of yesterday. Vaughn chucked him off that cliff when we rescued Mariah several days ago. Saw the guy fall with my own eyes. No one could survive that drop."

Kerr ran a hand over his head. "Maybe it wasn't as far down as we'd thought."

Garrison tilted his head toward Vaughn. "Doesn't much matter how, I guess. Somehow, though, Wyatt's back, like a bad penny."

"That's bullshit," Vaughn snapped. "And fuck that bastard. If Wyatt gets anywhere near Mariah—"

"Whoa there, Trigger." Kerr eased into a spindle-backed chair at the table and stretched out his legs with a groan. "Yes, yes. You'll kill him all over again. Got it." He grinned at his brother's black scowl. "Not that I disagree with your sentiment, bro. Too bad we have no legal recourse."

"Not as long as his brother Tommy is the sheriff and all." Vaughn *thunked* the butt of the spatula on the countertop, splattering egg. He cursed, then wiped the counter with a paper towel.

Garrison rubbed his jaw. "Son of a bitch, everything about that family stinks to high heaven."

Not everything. But Kerr kept his mouth clamped shut.

Big brother Vaughn attempted to glower the bacon into tapping out. "Fuck me. When is all this crap going to end?"

All this crap.

The unsaid issues thickened the silence. Pops and his stroke. Garrison's ex-wife deserting her son and husband. The destruction of the Taggart ranch's main barn. The loss of cattle.

And now the Taggarts had a monstrous entity trying to kill them all.

Shit. What angle could Kerr use to stop this creature from destroying his family?

Garrison leaned a hip against the counter. "Shelby at Eric's today?"

Kerr nodded. Thanks to the monster out there and its promise to destroy the Taggarts—but only when they were all four together—the most obvious temporizing measure seemed awful darn simple: Don't be all in the same physical location for any length of time. If that meant Kerr didn't see his twin sister for a day, he'd deal with the stress of separation. At least they were all still alive.

At some point, though, either the creature would get tired of waiting or the Taggarts would go on a monster hunt. The unworldly thing was big, mean, fire-shooting, and totally focused on annihilating the Taggarts and anyone they cared about. Why it hung out around the ranch was anyone's guess.

A zap of cold lanced through Kerr's spine, as it did whenever he thought of the shadow creature stalking his family. Shelby had nearly died when the dark force tried to kill both her and her boyfriend, Eric, a few weeks ago. Only Vaughn's timely arrival had pushed the creature away.

For now, like shells in a carnival game, Kerr and his brothers and sister moved around, passing each other, shifting positions and responsibilities. A shell game of a life. Until they could eradicate the creature once and for all. Kerr wanted to do it himself. If possible.

He rubbed his neck. Not being in close proximity to his twin felt weird, like a rubber band pulled too tight. Never comfortable. Never secure. At risk of breaking.

Garrison pushed away from the counter and held his plate out for

Vaughn to pile full of food. He repeated the process and took a plate over to Kerr. "Can you make a run to the hardware store today?"

"Since you delivered food with that request? Yes." Kerr's stomach rumbled until he got the first two forkfuls of bacon, eggs, and pancakes halfway down his throat. Ugh. "Vaughn, you've outdone yourself, bro."

"You want food? You got food. You want high quality, gourmet cuisine? Tough titties, little brother." Vaughn stomped over to the table with his plate. "You get what you pay for." He propped his thick forearms on the table, speared a bite, and made a face as he chewed. "Man, you're right. This is low-grade dog food."

"It's edible." Kerr grinned as he shoveled another bite. "I've eaten way worse. And, I do appreciate the ability to eat, any day of the week."

Silence, awkward and heavy, pushed down on them. A blast of memories assailed Kerr. So many tubes had snaked all over him in that military hospital, dripping fluid and drugs. He'd take Vaughn's Cordon Bleu gut bomb over a stomach tube any day of the week.

After gulping a swig of milk, Garrison leaned back in his chair. "So. Hardware store in Jackson?"

"The road this time of year is iffy. Let me check." Kerr tapped on his smartphone, pulled up the Wyoming DOT site, and swore. "Rock fall at Battle Mountain on Highway 191. Road to Jackson's closed until further notice. How soon do you need the items?"

"Soon," Garrison curled his hand into a fist.

"I'll just go to Copper River Supply here in town."

"Wyatt Brand banned us from there." Garrison frowned.

"Technically, he only banned Shelby and Eric." Kerr ignored the zip of adrenaline that woke him the hell up. Izzy sometimes worked in the store. Besides, it had been, what, four hours since he'd seen her?

Vaughn swiped his face with a napkin, a move that triggered Kerr's déjà vu as a superimposed image of their dad at the end of a family meal layered on top of his brother's face. Their previously healthy dad, that is.

"I don't know if going there is a good idea," Garrison said.

Winking, Kerr quipped, "Hey, they're capitalists. Money trumps blackballing. Besides, if things get bad, I can become scarce."

"Well. Be safe." Vaughn stared at his plate of half-eaten breakfast like his favorite pet had run away.

"Safe? I resemble that remark." Kerr's leg made a light *thunk* as he walked over and dropped his plate off at the sink. "Besides, what's the worst that could happen?"

CHAPTER 5

"*I*t's just for a few nights, Butch." Izzy stood on her oldest brother's porch, freezing her bagels off this frigid morning. "You have extra time, what with school being out for the holidays and all. Please."

Her hopefully still responsible brother ran a hand over his balding head. "I don't know, Iz." Behind him, twinkle lights and tinsel sparkled on his Christmas tree in the center of his bright living room in his large, welcoming house on the outskirts of Copper River. Somehow, Butch had managed to stay out of the knee-deep insanity at the family ranch. Until Izzy came a-knockin'.

"Did you ask Tommy?" he said.

"No good. He has to work a bunch over the holiday. Sheriff department stuff and all." *Please don't bail on me.*

"I don't know..."

Time to hit him in his guilt complex. "You don't know how it is. I need a break or I'm going to be committed," she said, with a no-fail hitch and quaver in her voice that only baby sisters could get away with. "It's been so stressful since Hank disappeared. And it's 24/7, caring for Mom the last week, with her coming home from the hospital. And...you know how she is..."

As if on cue, a muffled shout and curse came from the minivan. Good ol' Mom, pleasant as usual.

Butch hesitated. Glanced back over his shoulder. Shook his head.

What? He hesitated? No way was he going to bail on her. Time to play dirty.

It was way too easy to generate tears, given the stress she had been under. But Izzy poured on the waterworks, even doing the move where she pressed her fist against her mouth and pretended to not-cry. Which, of course, made the whole production even more effective.

A few more shaky breaths, and she had her squirming brother right where she wanted him.

"Okay, okay, Iz. Stop crying. Please." He gave her an awkward hug. "We'll watch Mom for a while. Don't worry." Pat, pat, pat on her back. She made certain to give a shuddering heave for good measure. "You get some rest. Maybe go shopping or something."

She so wasn't the go-shopping type of woman. But now wasn't the time to correct her brother and his stereotyping. She just needed him to feel like a hero today, and whether it took guilt or flattery, made no difference to Izzy.

"Thank you." She sniffed again, feeling only a little guilty for manipulating him. Perk of being the baby sister. "You have no idea how much I needed this. It'll just be for a short time, I promise."

His expression serious, he nodded. "Take the time you need. School doesn't start back for another two weeks. We'll take good care of Mom."

Izzy turned back to the minivan. In the early morning light, Mom's clawed hands waved from the depths of the vehicle. If the multiple sclerosis hadn't limited her dexterity, no question she'd be flipping Izzy the bird. She squinted. Make that two birds.

Butch threw on a coat and crunched in the rimed snow to the van. They started the process of unloading Mom, her equipment, and luggage.

Izzy hated to use him like this, but at least Mom would be safer here.

Next step? Gain Wyatt's trust so she could get the inside scoop on whatever plan the guys had brewing. The sooner she figured it out, the better she could help her family snap out of whatever was wrong with them, and the sooner she could help the Taggarts.

And the sooner she could put this bizarre chapter of her life behind her. Like in the rearview mirror, behind her.

The hardware store was cold enough to freeze the balls off a brass monkey. Whatever that meant. Izzy didn't have balls, and she was a hell of a lot higher up the evolutionary chain compared with some people who did have them.

Stomping her feet, she blew on her gloved hands as she prayed that the heating unit in family's hardware and supply store would kick on soon. Seriously, though, what idiot shopper would be out in these arctic temperatures, much less want to buy equipment and supplies? Seemed like most normal customers would rather stay in their cozy houses and be considerate enough to let her do the same.

Good grief, it was almost too cold to snow. God help anyone who asked her to pull lumber today. Stupid ideas like that could wait until spring.

Everything had frozen solid, which meant she got to warm up today with a brisk shovel-and-salt routine in front of the store, pickling the sidewalk. After one last lackluster scrape of the tool and a sprinkle of snow melt, she stomped her work boots on the mat inside the front door, tucked the shovel nearby, and flipped around the sign so it read *Open*.

Remember the plan. Gain Wyatt's trust.

Across Main Street, Izzy spied a couple, the man carrying a bundled baby, heading into the coffee shop. Something twinged deep in her belly. A reminder of her life and dreams, suspended.

Normal life would have to wait. She had business to take care of, and she didn't mean the store. One day, she would have that life.

Hopefully, Kerr had gotten back to the Taggart ranch safely last night. And no way would she analyze why the thought of Kerr popped into her head right as she was longing for a certain kind of happy ending to her life.

Per Wyatt's instructions, Izzy flipped on the pitiful string of Christmas lights around the front window. Instead of cheering her up, the circa-1990 colored glass bulbs made her chest tighten. What a joke, celebrating the holidays. What was there to celebrate? Family? Hope? Pretty sure tis-the-season wishes weren't supposed to involve wishing that her brothers and cousin would disappear.

What about her mother?

Aaaaand for the grand prize, there it was, the 10,000-pound elephant in the room. Izzy's eyelids burned. At least Mom was tucked in at Butch's for a while.

Good. Because Izzy had a plan, and being a star employee played into that plan. If she could gain Wyatt's trust, he'd let her in on the scheme he had cooking. Whatever it took to get him to open up to her, she'd do it.

By God, she would help the Taggarts. Kerr.

Then she was leaving town. For good.

In the storeroom, she hung up her worn winter coat and pulled a dull brown canvas apron over her jeans and old sweatshirt. Patting the pockets to make sure she had tape measures, pencils, and a pad of paper, she shuffled toward the front of the store. The large street-facing windows revealed freezing, gray skies, which spit out freezing, gray flakes.

Entering an aisle to check the inventory of Tormek blade sharpeners, she paused and rechecked her count. Missing one. Maybe Wyatt sold a grinder recently and didn't mark it down in his antiquated paper inventory system. She shook her head. He might be a surly mess, but he kept a tight rein on the supplies.

Before she could head back to the office and look through his papers, the front doorbell clanged. She groaned and walked toward the cash registers. First idiot of the day. Time to start this party early.

A Stetson hat bobbed behind several racks near the front of the store.

In the split-second the customer's face and a hint of orange hair curling over the nape of his neck came into view, Izzy froze and ducked back into the aisle, her heart pounding.

Kerr? Here? Not good. Hadn't he heard the part where he was in danger?

For one thing, Wyatt had banned the Taggarts from the store. If her brother caught Kerr here, the response wouldn't be pretty.

Second issue, why the heck was she acting like a middle-school girl, cowering in the bathroom at the school dance? Fine, so Kerr had showed up at her house, kissed her, and disappeared—literally. Granted, it was a good kiss. A very good kiss. Not that she had laid in bed and ran her fingertips over her lips, imagining more kisses from him.

Wake up!

He couldn't be here. Not today. Not when Wyatt might show up.

"Hello?" he called out.

Her heart skidded. Starting way back in high school, she'd always kept a proverbial light on for him. A little one. Just in case.

Then life had gotten in the way for both of them, and years later, here she stood, lurking in the aisles of the family hardware store in Frozen Tundra, Wyoming, keeping company with some wrenches and screwdrivers.

Grow up, Izzy. She straightened her apron and took a step toward the main aisle. A hint of cedar and sage tickled her nose.

"Izzy?"

She spun around at the mellow voice behind her. Kerr, lean and tall, stood a few feet away, his dark, oilskin duster jacket shifting, as if he'd just stopped moving from a dead run. That cheeky grin, half-cocky and half-deprecating, sucked the air out of her lungs. The auburn shadow on his hard jaw tempted her to survey the rough texture with her fingertips and see if it rasped like she imagined it would.

Or she could use her mouth. Last night was only a tiny taste. A parched gal needed more than a sip of water to cross the desert, right?

She blinked.

Kiss or no kiss, he was still a customer. Besides, if she was going to keep Kerr safe from her brothers and cousin, she had to steer clear of the guy. And the steering started now.

"H-hi. You came out of nowhere. Kind of like last night." Since when did her voice come out all soft and whispery?

He pressed two fingers to his temple and winced, like he had a bad migraine. "Yeah." Then he blinked those amazing brown eyes speckled with gold, rimmed with dark orange eyelashes. She hadn't properly appreciated his eyes in the darkness of her bedroom last night. "And remember, I'd like that little extra skill to remain secret."

His crooked smile made breathing difficult.

Sweat prickled her chest. The darn store heater must be set too high. She surreptitiously rubbed her palms on the canvas apron.

Who was she to debate the need to keep a secret? "As I mentioned earlier, my lips are sealed. Promise." Her cheeks warmed. "What are you doing here?" she managed.

His grin grew. "Well. Let's see. I have a shopping list of hardware items." He lifted a folded piece of paper. "By coincidence, you happen to have a hardware store. So I figured..."

"Right." She popped her palm to her forehead. "Brain locked up there for a second. Cold morning, no sleep last night, and all that junk."

It might be winter, but nothing about this interaction made any portion of her body cold. Quite the opposite. She needed to get some space between herself and Kerr.

She turned to go, but he tapped her on the arm. She jumped.

"Sorry to startle you," he said.

Despite the dry mouth, she said, "Not your fault."

He searched her face long enough to make her squirm. "Everything okay with you, Iz? And after I left?" In the space of a second, his voice went from teasing to concerned.

Any rational reason for why her insides quivered when he called her Iz? Or the fact that it sounded like he cared about her? Of course not.

"I'm good, thanks." She spent the next uncomfortable few seconds memorizing the strong curve of his mouth and wishing...Nothing. Wishing nothing.

"Just 'good'?" His mellow voice penetrated her solid emotional defenses like a hot knife through butter. "No one else threatened you?"

A lump formed in her throat. The urge to lean on him was so tempting...No. She would not drag him further into her family's mess. Shouldn't even be talking to him, much less texting in the middle of the night from Dysfunctional World.

And letting him into her bedroom at dark o'clock? Well, it would have been rude to let him hang there forever.

To be fair, though, Kerr didn't have extra time and energy to spend on her crap. He had more than enough on his plate. And she might be lumped in with the rest of the Brands, but Izzy still intended to make some things right before she left town. "No. It's all good."

"It's just—things feel, um, wrong at your ranch. Be careful." He shifted from one foot to another...foot.

With him wearing those well-fitting jeans and boots, you'd have to be in the know about his fake leg to pick up on that detail. He looked fine to her, complete with his solid shoulders and confident posture.

Very fine.

"You too," she mumbled.

"No, I mean it." He crossed his oilskin-clad arms. Seriously, did he even know how good he looked in that dark brown duster? Rugged cowboy chic. That garment on Kerr should be labeled as flammable in the presence of estrogen.

"You mentioned that"—she glanced at her watch—"a few hours ago. Don't worry. I'm careful. I know the deal."

Cocking his head to the side, he said, "No, I don't think you do know."

"Gee, thanks."

He cleared his throat. "I meant what I said earlier. Let me know. If I can help. Ever. You know. Call." The list fluttered to the floor, and with a grunt, he bent and picked it up.

"Sure. Of course. Because with the texting, I have your number and all."

He gave her shoulder a too-brief squeeze, then slid his hand down over hers. "I'm really glad you do."

Did she have a sudden virus that triggered a fever? Izzy tugged at her sweatshirt neckline. "So, um, let me know if you need me. To find anything for you. In the store. Hardware." She stepped back and flapped her hand in front of her. Her itching hand. What the heck?

Those golden eyes locked back onto her. "You'll be the first one to know if I need anything." He winked.

Seriously, was he flirting with her? Why yes, yes he was. And she enjoyed it far too much. "Okay. Well. I'll be over there for you to check out. Uh, for when you need to check things out. At the register. Oh, hell."

His goofy smile lit the gray day better than a bright beam of sunlight. "Absolutely."

Like a coward, she scurried away.

CHAPTER 6

*H*ow long did it take a man to go shopping? Scraping her hair back, Izzy chewed her lip.

Dumb question, but good God, Kerr needed to hurry. Wyatt could show up at any time. No telling what her loose-cannon brother would do to a Taggart who dared to enter the Brand family store.

Actually, she had a graphic idea of what Wyatt would do.

No way was Kerr getting hurt on her watch. But if she wanted to find out what was going on at the ranch, she needed to play nice and get on her brother's good side. She tapped the carpenter's pencil on the register.

Come on, Kerr, wrap it up. After rechecking her apron pockets for the tenth time in five minutes, she glanced toward the back door. Nothing. Yet.

But enough time had passed that she now qualified for AARP.

Another several minutes ticked by. Finally, he pushed a squeaking cart to her register, taking an agonizingly long time when he paused five times in as many feet and studied the checkout displays. After forever, he stopped in front of her.

When he shot her another rakish smile, not only did she forgive him for being the slowest shopper in the universe, but jolts of *ride 'em cowboy* galloped straight to her pelvis, challenging her vow to avoid entanglement. She'd be okay with being entangled with Kerr. And just like that, an inappropriate image of what they would look like... entangled...took up residence in her mind. Damn that Stetson and duster.

"What?" she stammered.

He did that libido-boosting thing again where a corner of his mouth rose, which made her think about things like his lips. And how those lips would feel against hers. "I didn't say anything."

Oh boy, this situation was bad. All of it.

Ducking her head, she concentrated on swiping the items over the temperamental scanner and passing them to the holding bin. When she grabbed a spool of twine, his hand brushed over hers and stilled her movement. A jolt zapped up her fingertips at the touch.

As air stalled halfway up her throat, she snapped her head up. Man, his eyes were beautiful, with those flecks of gold on the rich brown background. *Quit thinking that stuff.*

He tilted his head to the side. "Good. I thought you were ignoring me over here."

"I...um. No." Another glance behind her. "Just trying to be efficient."

"Because there's a long line?"

Tumbleweeds could have rolled through the store and it would appear less deserted.

"Something like that."

He curled his long fingers around her wrist, sending itchy prickles into her fingertips. A hint of his sage and cedar scent turned her knees to goo. "Iz. Last night—"

"The breaking and entering?"

"More like trespassing and stalking. But sure."

She smiled despite herself. "Go on."

"Uh, I was thinking, maybe...maybe one day we could go out. Together. You know? Like normal people on a date."

An effervescent bubble formed in her chest and lifted her up. Wow. A date. With Kerr. "That would be—"

Horrible. The worst decision ever. Dangerous for him. Useless for her, considering her Copper River exit plan.

That bubble sure did sting as it burst.

He rubbed the pad of his thumb over the back of her hand. Damn him for how good that simple touch felt. Damn her for needing that kind of contact so much.

He stopped the gentle movement. "Is there an issue talking about an...'us'? What's really going on?"

Pulling away from his warm grip, she rubbed her tingling palm on her apron, then fumbled for a paper bag and waved it open, the crinkling sound harsh in the empty store. "Nothing. Let's get all this packaged up and you on your way, okay?" Her voice came out too pinched, too chirpy.

The impish light drained from his eyes. The corners of his mouth flattened. "Got it. Should have figured it out sooner, but I'm slow. Shit, and I even went to your house. And the kiss...My bad. Message received."

"What? Wait. No. Kerr, you don't understand at all." Especially not about the kiss. "We should probably stay friends, that's all."

He rubbed the leather coat material that draped over his thigh. "Yeah. I get it. Hey, no harm no foul, Iz. Friend zone. I understand. I'll stop bothering you from now on."

"You're not—" The bang of a door in the back room spiked every one of her nerves into high alert. "Damn it."

She crammed the last few items into a too-full paper bag and hit the button on the register.

The twenty-year-old machine beeped *error*.

Are you flipping kidding me?

She tried again.

Come on. Come on. The stomp of thick work boots got louder as she punched the button again. The register slowly opened and she made change, spilling some coins onto the conveyor belt.

A furrow formed between Kerr's brows. Beneath the brim of his hat, his shadowed eyes narrowed as he glared over her shoulder. As he opened his mouth to speak, another voice blasted out from behind her.

"What the fuck are you doing here, Taggart?" Wyatt loomed behind her shoulder. His raspy breathing irritated the space she occupied. But she had to appease him if she wanted to earn his trust and then help the Taggart family.

Kerr lifted a shoulder. "Just a little Christmas shopping, dude. By the way, might I say you are looking healthy today, considering the little spill you took recently."

Twisting her head, she peered up at her brother. "Spill?" she said. "What's he talking about, Wyatt?"

"Nothing," her brother ground out. An eye twitched. He batted at his disheveled dark brown hair and tugged at the work shirt that smelled like it hadn't been washed in a week.

"Want to try for another answer, bozo?" Red blotches tinted Kerr's neck and cheeks. His knuckles turned white as he gripped the bags full of supplies.

He leaned forward.

A cold weight blanketed her. She craned her neck to search her brother's burly frame. "Wyatt, does his comment have anything to do with the extra bruises you and Linc had the night after Doc West did that second 'house call' for Mom?" Good God. The rumors in town might all be true. Had Wyatt truly kidnapped that woman?

She was truly stuck. If she protested the apparent kidnapping of Dr. West, then Izzy would lose the chance to find out what exactly her brothers and cousin were up to. If she bit her tongue to get the needed information, she would look like a wimp in front of Kerr? Or worse—complicit. Her stomach churned.

A red glow coated Wyatt's eyes, something she'd seen hints of before with him and last night with Linc. Weird. She looked up again and the redness was gone. Maybe she had imagined it. A faint scent of uncooked eggs and a wave of heat poured off of him, followed by a bone-deep sense of *wrongness*. Being close to him was like having a hot poker hover one inch from her twitching skin. One inch in the wrong direction and...sizzle.

Fiery breath washed over her neck, making the hairs stand up on end. Wyatt completely ignored her. "Taggart, you have one chance to get the hell out of my store. Anything short of that, and I will call the police."

"Right. The same police my family called to report a kidnapping? The same law enforcement that happens to include your brother, Tommy? Super not helpful."

"What of it?"

Kerr straightened up to full height, equal to her six-foot tall brother. His voice dropped to a low, dangerous tone. "Listen to me carefully, my friend." His icy calm chilled her blood.

Holy cow. She'd never seen Kerr this furious, ever. But the high color in his face and the pulse pounding at the base of his neck? His blanching knuckles? They were the tell: Kerr was one twist of the peg away from his wire snapping. Her knees shook as she clutched the metal edge of the counter, wanting to be anywhere else but here. God, her palms itched like crazy. She glanced down. No rash. The skin was just irritated and itchy.

Gold glinted in Kerr's narrowed eyes. "You're lucky that you have the law in your back pocket, Wyatt. Understand that we have taken all of these matters to the county commission and hired an investigator." Sweat popped out above his upper lip. "You and your family are done pulling all this shit—everything over the past month." He leaned in. "And let me be clear: Law enforcement or not, I will personally see to it that justice is served. I will fight you with whatever force is necessary."

She choked as her heart slammed against her ribs. Would he do it? Would he investigate and prosecute her family? He had good reason. Her absentee brother, Hank, had kidnapped little Zach Taggart. Add in today's confirmation about what happened to Dr. West. What else had her brothers hidden from her?

Wyatt snorted. "Good luck fighting with anyone, gimp."

Every cell in her body froze. Her knees locked into place.

The right answer was for her to go to the police and share what she knew, but she hadn't witnessed any of the things that had happened. Also, the retaliation from her brothers would be unimaginable.

No. At this moment, the right thing to do would be to tell Wyatt to back the hell off and quit being an asshole.

Kerr glanced at her. Waited for her to do the right thing.

She didn't move.

Then the light in his eyes went out.

Izzy wetted her lips. Damn it, she also needed to gain Wyatt's trust. She had to look at the bigger picture, and that meant bailing on Kerr. For now.

The bigger picture twisted her stomach into knots.

His hard jaw tightened as his expression turned to pale marble. The words barely escaped his clenched jaw. "You have no idea what I'm capable of, Brand."

Wyatt shrugged. "Fine. Then you'll go to prison for attacking us."

"Do I strike you as a guy who cares about something as trivial as prison?" He barked what passed for a laugh. "Look, dude, I've been to hell and back. I've lived in a different kind of prison for the past two years. Trust me when I say that four walls and some bars will make no difference to my existence." He drew in a big breath. "But if that's what it takes to keep my family safe, I'll risk incarceration to end you and yours. And screw any repercussions. Got it?"

"Whatever, asshole," Wyatt spat.

"Do you even know why you hate my family?"

"Sure I do. You all are pricks."

A snort. Kerr touched the brim of his hat. "No. Real reason."

"Uh…"

"Exactly. Our dads had a disagreement years ago. Your father instilled a hatred in you for everything Taggart. You don't even know why you hate us."

"Don't need to know." He sniffed. "Anyway. You better understand what punishment waits for you if you keep messing with the Brand family. And while I'm at it, stop sniffing around my sister."

Izzy sucked in a breath and held it. Did he know about last night?

Also, hello? This wasn't the Middle Ages where women had to be locked away in a tower. Time to wake up and smell modern life.

But did she say a word? No.

She glanced up in time to see spittle forming at the corner of her brother's mouth. "She's too good for a guy with…issues…like you." He pointed in the general vicinity of Kerr's legs.

A cord popped in Kerr's neck as his stare flicked over her again, like the lick of a whip. "It was over before it started."

"Kerr," she whispered.

"I want nothing to do with *any* of you…people," he gritted out.

In Kerr's view of things, she was no better than her jerk brothers. Didn't matter about her nighttime texting with him. Or her true intentions.

All that remained of that little candle she'd left lit for him all these years puffed out, leaving behind only smoke and a sickly burnt smell.

Izzy's face went numb.

Tried and convicted, along with the rest of her dysfunctional family. And why not? At least two of her brothers were now felons. Maybe three. While she hadn't helped them, she hadn't stopped them. So there she was, lumped into the steaming pile of manure.

Izzy might never be reformed into something good in Kerr's eyes.

But Izzy couldn't leave the Taggarts vulnerable to attack from her family. She might be lumped in with the rest of the Brand family in Kerr's eyes, but she could prove that she wasn't like her siblings.

And maybe—just maybe—doing the right thing would one day lead to a second chance with Kerr. He had served in the military. He had to understand a no-win situation.

First, though, the sell-out.

Swallowing, she forced her elbows to bend as she crossed her arms over her chest. "You'd better go now. L-leave us alone."

Kerr flinched. "Really."

Time to nail the coffin shut. "Look, I was nice to you because, uh, you're a customer."

He sucked in air. The glare he gave her made the snowy weather outside seem downright balmy. Then he shook his head like a man trying to wake the hell up.

Wyatt's nasty chuckle rumbled through the soles of her feet.

Get out of here, Kerr. Please.

"Be safe, Iz," Kerr muttered. He hefted the bags, spun on a heel, and with a swirl of the duster, banged open the front door with a harsh clang of bells.

She didn't dare move. The anemic heating system chugged and growled in the otherwise silent store.

The muffled roar of a diesel engine faded away.

Her stomach churning, she spun around. "Do you believe me now, Wyatt? I'm on your side."

A feral growl came from her brother. Rearing back, she pressed her hip against the dead end that was the register's holding bin, her heart clattering against her ribs like a rabid animal, desperate to escape.

His smile twisted. "There's much more going on here than you know." He gripped her shoulder and squeezed.

Forcing herself to hold still, she muttered, "Why don't you fill me in?"

"Are you interfering with my business?" His voice echoed inside her skull.

"Ow. Quit it," she squeaked as his grip dug into the muscle, triggering numbness down her arm. "How could I interfere? I just helped you out by taking out the no—uh, no-good Taggart trash." Tears pricked her eyes.

"Yes, at least you kept him here long enough for me to take run him off. Good job. Maybe later I'll share our plans with you." With one final squeeze that would leave more bruises, he turned in a herky-jerky movement and walked away, like a marionette whose strings were getting yanked. "Later."

She didn't move until the back door slammed.

CHAPTER 7

*S*logging through the midday ranch chores in the sub-freezing temperatures and snow showers did nothing to improve Kerr's black mood. With every pound of the nail on the shell of the replacement barn, Wyatt's words rang in his head.

She's too good for a guy with issues like you.

Issues.

Like a raging case of PTSD and a missing limb?

Or perhaps the lack of viable livelihood and the family ranch bordering on bankruptcy.

Or maybe the stellar family track record: date a Taggart and risk death.

None of those attributes screamed *pick of the litter*.

Despite the verbal pile-drive Kerr had weathered in the store, all he had wanted to do was come across that checkout counter and cold-cock Wyatt. And not for what the guy said to Kerr. Whatever. He'd heard worse.

No, Kerr wanted to punch that dude for how he treated his own sister.

Call a spade a spade—Kerr might not have quite as much muscle or spring in his step, but fury, a heaping helping of fuck-it-all, combined with military training, could still render some serious damage to your run-of-the mill asshole.

He pounded the next nail in with one slam of the hammer.

But right when he was ready to take on Wyatt back at the store, Izzy stepped in and leveled Kerr with a few choice words. It wasn't even a case of "what might have been" because no relationship had ever existed. Stupid to think otherwise.

Or was it?

He put himself in her shoes. What if Izzy was trapped in her life like Kerr was trapped in his? Sure, her words hurt, but he hadn't imagined their friendship. Or that kiss that would have knocked his hat off if he hadn't already removed it. Nothing pretend about the sparks when their mouths touched.

Even with what had gone down in the store this morning, he still cared about what happened to her. Not sure if that was a testament to being a glutton for punishment or his ability to read between the lines. Even now, he fought the urge to return to the hardware store, if only to make sure she was okay. Maybe he would drop by later today, when Wyatt wasn't there, and find out what was really going on. She'd tell him.

This was Izzy he was talking about, right?

Gravel popping under car tires stopped him in mid-hammer swing, and his tension dropped down a few notches. The familiar link with his twin clicked into place, like one puzzle piece fitting with another. He and Shelby always had a sense of the other one, but proximity enhanced the low-level connection. Several days ago, they had used their bond and worked together to find Mariah when she was lost in the woods as she fled from the Brands. Shelby couldn't travel due to injuries from a fall a few weeks ago, but she stayed at the ranch, homed in on Mariah's location, and used the twin link to provide Kerr with a destination to focus on. The connection worked perfectly.

But today that bond also meant that Kerr needed to *not* think about his plan to check on Izzy. Or how he felt about Izzy. Or his ever-present desire to stop the Brands from hurting his family. If Shelby got a whiff of any of it, his sister would blab. Her psychic power to detect strong emotions and her general nosiness combined poorly with an inability to keep her mouth shut.

A different truck engine revved and faded away. Ah, yes. Vaughn leaving to spend the afternoon with Mariah.

Because all four of the Taggart siblings couldn't be in the same place without that black blob of a creature trying to kill them and everyone they held dear.

This insanity was getting old.

Kerr worked for another half hour, then picked up his tools. The flat light in the cloudy afternoon gave every structure a strange cast as he walked from the half-constructed large barn to the smaller temporary barn where all the animals and supplies were crammed for the winter.

As he put a hand up to open the door, he caught a flicker of movement out of the corner of his eye. He flinched and stiffened. Was it something real or his PTSD? Always hard to tell.

He rotated slowly, planted his feet, and stood still, straining to make out anything in the shadows. A whiff of rotten eggs on a carcass-smelling breeze tickled his windpipe, and he stifled a cough.

Over the whickers of horses in the barn and lowing cattle behind him in the field, the rumble of a sadistic chuckle strafed Kerr's ears. Following the sound, he edged down the side of the barn. A finger of warm sulfur air scraped by him, making his skin twitch. His senses went on high alert.

He might not have Vaughn's radar for danger, but Kerr had a well-honed instinct for self-preservation. That particular instinct had served him well. He stubbed the boot containing his prosthetic.

Except for that one time.

Pay attention.

Wind-whipped snow obscured what poor visibility he had in the gray afternoon.

He could be walking into a trap.

How paranoid did a guy have to be, expecting to be jumped on his own property?

After the last month they'd had here at the Taggart ranch, not very paranoid at all.

Easing around the corner of the temporary barn, Kerr peered down the side of the building. Nothing. A few snuffles and whinnies coming from inside the building, but that was it.

With a sliding step, he eased down the length of the structure, his ears straining to detect anything beyond the normal ranch sounds.

Was that another chuckle?

Kerr went around one more corner.

A dark, blank area absorbed light.

The hot scent of burnt volcano mixed with road kill grew stronger. Two glowing spots appeared within the blackness.

Shit on shit.

Yep, he had seen that before.

And nope, he didn't want to hang around and swap recipes.

He activated his power, ignored the typical headache, and went invisible. At least that bastard wouldn't have an easy shot.

Kerr knew the adage all too well: *Don't bring a knife to a gunfight.*

Alone, he had limited tools to slow this creature down. He wasn't too proud to lay low and survive to fight another day. He gritted his teeth to hold the fading effect. His pulse pounded in his temples.

The thing hovered. What passed for the area of its head moved from side to side. The hint of a human body inside the thing made Kerr's stomach turn. Acid coated his tongue as the figure inside the creature made a weak movement. Did he really see it move, or was the fact that Kerr's vision blurred when he became invisible obscuring his view? Either way, not good.

A screech, like an inhaled howl, ripped past Kerr. He clapped his hands to his ears and hunkered down next to the barn.

Then, nothing.

Maintaining the invisibility, Kerr lowered his hands and sniffed. Clean, cold, snowy air. No unusual sounds. Nothing else out of place. Standing, he dropped the fade and staggered against the barn wall. Damn it all. Using his power hurt like hell.

But he had a way bigger problem than a little migraine.

Rubbing the back of his neck, he grimaced. End game was coming. He could feel it. The Taggarts would all have to face that thing. Together. Or be destroyed.

Decision made. By God, Kerr would figure out the connection between that creature and the Brands, and then he'd come up with a way to destroy the thing.

After circling the barn once more, he entered the house, ready to update his siblings on their nasty blob of a visitor. Strange how the bizarre had become an everyday occurrence. He took his hat off and scrubbed his hair.

The warmth and comfort of the bright kitchen embraced him, as always.

Dad's nurse, Ruth, stirred the pot on the stove, and a fabulous aroma of savory meat and spices filled the room.

Her hello struck him as more of a formality. Given the quirk of her raised brows, it always seemed like she knew before he entered and she had a bead on the tenor of his mental state.

Holy nervous breakdown, Batman. Time to take a break. Now he was imagining weird stuff everywhere.

Stranger still was the fact that Ruth and her husband, Odie, knew about the creature. Knew *of* it, to be exact. Or knew of something "just like it."

While it was tempting to press her for more information, Kerr and his siblings didn't want to alienate Ruth. The woman had helped their father recover from his stroke. No one wanted to guess what would happen to Dad's health if she left. Besides, she claimed to have told them everything she knew about the creature.

For his money, Kerr didn't care about what she *knew* about the creature. He wanted to know what she *believed* about the creature.

Kerr believed the whole Taggart clan was screwed.

The nonplussed expression on Ruth's sculpted features gave away no secrets. That is, until her husband, Odie, entered the room. As her gold-flecked eyes flicked toward the rakish, dark-haired Cajun, a slight smile curved her mouth. Color bloomed in her cheeks.

"Kerr." Odie nodded. Then he turned to his wife and breathed, "*Chérie.*" Amazing how that one word came out like a benediction. He snaked an arm around her waist, holding the tall, solid woman like a rare piece of art, his smile visible within his closely trimmed beard and moustache.

And just like that, there wasn't enough space in this big kitchen for three people.

Kerr shot them what he hoped was a polite smile, used the mat to stomp the clumps of mud off his boots, mumbled something marginally pleasant, and hurried through the kitchen.

Pausing on the other side of the kitchen door, he caught a few words from the couple.

"…still think we should do the paperwork?"

Her cool, calm voice held a new tension. "Yes. I want everything in place—" Her voice cracked.

"Just in case? Oh, *cher*, are you certain?" Odie murmured.

Kerr could imagine the man pulling Ruth into his arms.

"Am I usually wrong?" she asked. Final. Too much of a conclusion.

Quit eavesdropping. No. He needed to eavesdrop. Anything to get more information out of those two.

Unfortunately, their conversation had moved to nonverbal level if the light kissing sounds were any indication.

He had too much shit to wrangle. Time enough to work on the mystery of Ruth and Odie later. Right after he checked on Izzy. Right after he figured out what was going on at the Brand ranch. Right after he destroyed that monster.

Suddenly, it took too much effort to remain upright.

Another few steps brought him into the living room.

His dad occupied a recliner, where he'd nodded off, probably after a long day of therapy, thanks to Nurse Ruth. At least Pops was out of bed and enjoying time with the family again. That was a big improvement from the man who had been dwindling toward death a few weeks ago.

Nevertheless, Kerr couldn't stop the impulse to double-check that his father breathed, as he watched the once-muscled chest rise and fall.

Pops smacked his mouth and blinked his eyes open. "Vaughn, is that you?"

A lump made it hard to swallow. "No. It's Kerr." As usual. The second-place trophy winner. "Vaughn's away today."

One side of Pop's mouth rose when he spoke. "When will he be back?" The words slurred, but Kerr understood them.

The ugly twist in his midsection made it hard to answer. "Tomorrow morning. He'll spend time with you then."

"Very good, son. Thank you." He tugged the quilt up and within seconds was snoring once again.

The family update Kerr had planned died on his tongue. He inhaled the scents of a wood fire crackling and the freshly-cut spruce Christmas tree that Garrison's son, Zach, currently decorated. Kerr refused to ruin his family's rare moments of peace with the story of his encounter with that rotten-egg scented monster. The news could wait until after dinner, at least.

Garrison sat in a rocking chair, a half smile playing across his weary face as he watched his girlfriend, Sara, help hang ornaments. Garrison was whipped. And with good cause. Feisty teacher Sara Lopez fit in perfectly with the Taggart clan, but it was a miracle she still wanted to be around them. She had almost died because of the Brand-Taggart feud.

But with her dark hair piled up on her head and a dimple winking in one cheek, that woman had Garrison's attention, now and maybe forever, judging by his brother's riveted expression. Happy murmurs drifted through the living room.

Eric, Kerr's hunting guide business partner, looked up from where he sat on the middle cushion of the couch. "How're things? Ready for another trip into the backcountry?"

"Good, Humpty Dumpty. Are you released to full duties yet?" Kerr asked, knocking on his own skull. His friend had been in a coma not even a week ago. Thank God the guy was even alive, much less able to consider working.

"Should be a free man after my visit with Doc West coming up. A little coma won't hold me back."

"Yeah, but your girlfriend sure as heck will," Shelby piped up from the end of the couch, her legs draped across his thighs. She was one to talk. To save Eric from that evil creature that had attacked them, her power had grown and warped. The side effect of the change rendered her temporarily blind. Then when she dove into Eric's mind to bring him out of the coma and back to this world, sis had gone into a coma herself.

Made for one messed up game of hot potato, trading conscious-ness for consciousness. Thankfully they had both survived.

Shelby scowled at Eric. "I'm not happy with you working. You still get headaches from that fractured noggin." Raking back her wild, orange curls, she said, "Not like he needed another hole in his head." She crossed her eyes.

Kerr snorted. Too bad it didn't matter how hard he and Eric worked on their guide service. After the disaster of the missing client who had been terrorized by the nasty monster, trip reservations weren't exactly pouring in. He jammed his mouth shut. Later. Right now, he would simply be happy that his childhood friend had survived.

Eric lifted and then kissed the back of Shelby's hand. "So nice, the deep concern for my welfare and employment, darlin'. Trust me, every day I'm with you, it's a full-time job."

"Hey!" she protested.

Eric looked up to the ceiling with his hands raised in supplication, then back to Kerr. "You have no idea, man."

In spite of his dragging fatigue, Kerr smiled. "I have a pretty good idea." The whirling dervish of his sister might be limited by the compound fracture of her leg, but it hadn't slowed down her nonstop commentary. If anything, all the sitting around meant that she had more energy available for the barrage of stream-of-consciousness observations.

Kerr pointed. "Hey, sis, your leg's casted now."

Moving the leg with a green wrap on it, she grinned and shot him a thumbs up. "Had the external fixator taken out this morning in the hospital."

"No problems with anesthesia?"

"Nope. In and out, quick procedure. Over early." She rocked her leg back and forth. "I can start bearing more weight on it now."

Eric gripped her arm. "Not too much."

She pulled a face. "Got it, Nurse Eric." Holding up a hand, she gave a fake aside. "Between you and me, he's a really bad nurse."

Eric's face fell. "But I try so hard, what with the enemas and sponge baths—"

"Enough. God, stop." Kerr could only take so much sap from his former military brother. The guy was headed over the waterfall's edge, with Shelby at the helm of the ship. Poor guy.

Shelby laughed, then stopped. Her eyes unfocused and then she winced. "Hey, what's—? What happened, Kerr?"

"Quit using your power, Shel," Eric snapped. "You know that's dangerous."

Her jaw jutted out. "No. Me climbing fully into someone's head is dangerous and almost killed me. If I pick up projected emotion, that's fine. Just a little headache for the ol' radar dish." She pointed at her head. "No big deal."

"I'm not happy with it." Eric shook his head.

"Yeah. I can tell." She rubbed her temple and closed one eye as she glared at him. "Obviously. Right?" Turning back toward Kerr, she sniffed. "So what's the story?"

He stared at the crackling flames. "It was an interesting trip to the hardware store."

From decorating the tree, Sara called out, "Izzy there?"

Damn it. Even the mention of Izzy's name made his heart do that teenage pitter-patter crap. Even after he'd had his ass handed to him. "Uh. Yeah."

Shelby raised an eyebrow. "Yep. Way more to that story. Spill it."

"Nothing to spill."

"Clearly."

Sara asked, "Is Izzy doing okay?"

Garrison's glare nearly flayed skin off Kerr. Having his son and girlfriend kidnapped by the Brands would make a guy surly when the topic of that family came up.

"Izzy's family is causing her problems." Kerr shoved hands in his pockets and shrugged. "But hey, she should join the club. We've all got troubles, right?"

"Nuh uh." Shelby tapped the back of his hand that rested on the cushion. "More. Out with it."

"Fine." He braced himself on the back of the couch, taking pressure off his leg. "Wyatt showed up at the store and ripped me a new one."

"What?" Garrison whipped his head around, eyes narrowed and dark, searching.

"Not literally." Kerr checked to make sure Zach was occupied with tree decorating and not paying attention to the adult conversation. Dropping his voice, Kerr stopped joking around. "Wyatt also made more threats about what he wanted to do to our family. In enough detail to piss me off. And then he warned me away from Izzy."

"Why ever should he have to warn you away?" The corner of Shelby's mouth rose.

"No reason." At her opened mouth, he lifted a hand. "Seriously. There is zero reason for me to be around her."

"But she's so nice," Sara protested. "You guys would be perfect together."

"Not gonna happen," he quipped. "Therefore, end of story."

Garrison pushed to his feet and lifted Zach to place ornaments at the top of the tree. "I agree. The less interaction with anyone in the Brand family, the better."

Kerr turned his hand palm up. "See? The voice of reason. Case closed. "No way would he let anyone in this room know about his harebrained midnight rendezvous and lip-lock session, either. Or his plan to go back to the store and make sure she was okay.

"Only it's not closed, is it?" Shelby squinted at him.

"Put the shovel down, sis. There's nothing to dig for here."

"Don't have to dig." She paused. "I wonder if we can help her with those nasty brothers."

"You first," Kerr tried to sell the nonchalance. "I don't want any interactions with those missing links."

Oh, but he did, not that he'd cop to that plan. He would interview Izzy and obtain more information about what was going on at the Brand ranch. He would complete the mission to get intelligence, because those folks were brewing up something. Something that might hurt his family. Something that could hurt Izzy. Maybe there was even a connection to that creature. By God, he'd figure it all out.

"So, do you want to try for a future with her?" Shelby asked.

"You're like a Hatfield playing messed up matchmaker with a McCoy. To clarify, that would be a big ol' nope on any possible future." And that was God's honest truth. It didn't matter how he felt; nothing could come of a relationship between Izzy and him. At least not with the bad blood between their families.

Eric clasped her hand as he looked up at Kerr. "Sometimes you have to take the risk. Put yourself out there."

"Okay, against-all-odds inspirational couple of the year, easy for you to say. You two are like the living embodiment of a sappy movie, minus the obligatory canoe ride and ridiculous handwritten letters. This is a little different situation."

Shelby's eyes narrowed. "You seem to know a lot about sappy romances."

He patted his leg. "Lots of free time a while back. Don't judge. Several of those movies helped me recover from my skin graft surgeries." He batted his eyes. "Those heroes. So dreamy."

With a sigh, Shelby said, "So. You like her?"

"Irrelevant." He concentrated hard, blanking his mind. Anything to keep his nosy twin from rooting around in his head, pulling a hound-dog act, and sniffing out his true emotions. Or his plans.

"Disagree." She pursed her lips and drew in a solid lungful of air. Oh, shit. She was gearing up to give advice. "You'll never know if you don't put yourself out there," she said.

"Really? Do you really think I need that lesson?" He lifted his leg and let it *clomp* on the hardwood floor. "I am a sixth degree black belt in taking risks. See where it got me?" He prayed the amputated leg shtick would be the conversation stopper he needed.

Eric didn't meet his eyes. "Man, I—"

Kerr's hand chop through the air cut off his friend's words. "I'm not blaming anyone, dude." He hated how his squad teammate still carried guilt about that terrible day outside of Jalalabad. Hey, shit happened.

"But—" Shelby sputtered.

Kerr lifted a hand. "Look, even if this bizarre cross-valley rivalry weren't happening, the situation is so clear that a blind man could see it: I don't fit with someone like Izzy. Not with anyone." He ignored

Sara's open-mouthed stare from the other side of the room. "Not the way that I am, inside and out. And that's cool.." Before anyone could interrupt his pity party with more bad advice, he glanced at his watch. Four thirty p.m. He'd give his siblings the beta on that creature after dinner, then head to the hardware store. "Besides, I believe dinner's almost ready."

"Really?" Zach whipped around, eyes wide. He licked his lips. "Let's go!"

CHAPTER 8

*A*t seven p.m. it was full dark when Izzy flipped off the store's
lights and locked the back door. Zipping her worn coat to
her chin and shoving on her gloves, she flinched as the frigid air sliced
right through the materials. She might have grown up here, but when
the air hurt to inhale, no amount of "Wyoming tough" made breathing
in shards of ice any easier. She'd had about as much as a gal could
take.

From the shadowed alley behind the store, a voice reached her.
"Why are you still here?"

She jumped at the grinding voice that scraped like a coarse metal
file over her ears. Linc. His spectral-pale face surfaced out of the
darkness near the dumpster. Her skin crawled.

Soon. She just had to stiffen her spine, help the Taggarts get clear
of her family members, and then she could leave for good.

Crossing her arms, she glared at his face that was shadowed by the
wimpy alley lights. "Why are you here? Shouldn't you be out beating
up inanimate objects? Or doing sit-ups or something?"

"Took the week off after the fight," he mumbled.

The fight he had lost, thanks to Vaughn Taggart. Linc probably deserved the butt kicking. "So then...what? You're bored and decided to hang out in cold at the back of the store?"

"No. Making sure you're legit. With wanting to help my family." Ah, yes. Linc, the third stooge of the trifecta hanging out at Crazy Ranch.

"'Legit'? What are you, a teenage gangster? Also, it's *my* family more than yours, cousin. Don't you have a home base back in Cheyenne? You should return there."

The nasty growl shuffled her backward in the ice-rimed snow. Okay, that comment pushed him too hard. Duly noted.

He crossed his thick arms over a barrel chest. "We need to know that you're on our side. The correct side."

Squelching the retort, she stuck with bland and safe statements. "Of course I am. That's what I already told Wyatt this morning."

He leaned in. His block-toothed smile turned into a feral snarl. "We need to know for sure."

Izzy crossed her own arms, like doing so might buffer her from the hulking MMA fighter. "And you need to invade my personal space to figure this out? Step back, Linc, you smell bad." She peeked around him. Quiet alley. Empty. What she'd give for her nice brother, Tommy, to stop by and help. Although, the way the guys were acting, she might not be able to count on him. She looked around one more time. Alone. The only tool at her disposal tonight was bravado.

A finger of sulfur whipped around her, warming the air and tainting it at the same time. Linc's blue eyes turned a dull, ember-like red.

Okay, seriously? His weird eyes looked like a special effect in a horror movie. The goose bumps on her arms had nothing to do with the cold weather. Something was horribly wrong here.

"Do not trifle with us." His fingers gripped his jacketed upper arms, the knuckles turning white. Spittle formed at the corner of his mouth.

Us? The skin on the back of her neck twitched, like a hand hovered above it. "Wouldn't think of it."

He stared at her and licked his lips. "Prove it." He uncrossed his arms.

Whoa. Rocking back on her heels, she exhaled a puff of frozen air as her spine bumped against the brick wall. "Pardon?"

"Provide information about the Taggarts that we can use. And I'll pass it along. It'll help us decide whether to let you in on our little secret. If you're nice, I'll help you personally. If you know what I mean."

Her blood flashed hot then cold as her stomach went into a tailspin. "Uh, no, I don't know what you mean, *cousin.*"

She pretended to drop her keys in the snow to buy a few seconds. *Think.* Somehow she had to keep him at arm's length but not piss him off. All while getting the necessary information. Simple enough.

She stood and shoved the keys into a pocket. "Fine. I'll meet you all back at the ranch in a few hours with new dirt." What new information? She had nothing. Literally nothing.

His hands dangling loose and dangerous at his side, he stepped a foot closer. "How are you getting it?"

The cold air sawed through her throat. *Keep him talking. Make a plan to get away.*

Going for flippant and familiar, she quipped, "Don't question my methods. Just sit back and appreciate the results. Cousin," she tacked on as he leaned in far too close for familial relations. Maybe he'd get the hint. She peered at his leering mug. Nope, the hint didn't register with Linc. Gross.

Despite the frigid temperatures, sweat rolled between her breasts.

She was literally backed against a frigid wall in an empty alley in Nowhere, Wyoming, with a half-baked cousin who didn't let a little thing like consanguinity get in the way of making a move on a potential partner.

Izzy was screwed.

All this because she had some dumb idea that she might help the Taggarts. Why? Because she had a stupid idea that in doing so, she might have a snowball's chance with Kerr one day.

Well, that sort of thinking took a special kind of stupid.

Screw ingratiating herself to her own family. Screw getting information for the Taggarts. She wanted to get out of town. Every woman for herself. She should have come to that conclusion at the humiliation-fest in the store earlier today. Better late than never.

"What about some help?" He was too close. Far too close.

A virtual bubble burst, sending prickles through her body. Her heart beat out of her chest. "Seriously? Go. We're done talking." A too-casual flick of her wrist punctuated her words. Hopefully he wouldn't react and pull a sick MMA move on her.

Another red flicker in his eyes. "You can't fail."

"Or what? I can't be in your club? Good night. See you later." She pushed against him, her hands becoming oddly itchy all of a sudden.

Only, Linc didn't move. A grunt, and he thudded a meaty fist against the brick as he leaned in.

Then her cousin laid a hand on her.

The walk from the nearby Laundromat to the back door of the Copper River Supply was like approaching a horrible highway accident. Kerr was pretty sure he wouldn't like anything he found at the hardware store. Not that he expected confetti and kisses.

But beyond the garden-variety dread, something else was wrong.

The muscles between his shoulder blades twitched. Nothing felt right as the flurries struggled to fall in the still, quiet evening. He hunched into his duster and flipped up the collar. Man, it was colder than a polar bear's ass on an iceberg tonight.

At the sound of low voices up ahead he slowed his ice-crunching steps and winced as he activated his ability. The pain was worth the tactical advantage.

The sounds of a few cars puffing down Main Street on the far side of the building echoed between the brick wall of the hardware store next to him and the high wooden fence across the alley. Shadows floated in odd places, like someone slinking around, visible only out of the corner of his eye. But when he squinted, his eyes blurred by the use of his invisibility power, he saw no one.

Reality or PTSD?

Damn his brain.

The scent of burnt eggs irritated his nose.

Nothing good came with that smell.

Before he could track the scent, he slunk around the dumpster and had to blink his filmed eyes to make sure he was seeing correctly. Even six feet away, Izzy's wide-eyed expression hit him like a jab to his gut. Against the dull gray ground around them and the harsh light over the back door of the store, her bright blue eyes glinted, tiny beacons of color in a blurry, dark world. Linc loomed a few inches from her, his tight posture radiating nothing but trouble.

"Get back." Her voice came through muffled, but he still picked up the undercurrent of determination. And fear.

"You going to make me?" the jerk said with a chuckle that tempted Kerr to put his fist through the guy's head.

Her reply came out as a gurgle.

Dammit. Although he dearly wanted to, no way could Kerr run over, half-cocked, or the guy would pulverize him. He sidled back behind the dumpster and dropped the fade, staggering and blinking as his vision cleared and the headache ebbed.

The pitch of Izzy's voice went up an octave and tightened.

Kerr needed to hurry. Rifle on the gun rack back in the truck? No. Would take too long to run back and get it.

A chuckle, thick and malevolent, reached his burning ears.

Kerr searched the debris between the dumpster and the alley. Broken pallets lay crumpled in a pile. Selecting a sturdy-looking piece of wood, he pulled it away from the pallet frame with a crisp crack.

"What was that?" Linc shouted. Crunches of heavy footsteps on frozen snow grew louder.

Kerr faded. His fuzzy vision couldn't see the details of Linc's ugly mug. A bonus in this case.

Taking a few slow, careful steps to get in position, Kerr raised the piece of wood.

Linc peeked in the dumpster. Looked down the alleyway. Scratched his head like a monkey doing a math problem.

Kerr glanced up at Izzy. She'd frozen in place next to the brick wall, pulling in deep, gasping breaths. Any question about the ethics of his decision went out the window when Kerr spied red marks on her neck. Dark, Linc-finger sized marks.

Kerr ignored the splinters digging into his palms as he gripped the piece of wood, and let the beefy genius pass by.

Was this cheating? Using his power to gain an advantage?

Izzy knelt down in the snow, coughing.

Who cared about Geneva Convention. That bastard had hurt Izzy.

He braced one foot behind the other, pivoted, and swung the wood against Linc's head. The guy dropped like a lead weight.

He dropped the fade at the same time he dropped the piece of wood.

Izzy stared up at him from where she knelt on the ground. "What did you do?" Her voice came out thin as she wheezed. "Where did you come from? What are you doing here?"

"Which question did you want me to answer first?" He closed the distance between them, cupped her elbow, and helped her to stand.

"Like your disappearing act the other night, huh?" She sagged against the building. The coughs ripped from her throat. The sound scourged him. "Oh man, he was going to…"

Even in the shadows, the wide, blank expression told the rest of her story.

"So, what's the deal?" he blurted. No preamble. *Smooth, buddy. Smooth.*

She bit her lip. That tiny act made the muscles in his stomach clench. This woman had control of him and she didn't even know it. "Should we, you know, call someone about him? He is my cousin and all."

He shook his head. "Wait. Now you want to help him?"

"Even jackasses don't deserve to die of hypothermia."

"Not so sure about that, Iz. But if you want me to get help on the way, I'll do it." He punched in three numbers on his phone and spoke to the dispatcher while she bent and checked on Linc. Ending the call, he turned back to her. "They'll be here in fifteen minutes."

"So, um. Looks like he's just out cold." Standing, she swallowed and grimaced. "Thanks."

"Iz. Can I get you away from here or something?"

"Away?" When her eyes locked onto his, stupid shit like sunshine and fairies danced in his stomach.

"Surely you don't want to stay in this situation."

Her jaw dropped. Then she closed her mouth and pressed her lips into a line. "One more night. I need to find out what Wyatt and the guys are doing."

"Why would you want to do that?"

She reared back like he'd slapped her. "No offense, but number one, they still are family, crappy as that fact is. And two, I had planned to find out more regarding their plans."

"Why?"

She planted two hands on her hips, emphasizing the form-fitting denim. "To help you all out, you numbskull."

So slow, his thoughts, as he tried to process what she told him. "Wait. You're doing all of this…for us?"

"Well, no. Not the fending-off-advances-from-my-cousin part. That's plain gross." With a wince, she trailed her fingers over the skin of her neck. "But if I figure out what the hell their plan is, maybe your family can stop them."

"And then you will…?"

"Be gone from this dump." Another heaving sigh got his attention. As did the groan from the big guy on the ground. Good. At least the bastard was breathing.

"You're leaving, Iz?" *No, you can't.* Because. Because…

"Can't stay around these idiots."

"There are other places to go in town." Why shouldn't she leave?

He had no good answer to that question.

"You don't get it. I'm done with all of it, Kerr. Finished."

"So as your last act, you'll put yourself in danger, all to help my family? I still don't get it."

"I don't strike you as the altruistic type?"

"No, because that's a scary mission. And you usually have a better head for danger."

She blinked. "Wyatt, Tommy, and Linc are acting so strange. I wanted to gain their trust to find out more, so…" The shuddering breath she took shook him to the core. "I'm so sorry about earlier in the store. I completely sold you out." Her eyes shimmered.

Real tears or fake? He rested a hand on her shoulder.

The tremors vibrating through her frame? Real.

"So what's the deal?" Pretty sure he didn't want the answer.

"I'm going to find out more. Tonight. But I need some help."

"O. Kay?"

"To prove that I'm trustworthy, I have to provide inside information about the Taggarts."

He pulled his head back. "So you want me to give you information that makes my family vulnerable to attack? Then you'll pass this information along to your brothers and cousin...who want to destroy my family?" Sirens began to filter through the air toward them. "And somehow this is going to help us?"

She chewed her lip. "Sounds bad when you say it that way."

"How the hell else should I say it?" He let go of her shoulder and rolled a hand into a fist, resting it on the wall. "You know what? This was a mistake. Maybe Garrison was right. I don't need to get mixed up with you and your crazy family."

"But I'm trying to help."

"See, now, you lost me there, back where you wanted a secret Taggart ingredient to sprinkle in the recipe of your nut-job family members."

"Kerr," she breathed.

No. *Do not cave.* Do not look at the quivering lower lip that would taste so good. Like pillowy soft wildness and joy all rolled up together.

Focus, dammit.

She took her gloves off and stuffed them in her pockets, then sniffed, her pert nose red as she rubbed it along with her cheeks and forehead. "I'm on your side. Or rather, I'm on the side of not-crazy. And for your information, yes, I'm sticking around this joint long enough to help you all out. Because I can't take the insanity any more. I'll be damned if good people get hurt when I can do something about it." She pressed her lips into a tight line, like doing so could hold her shit together.

Here he stood, two feet away from the woman he wanted with a hunger like he'd never experienced before. The same woman who had stood there while her brother had verbally eviscerated Kerr in the store. The woman whose family wanted his family dead.

The same woman whose shoulders slumped as she tried not to cry. Great.

Afghanistan all over again. Kerr knew a trap when he saw it.

But like in combat, he could never resist doing what was right. Hopefully, he wouldn't get fucked by this decision.

CHAPTER 9

Kerr pulled open his duster lapels and yanked Izzy into his chest. With a few tugs, he took off his gloves and stowed them in his coat pocket. Wrapping his arms around her narrow shoulders, he tried to resist the urge to surround her with every cell of his entire being. Where did that compulsion come from? Protecting someone from danger was Vaughn's ability, not his.

So the feeling of wanting to act as a wall between Izzy and anything that could hurt her? It had to be pure organic emotion. No power or weird ability influencing the feeling. Plain and simple, he needed to keep her safe. Needed to provide comfort.

Her mouth and chin tucked right in next to his neck. When she shifted and brushed her lips across the sensitive skin, he groaned. A stab of male interest begged him to drop the altruistic, hero crap, like, now, and go after what he'd wanted for so long.

It was too bad that by hanging out with him, Izzy was in even more danger from more than her nutty family members. That creature had a connection to the Brands. The same people who hated Kerr's family and wanted them gone. What about the creature? It wanted to destroy the Taggarts and anyone they held dear. Christ almighty.

Another layer of complexity? If Hank Brand's carcass somehow lived inside of that monster, then Izzy was somehow related to that creature. To destroy the creature, he might have to kill her brother.

Talk about a fucked up mess.

He let out a slow breath while she snuggled into his neck and chest. The simple action dropped his blood pressure but ramped up his pulse.

He still needed to pump her for information. But in a minute. For now, he'd enjoy the moment he'd fantasized about for years. Back at her house last night? That was a small taste. An appetizer, really.

He'd fantasized about way more than this simple act, but holding her in his arms in sub-zero weather made for a good start.

The exact moment when she sighed and her soft curves melted into his body was pure perfection.

And when her lips brushed over his neck a second time? He froze, torn. He wanted her to do it again. Needed to know that the feather-soft touch wasn't an accident.

Needed to know that she was okay if he returned the action.

Needed...more. He inhaled her lemon and orange scent. His mouth watered.

When her lips swept back over his neck once more, he groaned and pulled back, gazing down at her face. The moment her eyes opened was like watching dawn break after a long night.

Inches. Her mouth was only inches from his.

"Iz," he breathed.

"Hold me." She rubbed her damp cheek on his flannel shirt. "Please."

He slid a hand up and tilted her jaw. Her face glowed, even in the shadows.

Lowering his head, he paused, a millimeter from what he'd wanted. Last night was a dress rehearsal, a hasty pressing of lips, only skimming the surface of what was possible.

"Can I—?" he stammered. For God's sake, the woman had been threatened by her cousin mere minutes ago. Kerr couldn't take advantage of her. "I want—But not if—"

"You talk too much," she said, rolling her lips together.

With a harsh sigh, he thumbed the brim of his hat up and brushed his mouth over hers.

She tasted like life and fresh air and hope. Sweetest thing he'd ever experienced. That mouthwatering scent of hers surrounded him. With a tilt of his head, he changed the angle, and she responded, arching into him and wrapping her arms around his neck.

Like he was king of the entire world.

On and on the kiss went, each new angle an amazing discovery. Her light, citrus essence worked itself into the cells of his body. Every taste of her mouth quenched his parched soul, made him want so much more.

He should care about Linc, lying in the snow. A random groan reached Kerr's ears. Good enough for now. Sirens growing louder assured him that the ambulance should be here in a few more minutes.

When she tightened her fingers in the hair at the nape of his neck? Wow. Screw crazy family feuds and bad blood.

He had come here to check on her, but all he'd discovered was his own blind spot when it came to Izzy. Now she wanted to leave town. Couldn't blame her.

But now he wanted to convince her to change those plans.

She sighed again.

Anticipation, like the split second before his first parachute jump, shot through his chest. Pressing her flush against the building wall, he leaned into her, molding her torso to his. Perfect fit. The curves of her hips? Perfect, cradled against his. Despite the layers of clothes, the sensation of her full breasts pressed against him made his mouth go dry.

Defenses down, his universe narrowed to the surface area where his body came into contact with hers. The way their breaths mingled. The softness of her skin beneath his. He needed to wrap this woman in his arms and protect her from anything that dared threaten her. Nothing else mattered.

Slipping his tongue along the seam of her lips, he shuddered when she opened to him, and he explored even more. Their groans blended as she wriggled against him. Damn, the rocking of her pelvis against his should be illegal. Even with layers of clothing, she made him hard as a two-by-four.

The air around them warmed.

Everything that mattered right now existed within the space of a few inches where their mouths and bodies met. The shush of fabric, the glide of his tongue over hers. The sighs and deep groans. The *scritch* of her coat fabric against the brick wall. The sweet sting of her hands clenching on his neck.

Bliss.

He shrugged off a painful pinch on his shoulder.

But the kidney punch that staggered him hard into Izzy, knocking the breath out of them both as his teeth scraped against her lips?

Spinning around, he put the pieces of reality together. Keeping Izzy behind him, Kerr stared into Linc's wild, bloodshot eyes. Kerr blinked the cobwebs out of his lust-fogged brain and focused on the asshole in front of him. Talk about pulling the parking brake while going seventy on the interstate.

Linc ran his meaty hand over his sandy buzz-cut and stretched his neck. Deep bone pops sounded like gunfire in the distance. How had the dude woken up? Kerr had clocked him with a solid piece of wood. It wasn't a love tap, either.

"Get the fuck away from her, Taggart." The guy winked. Like a beacon, indicating the perfect place for Kerr to punch.

Kerr's hand curled into a fist. "I believe that is my line."

The fighter rubbed the back of his jug head. "Where'd you come from, anyway?"

"Right behind you. Didn't you notice? Maybe you're losing your skills."

The indrawn gasp behind him fired up something primal inside of Kerr. Something he'd never experienced before, not at this level. Not only did he want to get her away from here, he wanted to keep this jerk from coming close to her permanently. And how fucked up was it that he needed to protect her in the first place? For chrissakes, the man was part of her family.

Izzy shifted with a scratch of fabric on brick.

"He hasn't done anything wrong," she said over Kerr's shoulder. "Go away."

Linc snorted and shook his head. Then he pointed a meaty finger. "Good job, cousin. Keeping him here until we could arrive."

Kerr's spine snapped tight. His head swam. The strangled squeak behind him barely registered.

Pieces of logic cracked into shards. No way. A trap? Had the guy faked the head injury and fall? Had she faked...?

A trap.

Air escaped his lungs, leaving him empty. Dizzy.

Linc threw a thumbs up sign and another wink.

She'd set him up? Holy fuck.

Linc grinned and puffed out his big chest. Then the fucker flexed—actually flexed—with muscles bunching up along his bull neck and chest. This was the guy who almost killed Vaughn in a recent bout. Vaughn, the scariest and hardest guy Kerr had ever known.

Also, chances were good that Linc remembered the beatdown Kerr and Garrison applied last week when Linc had helped hunt down Mariah. Chances were excellent that Linc wasn't a forgive-and-forget kind of guy. Talk about a shit sandwich. Kerr's stomach muscles tensed.

Payback was going to be a bitch.

Kerr swallowed hard. "We're two consenting adults here, dude. Move along." He'd deal with her betrayal later. Right now, he wanted to get Izzy away from this sucking whirlpool to hell. Then Kerr needed to make himself scarce.

Linc smacked his fisted hand into the cup of his palm and set his feet shoulder width apart. His eyes flashed a brief, lurid red glow. "I have good news for you. I'm a consenting adult as well, Taggart."

CHAPTER 10

One minute Izzy rode the thrilling rollercoaster of passion, immersed in the excitement of everything Kerr. His solid embrace shut out the world around her. The intense gleam in his gaze when he looked at her turned her knees to Jell-O.

The next minute, the coaster car jumped the tracks and crashed.

Still reeling from those world-tilting kisses, Izzy struggled to concentrate on what her stupid cousin said. His wild, red stare made her heart kick against ribs, knocking the breath out of her. So wrong. She needed to get Kerr out of here, and fast. Damn it, but her hands were driving her nuts with the itching. Later. She'd deal with it later.

Sliding out from behind Kerr, she snapped, "First of all, Linc, you were being a jerk and are lucky I didn't call the cops on you." She ignored his snort and shrug. "And second, it's not your business, but Kerr and I were talking," she said. Sure. If by talking she meant kissing the other person to where neither party could breathe. Then yes, talking.

Damn it. So much for swooning in a handsome man's arms. She inhaled the cedar and sage scent of Kerr's that made her insides quiver. No more of that, either. *Thanks a crap load for dumping ice water on my dream moment, cousin.*

So close but yet so far away from a normal relationship with a normal guy.

Linc shifted his weight from leg to leg. "Looked like a pretty intense conversation to me."

What she'd give to smack the leer off his face.

She flicked her hand. "Go on now. There's nothing that you need to discuss out here. Ambulance is coming. Let them look you over." Speaking of which, what the heck was taking the crew so long? Were they going through the drive-thru before showing up at their call?

"I don't need an ambulance. And you're right, we have plenty to discuss," Linc said. "How about how Taggart here is ruining my cousin's reputation? Wyatt's going to be very interested in what's going on here."

"The hell—" she sputtered. "Hello, twenty-first century? Besides, and I repeat myself, it's not your business."

Linc sneered, "It's my business if someone's turning you into a whore."

"What?" Her jaw dropped.

"Insults are uncalled for. Quit it," Kerr bit out.

"She's too good for you, Taggart."

The Stetson bobbed next to her. "I won't argue there, pal. But I'd add that Iz is too good for most guys. Deserves better than how you have been treating her."

On the one hand, she appreciated him standing up for her.

On the other hand, had she lost so much spine that she couldn't do it herself?

And did Kerr actually laugh? With an angry and unhinged MMA fighter a few steps away from him—a dry fuse begging for a lit match?

"Why don't you move on," Kerr said.

Linc's eyes narrowed. "Like hell I'm going anywhere."

Grasping at straws, Izzy said, "Hey, Linc. Remember what we talked about a little while ago? I can't do my job if you're out here, interfering."

Kerr's head whipped toward her. "What?"

"The information she was going to get for us about your family,

Taggart." Linc snorted. "Don't need it now, but thanks, cuz. I'll get the information my way." He took a half step forward.

Kerr eased over to block her again with his tall frame. The action was the equivalent of waving a red flag in front of that bullheaded ass. Oh, God.

As she ducked under his arm to stand next to him once again, the insanity of the situation hit her like a ballpeen hammer. Kerr snaked an arm around her shoulder. Support she didn't realize she craved.

The pop of muscle in his jaw told her that the support only went so far. Kerr thought she'd sold him out twice now.

"You still want to have that talk, Linc?" Kerr asked, the cords in his arm around Izzy went tight, ready.

"Not any more," her cousin said. "Let's skip to the part where I teach you a lesson."

"Well," Kerr gritted out. "This is kind of going to suck. For you."

Was he nuts?

Why didn't he disappear and run away? If Izzy had that power, she'd damn well be using it right about now. But she kept her mouth shut. She might be a patsy for her sick family members, but no way would she rat out Kerr's secret.

Linc's bark of a laugh wasn't a pleasant sound. "Fuck you."

"That's it. I'm getting help," Izzy said, pointing toward Main Street. Lights from vehicles threw brightness into where they stood. The ambulance would turn a corner and head up the alley. Another minute, and there would be too many witnesses. That was good, right?

She peered up at the determined set of Kerr's jaw. And the wink and lift to the corner of his mouth? He wasn't waiting on witnesses. He removed his arm from around her, and let his hands hang, loose but ready, in front of him.

Linc's punch whooshed high and—missed. When Kerr ducked, the fighter's knuckles impacted the brick in a bone-crunching smack. Her cousin howled and cradled his bloody hand as he staggered backward.

Then Linc shook his hand and fixed his beady pig-eyes on Kerr, stalking a half-circle in front of him. And back again. The smirk never left his ugly face.

Sweat popped out on her forehead.

Two jabs met air, but the third one slammed into Kerr's jaw, whipping his head back. His hat went flying. With a grunt, he backed against the wall, his eyes glazed.

Hatred twisted Linc's face as he leered at her with that reddish glow in his eyes. A whiff of sulfur made her want to sneeze.

Evil. Pure evil. Her hands tingled. She wanted to run.

But no way was she leaving Kerr in this mess.

Linc backed up a few feet and rolled his neck muscles.

Then charged.

"Stop it!" Izzy jumped in front of the meathead, waving her arms, trying anything to make him stop.

Didn't work out like she'd hoped.

Kerr's curse behind her preceded the snap to her cheek, and she flew into the brick wall and slid until she lay on the snowy dirt and gravel-covered ground. Stars burst in her vision and rained down over the scene in front of her.

The burning in her face? Never felt anything that awful before. Hoped to never experience this much pain again.

She lay on dirty, frozen slush. Rotated her head so the injury nestled deeper into the snow. At least the cold numbed the throbbing area. Freaking win.

She struggled to breathe.

Her sideways view of Kerr and Linc as she rested on the ground went fuzzy.

Fists and grunts.

Then Kerr doubled over.

He heaved back to a standing position and stepped away from the wall, walking into the blur of Linc's uppercuts and producing punches of his own. Linc staggered back a step.

Loud sirens and lights blended and banged around in her throbbing head.

Linc threw out a leg and tripped Kerr. With a grunt, Kerr pushed up to all fours. Another sweep took his propped arms out from under him.

Then, like a professional punter, Linc angled his hips, leg

extended, and blasted a booted kick into Kerr's side, lifting him and heaving him two feet away with a crunch that turned her stomach. Another series of punches to his head turned his face red. Blood burst from Kerr's nose.

"Yeah," Linc swaggered to stand over Kerr. "Like shooting fish in a barrel with a guy like this." He stomped on his hat, grinding it into the gravel and snow.

Clawing to her hands and knees, she used the wall to work herself into an upright position. Or as close to it as her spinning head would allow. Through her aching jaw, she screamed for all she was worth, "I said quit it!"

Linc stopped and stared at her.

Kerr pinned her with a terrible golden-brown stare, blood dripping from his nose. He pushed back up to his feet, then winced.

And winked out of existence.

She blinked.

Thank God.

The ambulance pulled up, spraying pieces of ice and gravel. Took them long enough.

"Damn you, Izzy," Linc muttered. "Coward ran away."

Coward? That brave guy had stood up to a big bully.

Izzy had had enough.

Enough of being used.

Enough of everything.

Ears buzzing, she shook the stars out of her vision and staggered a few steps. Near the building, two bright red drops of blood stippled a packed clump of snow. She whipped her head around, whimpering as pain shot through her neck.

Rubbing her eyes, she tried to focus, but there was a distortion right next to her. In front of the building. A faint aroma of sage.

Then behind her, Linc chuckled like the self-satisfied pig he was.

Her control broke.

The effort to hold his head together all but blinded Kerr.

But he had to remain still.

Couldn't yell or moan. Couldn't let out the rattling breath that was all the air remaining in his battered lungs. Couldn't make a sound.

Or else he'd be dead.

The veil that filmed his vision made it hard to see Izzy well. The effort to stay hidden combined with his aching midsection turned his gut into an unbalanced washing machine on the spin cycle.

His ears buzzed at the image of her curled up on the snowy ground. His hands rolled into fists again.

Her own cousin had done that to her. If Kerr hadn't arrived, Linc might have done worse.

But Izzy had sold Kerr out. Again. What the hell? God, he was the most gullible dude to walk this Earth.

Even knowing what had happened, Kerr didn't want to yell at Izzy. No. If he had another chance to beat the shit out of that animal, Linc, he'd gladly do it. But reality dictated a different route. Time to use his brains. Save the brute force, Neanderthal, fist-pounding action for big brother Vaughn.

Speaking of evolutionary throwback, that idiot who'd tried to serve him his ass? Wandering around and scratching his head like a real-life imbecile.

Good.

Kerr suppressed a painful whistle as he slowly let the air escape his lungs. The movement caused a nasty crunch, and a virtual icepick lodged in his side. That goddamned poodle fucker had cracked his ribs.

Remaining pressed tight to the building, Kerr winced as another wave of his power stabbed him through the temple. Damn it, he had to hold onto the fading effect. If he reappeared, not only would he get his ass kicked into the Happy New Year, but he'd reveal his secret power to the Brand family liaison as well as all of Sublette County's second-string EMS crew.

Enough town rumors swirled about the Taggarts without adding creepy supernatural powers to the mix.

How about those chances with Izzy now?

His demonstration in collapsing like wicker chair holding up an elephant would seal the deal on a future with her, followed closely by the harsh fact that she had used him.

Damn it. For a second, he had thought…maybe. Wow, those lips, her flashing eyes, those hips, the tiny sounds she made when they kissed.

He had thought for a second that they might have had a chance for something amazing.

Now?

Christ almighty, he wanted to hate her. Wanted to place blame for her part in the beatdown. Wanted to walk away and never look back.

That's what he should do.

Now she struggled to stand up. How badly had she been hurt? Maybe she was acting.

Because he had sure walked right into a damned trap.

Instead of artillery shells exploding and building beams falling, this time he'd been trapped by a sweet mouth and body that blinded him to the truth.

God*damn* it.

The veil wavered. Izzy came closer. So close that he could see the bluish purple swelling on her cheek. He curled his sore fists into balls again. *No. Wait.* He had to concentrate and stay hidden.

If Linc got his hands on him again, Kerr would require even more artificial limbs.

Muffled by his power, the sound reaching him came through indistinctly, like someone talking behind a thick curtain. However, the intent behind Izzy's pissed off, nonstop tirade wasn't indistinct. She stood mere inches away from her cousin as she screamed at him.

Holy blazing temper, Batman.

Even Linc shrank away. Smartest decision that moron had made all night.

As of right now, here in the back alley behind the hardware store of his family's enemy, even as he fought against the urge to sniff back the blood dripping from his busted nose, Kerr was done being trapped by his body, done being trapped by events out of his control.

Done being trapped by a pretty face.

As the EMS team separated Linc and Izzy and helped her to the back of the ambulance, Kerr tiptoed away, down the alley. Once he reached his truck, he bit the inside of his cheek to keep quiet against an agonized moan as he dropped the invisibility power. The action mimicked an embedded icepick sliding slowly out of his head. He sagged against the vehicle, the heaves of air making his ribs scream.

There wasn't enough Excedrin to fix this migraine.

Note to self: *This is why you try not to use this particular power.*

Second note to self: *Don't pick a fight with a dude who has beat people into the ICU with his bare hands.*

Third note to self: *For optimal health, steer clear of Izzy Brand.*

CHAPTER 11

*V*aughn's jaw dropped open as Kerr dragged his sorry ass down to the kitchen late the next morning and slumped in the chair, wincing as the movement jarred aching, creaking ribs.

"What the fuck happened to you?"

Kerr grunted and dropped his forehead onto the table and rubbed his bare head. Damn it, he had liked that hat.

His brother said nothing as he filled a plastic bag with ice and handed it to Kerr. Really, he should pack his entire body in ice, with all the bruises it held. Should have done it last night, but he was too exhausted to do anything more than limp up to bed. He motioned for Vaughn to load up another bag for his throbbing temples, the aftermath of using his invisibility power so much.

"Thanks, man," Kerr said.

A shrug from Vaughn. It was enough.

Big brother shook his head and whistled low. He snagged an apple from the basket before pulling a chair out from the table and spinning it around. Straddling the seat, he rested his thick forearms on the back of the chair.

"Talk."

"Not much to say."

"Ah. I don't believe you." Vaughn bit into the apple with a crack and chewed. "Tell me this: did you at least look good while you got your ass kicked?"

"Went down in a miserable blaze of glory."

"Strong work." His dark eyes narrowed until only a few gold glints remained. "Was it over a woman? Because that might almost make it worthwhile."

Kerr tried clamping his jaw shut, but quit when it hurt too damn much. He settled for counting the tiles on the floor.

Vaughn took another bite and smiled. "Well, isn't that interesting?"

What he wouldn't give to rip that annoying fruit out of his brother's grip, but that would take more energy than Kerr had. Also, moving hurt too much. So did breathing. "What are you, clairvoyant?"

"Only for danger. And little brother, if a woman is involved with this situation," he waved his hand at Kerr's battered body, "then you are in more danger than you know."

"It's actually worse than that."

"Do tell."

"The woman?" He blew out a creaking lungful of air. "Izzy Brand."

"The fuck you say." Vaughn paused, stared at the apple, then back to Kerr. "Did she beat you up? Because I wouldn't advertise that shit."

"No, bro. Way more complicated than that."

"Hold on, boys." Shelby clomped into the kitchen on crutches and her walking boot. She paused and peered at Kerr with unfocused eyes, then winced. He was busted. "I thought something was going on." She tapped her forehead, then studied him for several more seconds. "Well, I can tell that this story is going to be good. Might need some popcorn."

Vaughn snorted and got up to pull out a chair for her, propping her crutches against the table and ducking away when she scowled at him.

"Don't let me interrupt," she said, leaning her elbows on the table and resting her chin on her hands. Kerr didn't buy the innocent pose for a bare second.

"Where's Garrison?" he asked.

"Left early this morning to spend the day in town with Sara." Vaughn shrugged and sat again. "He's whipped."

Shelby raised an eyebrow. "You're one to talk, mooning after Doc West."

"Hey, I'm still healing from my fight. I need closely monitored medical care." He rotated the apple and took another chunk out of it.

She rolled her eyes. "I give up." Waggling her fingers at Kerr, she said, "Continue."

He shifted position but stopped at a stab of pain. "Went over to the store to check on Izzy last night. I got a feeling that she's doing poorly by that family. Boy, was I right. Linc joined us. It was not a happy reunion. I activated hide-and-seek mode. End of story."

"Nope. Nope. Sorry, but no." His sister pinched the bridge of her nose. "Way more going on there."

"I'm not getting into it," he growled. He and his siblings lived too much in each other's head as it was.

"Really? Like you think you can hold back from me?" Glaring, she straightened. "Fine. I'll do this the hard way."

"No!" Kerr and Vaughn both said.

She grinned. "Okay. If you don't want me to fry my brain, I believe it's sharing time for you."

Kerr leaned back with a groan. "So, Wyatt verbally handed me my ass yesterday morning at the hardware store. Something wasn't right in the way that Wyatt had treated Izzy in the store, and so I decided to go back there and check on her. I also wanted to find out more about what was going on at their ranch." He waved his hand in the general vicinity of the Brands' property.

"Which you knew anyway because you visited there a few nights ago on your own, right?" Vaughn muttered.

"What?" Shelby gasped. "You went over there?"

Kerr waved a bruised-knuckle hand. "Whatever. Ancient history. Anyway, I just know deep in my bones that creature is linked to the Brand ranch." And he had plans to return to the ranch for more in-depth analysis. He'd do it later, after his ribs healed.

"Agree." Vaughn's dark eyebrows lifted as a wave of malice

emanated from him. He set the apple core on the table and rested his fists on the wood surface.

Shelby cocked her head to the side and grimaced. "Quit it," she snapped at Vaughn. The blast of danger dissipated. "Go on."

Kerr tried to suck in a deep breath but failed when his crunching ribs screamed at him to stop. "The guys are cooking up something bad over there. Izzy suspects it, too. Last night, Linc assaulted Izzy behind the store. If I hadn't been there to stop it...shit."

"The fuck—?" his brother spat.

"Are you kidding me?" Shelby's pale face went paper white.

"Fuck that." With a shake, Vaughn stood and shifted into something that resembled a fighting stance, leaning forward, legs braced shoulder-width apart. He pawed at his neck with one hand, eyes darting around the room.

"What's wrong?" She rubbed her temples.

"Sorry for the emotional feedback, Shel." Straightening up, Vaughn ran a palm over his face. "I've felt like something's been coming for a while. Since that episode with the Brands kidnapping Mariah, my danger radar has been pinging like crazy."

"Yeah. I've gotten the strange feelings, too," she said. "But I figured that was due to general weirdness going around. Still doesn't explain why Kerr got beat up." She flashed a grin.

"I was getting to that part, thanks for staying on topic." He sucked a tooth that was thankfully still attached to his head. "When I went to check on Izzy, Linc was being a sick fuck. I stopped him with a two-by-four. Thought he was out cold. I was wrong. Then Linc handed me my ass."

His sister's eyes narrowed. "That's still not the whole story. What happened between knocking Linc out and him handing you your ass?"

"For one minute, just once, could you stay out of my head?" he groaned.

A Cheshire cat would be jealous of her slow smile. "I'm not in your head, doofus. Your whole face turns beet red when you talk about Izzy."

Kerr dropped his head on the table for a solid thirty seconds, then lifted it. "I give up. There's no privacy in this household."

With a lift of his jaw, Vaughn said, "You really like her?" He dropped into the chair again, arms resting on the spindled back. "Because that would be bad. She's a Brand."

"Okay, really? Is this fucked up Romeo and Juliet with rules and shit? No. It's a free country."

"Not if dating her means her idiot family could kill you."

"Point taken." He brushed a hand over his tender nose and winced. "But it doesn't matter."

"So how did you leave things?" Shelby asked.

"Bleeding, with my spleen ruptured."

Vaughn snorted. "Nice."

It hurt to laugh, so Kerr quit trying. "Thought there might have been something there between Izzy and me. Then her cousin tried to drop-kick me into next week. Then I realized that she had been in on it, luring me into a trap. Then I pulled a disappearing act." Playing with the bag of ice that rested on the table, he said, "Never thought Iz would set me up for Linc to attack."

Vaughn rubbed his chin like their father used to do when working through a problem. What Kerr would give for his old man to be here at the table, helping with this mess. Maybe one day, he'd do that again. "I'll say," big brother muttered.

His sister's mouth dropped open. "Wait. How do you know she had anything to do with it?"

"Uh, Linc said so."

Vaughn scowled. "And you believed that moron?"

"Um." Shit.

"How did she respond?" Shelby asked, eyes narrowing.

"How you'd expect? She denied it. Of course. What, you think she wasn't involved?"

"Maybe someone else. But Izzy? She and Sara are best friends. Izzy's solid. She wouldn't have led you into a trap," Shelby said.

A nasty sensation twisted his gut into a knot. Had he been wrong about her? Twice? "Well. Linc did hit her, too."

"Is she okay?" His sister's eyes bugged out.

"I think so."

"You didn't check?"

"Well, I was digging teeth out of the back of my head, so…"

"That's no excuse!"

Kerr had to take a breath so he didn't strangle his sister. "After I disappeared, she got up and yelled at her cousin. Then I left." He shoved a hand through his hair. "Shit. I assumed…"

Vaughn tightened his fingers around the chair rail. "You know what they say about assume. You make an ass out of—"

He cut his brother off with a swipe of a hand. "Thanks. Don't need the lecture. Already flunked the class. Here's the report card." He pointed to his busted nose.

"So, let's see if I have this straight." Shelby drummed her fingers on the table while Kerr's stomach dropped. "You like Izzy. And I bet if we checked into it, the feeling is mutual. Right?"

"Maybe."

"That's a yes." She held her hand up to stop him from rebutting anything. Even Vaughn had checked out of the lecture and spectated from a safe distance. No one challenged Shelby's assessments and lived to tell about it. "I'm going to assume you two have chemistry."

"Seriously—" Privacy? At all? Anything? No.

"Mmm hmm. That's also a yes." She blew an orange curl off her forehead and pinned him with the same gold and brown stare that he saw in his own mirror every morning. "And she's a nice person dealing with a shitty situation. Whose same situation might have gotten shittier because of your rendezvous, which puts her in more danger."

"Uh." Air moved in and out of his mouth, but no sound emerged.

"You know the answer to that question. Okay. The creature is likely on the Brand ranch or somehow linked to those guys. Izzy's relationship with her family members, which was already bad, just got a hundred times worse. And you still like her." She sniffed. "Have I missed anything?" Holding up her hand, her hard glare softened. "One more thing. On top of all that, you're still fighting your own personal demons, aren't you?"

Well. Shit.

The imperious lift of her jaw meant one thing: an unpopular conclusion was headed his way. Reminded him of Mom years ago, before she'd gotten sick with cancer. Someone else he wished could be helping out with this situation. "Seems like you have a choice, dude. Take a chance and step out on that limb. Or cling to your insecurities and let what might be the best thing in your future walk away."

"I hate you," he mumbled.

With a shake of his head, Vaughn said, "She did the same head-games mumbo-jumbo thing to me when I was being stupid about Mariah."

"It's a gift." She smiled. "So, what are you going to do about it?"

Kerr shoved back from the table and tried to ignore the painful reminder of his stupidity. "I'm going to do chores."

"Good idea. I'll help," Vaughn said.

"You guys are two ridiculous peas in a pod." Shelby pushed to stand and positioned her crutches under her arms. "I'll be working in the office if you want to go for another round."

After his sister had left the room, Vaughn grimaced. "She's a nightmare."

Kerr made the sign of a cross. "All I can say is that Eric? He's a saint."

CHAPTER 12

*A*fter a visit to the ER for x-rays of her face, a chat with the police, and an overnight stay with her friend Sara, Izzy was, well, not rested but at least more focused this afternoon.

Mom was safe at Butch's house.

Linc would hang out in jail until Monday, according to the officer.

No disasters had occurred overnight. To her knowledge.

So that would give Izzy enough time to pack her stuff and get out of Copper River.

She had nothing tying her to this place anymore. She paused and breathed through the twist in her chest. Nothing. Nope. Not after last night.

Altruism was one thing.

Hanging around after being rejected was another stupid move altogether. Actually, strike that. Kerr hadn't rejected her. During that bizarre situation behind the hardware store, there hadn't been time to go into the details regarding the backward way she was trying to help the Taggarts. At this point, though, not only was it water under the proverbial bridge, the bridge had collapsed.

So basically, the only energy she could put into helping the Taggarts would have to occur on her way out of town.

Rolling up in the minivan, she put the vehicle into park and stared at her home. Memories, some wonderful and some frankly awful, jumbled together. She remembered tagging along with her older brothers as they had worked in the barns. They fussed at her for not really helping, but they never made her leave. Her favorite brother, Tommy, made sure she was a part of their adventures, and he always stood up for her when Wyatt picked on her. Well, stood up for her in the past, at least.

The memory of the day Dad passed away made her choke. With the whole family, including then-healthy Mom, by his side, Dad had died, surrounded by a houseful of love. "My little girl I never deserved," he had said the day before. "I will always love you just the same." Izzy had asked what he meant, but by then, the pain meds had pulled him into a deep sleep.

As bittersweet and happy as those times had been, more recent events steeled her resolve to leave this place. She recalled the cruel twist of Tommy's mouth as he yelled at her only last week to stay out of his business.

Never would she forget how Wyatt spewed insults at Kerr. And Izzy had stood there and done nothing. That made her almost as bad as her brother.

Even though she knew Linc cooled his heels in jail, she still hesitated to enter the house alone.

Glancing up at the cloudy, heavy sky that cut out most of the light, she sighed. She had to concentrate to make her ribs expand so she could take a breath. Even the act of getting out of the van took far more energy than it should have.

The house was cold and dark as she trudged through the front door. No Christmas cheer in this place. An anemic smattering of holiday cards cluttered the scratched dining room tabletop. A few drooping decorations hung from the sooty mantel edge. The living room with the worn couch and chairs was deserted.

Christmas. Good grief, just over a week away. She was too tired to think about it.

A big sigh hitched in her chest.

Come on, now. Get going. But all she could do was lean against the back of the worn chintz couch. She rubbed the fabric, trying to collect enough energy to do anything. Something.

Every time she had returned home over the past month, it was like gravity had been turned up to double strength. Each step was a climb up Mount Everest. Right about now, she could barely lift her arms. The idea of packing was too much to think about. Maybe she would leave tomorrow.

A heavy tread down the hall got louder, every step amplifying the virtual lead balloon dropping to the bottom of her stomach.

"'Bout time you showed up," Wyatt said, stopping a foot in front of her. Hello? Personal space. How about asking what the hell happened to her? The guy looked right at her and apparently ignored the purple, swollen mouse on her cheekbone.

His silence spoke volumes.

So did his odor. She wrinkled her nose. While no one accused Wyatt of being a neat freak, his appearance had gone to hell over the past few months. Unruly hair stood up on end. He hadn't shaved in several days. And man, what animal corpse crawled up into his armpits?

"Well? Where were you?" he asked.

Screw this conversation before it even started. "Getting patched up at the hospital because our cousin was an ass. Or didn't Tommy tell you?" Her brother, the sheriff, would have the inside details on Linc's incarceration. With Tommy and Wyatt thick as thieves, stinky brother probably knew that Linc was behind bars.

For now.

"Tommy told me. And don't worry. *My* cousin Linc will be out soon," he chuckled.

Weird choice of words. Her hands started itching again. Damn it. "Says who?"

Another half step closer. Enough with the looming already. "I just know," he said.

The desire to argue drained away. She had nothing left in the tank and only enough fumes left to...well, leave. Not even that much. She sure as hell didn't have time for Carnac the Magnificent and his predictions of the future. "Look, Wyatt. I'm tired. Do you actually have something useful to say?" A wild, reddish flash in his eyes, and she backed up. Things were so, so wrong here. Her neck ached as if a hand squeezed around it. "You know that I've been doing extra work at the store and here at home, ever since Hank disappeared."

A flicker of calm morphed his wide-eyed expression from crazy mean to crazy placid. Not much of an improvement. "As is required in these times."

She crossed her arms, more to create some kind of buffer. And to rub her palms on the fabric to stop the itching. "Tell me again why we're not pursuing the missing persons report and investigation." She hadn't been particularly close to Hank, who was nine years older, but still. He was her brother, and he had disappeared. Why didn't anyone around here seem to care about that fact?

"Trust me. He's gone." *Trust* was the last word that came to mind when she free-associated Wyatt's name.

"How do you know? And don't tell me that 'you know things.' That's B.S."

Another blast of red heat glowed from his eyes, then he blinked back to normal. Well, normal for Wyatt's recent state. "I have knowledge that you wouldn't understand. But we should share it with you."

"The little buddy club you guys are in? I'm over it. Count me out." She tried her best to ignore how lumping Tommy into this group hurt.

His shoulders widened. How was that possible? Her skin prickled like a snake slithered over it. "This isn't about you, Izzy." His voice dropped an octave. A whiff of sulfur made her want to sneeze.

Ignoring the bizarre signals from her brother, she stood her ground. Because, enough was enough. "If it involves Mom's care and my life, you bet that your business involves me. Otherwise, you and Linc and Tommy are three weird peas in a pod, plotting and planning. What are you all doing, anyway?"

An eye twitched. "Can't tell you."

"Really?" she snapped. "I'm your damn sister. I'm the reason Mom's not in a nursing home. Hell, I might be the only reason she's alive. If you'd been the one looking after her, she'd have died of neglect by now. And I'm probably the reason your store is still open." She sucked in a breath. "Hypocrisy has a bitter taste, Wyatt. You don't want me involved, but you enjoy the help. Well, you can't have it both ways."

His brows pulled together as he did that getting-bigger trick again. Freaky. Had to be her mild concussion. "No." His voice had deepened. The rumble should have warned her off. "You will not get to know."

"Why?"

"Because you associate with the Taggart family."

"There's no link. You saw that already when I backed you up at the store with Kerr."

"You saw him again last night. So says Linc."

"Micromanage much?" She raked her hair back, like she wanted to keep her head from flying into orbit. "I was at the store and Linc committed at least two crimes during the encounter."

"What about your friend, that teacher? The traitor, falling in with Garrison Taggart."

"Sara? Seriously, Wyatt? She teaches second graders for a living. Like, gives out hugs and gold stars and brutal crap like that."

Like a big, shaggy dog, he shook his head. "We don't trust her. You spend time with her. You might tell her something that will get passed along to the Taggarts."

Making a circle with her finger near her temple, she said, "This paranoia is clinical, you know."

"No." He paused, eyes darting back and forth. "We can never be too careful. All must be in order."

"For what?"

"For the coming sol—"

"The what?"

"Nothing." He clamped his mouth shut as he turned his back on her and exited the house.

In her musty, wood-paneled bedroom, Izzy turned away from the open suitcase that had taken too many hours to pack and shoved the window open. She took a deep breath of ice-cold air. Anything to wake the hell up from the invisible weight on her shoulders.

Fishing out the phone that she kept hidden under the worn floorboard beneath her bed, she flipped it on. A brief jolt of hope made her heart jump.

Then it plummeted.

No messages. No missed calls. No texts.

Nothing.

Peering out the window, she paused. One of the large, rusted metal storage buildings on the edge of the main ranch had a deep red glow filtering out of the structure's seams, visible even though twilight had just begun to fall. Then a rumble, like a machine firing up, transmitted through the soles of her feet. Maybe the sounds had more to do with that mining operation the guys had been working on for the past few months. Seemed weird to be doing anything in winter, but it was *anything goes* with her family members.

Another shudder of the earth beneath her. Stronger. More like an earthquake. What the hell?

She'd been told to stay out of their business.

Well, screw them. And screw that mandate to stop trying to help the Taggarts. Thanks to a good dose of pissed-off, Izzy had just enough energy to tackle this job. One more burst of effort to figure out what her family members were doing. Then she would drive away and not look back.

Stowing the precious phone safely in a jeans pocket, she shoved her suitcase to one side and sat on the bed so she could pull her boots and gloves back on. After donning her brown canvas coat, she pushed herself up to the windowsill. Easing her legs over the edge, she then dropped down onto the ground with a crunch of snow. She hurried across the open space, a hundred feet or so to the building.

A backward glance at the house showed only a few lights from the front room. Good.

But her tracks, plain to see, crisscrossed her brothers' larger ones. Damn it. She'd deal with that in a few minutes.

Groaning, keening, low noises came from inside the storage building, making the skin on her arms prickle. She crept up to the structure, the bottoms of her feet vibrating as the ground shook.

Finding a gap in the metal next to the garage door, she bent and peered through it.

Air stopped moving through her throat. Her heartbeat echoed in her head.

Red light cast a hellish glow on everything inside. The large drilling and ore processing equipment took up most of the space, starting from the back wall, leaving ten feet free closest to the big garage door. Between the large machines stood three figures: Wyatt, Tommy, and Linc. What? She rubbed her jaw. Linc was supposed to be in jail still. Damn Tommy. No doubt he pulled some strings.

In the middle of the loose circle that the men formed, a dark shape, like a puff of black smoke, emerged. Or maybe bloomed, if one could imagine a volcano-smelling cloud creature coming out of the earth like an emerging flower bulb. She couldn't move. Somehow, the indistinct dark form absorbed light but also radiated that strange red illumination.

Air got stuck in her throat. Even her ribs vibrated. Rubbing her gloved hands together, she tried to stop the worsening itching.

The red glow was more like a banked campfire. Only nothing about this thing invited a person to come closer, roast s'mores, or tell stories.

Quite the opposite.

A clatter of a chuckle rattled the metal of the structure. The three men bowed toward the red-glowing blackness. What the hell?

"Oh, Great One," Wyatt said, his voice too high, too loud. All wrong. "Your time is near."

"Yes. Soon I will be fully manifested in this world." A sizzling sound, which she took for an exhale, somehow oozed out of that thing.

"Soon, soon," Linc chanted.

"The longest night will be here soon," it intoned.

Longest night? Solstice. Right around the corner.

"What must we do, my Lord?" Wyatt asked.

"We need four," it hissed. "And I need the knife completed."

Four? Knife?

Tommy's head bounced like a Bobblehead. Tommy, the brother

who stuck up for her. The sensitive guy who gave her hugs and put Band-Aids on her scraped knee. The guy with integrity who worked in law enforcement. Heck, he even had kids. Now he'd become a lapdog. "Yes, yes. Anything," he chanted.

The creature made a horrible metal-shrieking noise. "I want all of the legacy. Together." A hiss. "And to do this, I need four of you."

She wrinkled her nose at the smell. Like hanging out at Old Faithful. But less scenic.

"We will draw the legacy to us soon," Wyatt intoned. "The four siblings of the legacy will be powerless before you, once we are four as well. On the longest night, you will have them."

Her brain short-circuited. Thoughts turned to sludge. Her world tilted off axis. Four siblings.

The Taggarts.

Kerr.

Her head spun.

Once we are four as well. Acid clawed its way up her throat, and she choked.

Tommy piped up, "If we bring you the legacy, will you release our brother?"

The blood drained from her face to her feet. The sound of wind rushed past her ears.

"Of course." The laugh was ghostly chains rattling together.

The itching on her palms increased in intensity.

Tommy crossed his arms. "Is he okay?" Most practical thing anyone had said in the past ten minutes. Maybe he wasn't as affected as the other two guys. Maybe she could bring him back from the land of zombie jerks.

"You dare doubt me?" the thing hissed, ice water hitting hot lava rocks.

"We want proof." Tommy waved off Wyatt's desperate gesture to shut up. Go, Tommy.

The creature's growl, like a train engine, shook snow from nearby tree limbs and the roof of the structure, dropping clumps onto her neck. Cold, liquid fingers melted down her back. But she didn't move.

"You want proof?" it roared.

If Tommy said something, she couldn't hear it.

She gripped the jagged edge of the metal with her itchy, gloved hands.

With another hiss, the thing peeled…itself…open? A wet, creaking, bone-snapping sound turned her stomach upside down.

A form emerged from within the creature. She took her gloves off, wiped her eyes, and stared again. What the hell was she seeing? Cloudy skin thinned and revealed…

Hot bile clawed up her throat. Oh, God. There, in the middle of the dark shape, suspended like a bug pinned to a board, hung a mangled form.

No bug. It was a limp human body.

Wyatt and Linc stared, jaws dropped.

Tommy clutched his chest, his own red, glowing eyes riveted on the thing.

Then the form inside the creature moved with weak, infantile movements. It waved gooey, skin-dripping arms.

Not human. Not human, right?

But then it opened what remained of its macerated mouth in a silent scream.

The thing opened its black eyes.

Hank.

Then the Hank and creature combo pointed toward her hiding spot. "Get her," they yelled in sick duet.

CHAPTER 13

Backpedaling from the metal building, as if touching the frame would somehow contaminate her with…whatever evil existed inside, she held down a gurgling scream. The harsh heaves of air that she forced in and out of her chest didn't help at all.

Oh, God. Hank. That thing had Hank inside. Could she somehow get him out of there?

Out of there. Which is where she needed to be. Now. Pushing to her knees, then to her feet with a scuff, she spun on her heel and went nowhere.

The grip on her shoulder made her arm go numb. She craned her neck.

"Tommy?"

Hope formed a bubble in her chest. Tommy.

The bubble burst. Hard.

His face was blank. His scarred eyebrow didn't move. He grabbed her wrists with a slow, strong tug and dragged her into the garage as her boots left twin tracks in the snow. He pulled her closer to that… thing. And Hank.

As she passed through the side door into the garage, the heated air buffeted her skin, taking her from damp cold to flash dried in a split second.

The cloud creature with the flesh-hanging body of Hank rose up on its—feet?—and approached. And by approach, it consumed all of the space and air in front of her. She backpedaled but went nowhere.

"My lovely dear." It closed the nebulous black chest cavity with a wet creak, and the image of Hank's rotting mouth, ceased to exist. "You're one of them?" A smoky hand waved toward her family members.

One of them, as in these mindless zombies next to her? Or as in just a plain ol' Brand?

She held her tongue.

"Get back." She managed to keep her voice steady despite every instinct to scream and run. What good would any action do? She couldn't go anywhere. Tommy had a vise grip on her. Linc and Wyatt stood as mirror image sentinels next to Tommy.

The black smoke washed past her face, filling her nostrils, burning its way down her throat. The skin on her palms crawled like a thousand bugs tunneled into her wrists. If Tommy didn't have hold of her arms, she'd dig the skin off her hands with her fingernails.

"It's time for you to join us," it said, in that reverberating split tone like Wyatt had used before. "Then we will have our four against the legacy's four. Ah, my minions. I love you all already."

"Is this what you did to them?" She pointed at her blank brothers and cousin. She needed to stall. "You made them follow your orders?"

"It's so much more than obedience, *mademoiselle*. It's a holy communion with power beyond imagining. I am life and death and all that resides in end times and beyond. Join with me."

Nothing to lose by arguing at this point. Nothing at all. "Um. Not interested. I'm going to take a pass on that offer. Thank you, though."

"*Mon dieu*. You have no choice. You will receive the blessing of the Great One."

"Kind of saving myself for someone else, actually." That blast of truth stiffened her spine. An image of Kerr's wry, sincere expression filled her mind's eye, blotting out the cloud of nastiness seething mere inches from her face. Would this be the last time she had free will to conjure up a memory of her own? To dream? God, she had wasted so much opportunity and time in her life. If her future disappeared today, she was going to be pissed beyond belief. "So, no thank you. Again."

"We have a destiny to fulfill: my second coming. My return to this Earth. I am ready to be with my one love. No one refuses the Great One. You will become part of me, just like they did. And then I can regain human form. For her."

It grew larger still.

The itching in her hands intensified to the point where she almost lost focus on the monster in front of her. Almost.

"Hold her," it said.

Despite her struggles, the guys took off her coat. Then more hands manacled her upper arms, weighting her, locking her into place a few feet in front of the mouth to hell.

A sucking vortex of a scream ripped past her ears. Hers? No, it came from that...thing. Then her brothers and cousin screamed, echoing the terrible agony of sound tearing out of the creature. Every inch of her skin vibrated and stretched toward the cloud monster. Unable to control the movement, she watched as her arms bent at the elbows, fingers spreading outward. Like he was one pole of a powerful magnet and her body the opposite charge. The skin of her palms begged to be scratched.

She had an overwhelming urge to touch the thing.

No. Don't.

Ember-hot eyes met hers, now only a few desert dry inches away.

She didn't dare blink.

Her bones rattled, echoing the Quonset hut garage walls clattering against the rigid bolts, as if the structure would fail. As if her bones would fail.

Another flash of Kerr's gold-glinting eyes filled her mind. She brought up memories of their kisses, the way their bodies fit perfectly, the sensation of being in his arms. The hope. The possibility of a future. Unlike the scorching furnace in front of her, a campfire-warm feeling expanded deep in her chest.

The creature raked a smoky tendril over her cheek. Fire bloomed over her skin. In the instant she opened her mouth to scream, hot smoke shot down her windpipe and into her lungs, substituting poison for air.

She couldn't breathe. Couldn't move.

Then warm happiness deep inside her core grew and pushed back against the suffocating furnace consuming her. Pressure against pressure. Izzy became a vessel, in stasis, suspended by her brothers and cousin, as the essence of the creature invaded every cell. Every pore.

No.

She held her itching hands out to the thing.

The moment of tactile contact...

Hellfire shot down her fingertips, up her arms, to burn from the outside into her body.

The drowning onslaught continued until her vision sparkled like a fully fired kiln. Her eyes couldn't tear up—every molecule inside of her had been stripped of moisture.

With a roaring engine inferno echoing in her head, she felt the creature push until she split into two Izzys: the woman with will and the vessel without.

Which would win out? She stretched to the point of breaking.

Then the agony truly started.

Flashes of screaming mouths of humans—men dripping blood, women torn in two by a glinting blade, children crying out for their parents—blasted through her mind, until all of the suffering blended into a white-hot burn that consumed her as a rocket blast would consume anything standing beneath it.

Her hands, connected to the creature, glowed red like lava, giving off heat and wavering light.

The barrage of hellish images continued. Blood and pain and terror.

No. She would not let it consume her. Slowly at first, she began to turn, inside of herself, spinning faster as each new torture was revealed. She became a centrifuge, flinging all of the poison to the edges of her body and soul.

Kerr. The sensation when she stood in his arms filled her heart.

She needed to survive this and help him. She needed to see him again. The joy and hope inside of her expanded, pressing back the evil.

Faster and faster her mind spun. Pushing out the madness as quickly as it filled her.

The creature's black contamination thinned out, out, until…

The hands that held her let go. She stumbled forward and flung her hands out, touching nothing. Then she paused. Stared. Her palms were scored, blistered, peeling. But they were no longer glowing. She blinked. Was she was still a human body instead of a crucible?

Was she a demon?

The creature whistled, piercing the air into splinters of pain.

"Now you are all four mine to command."

The guys nodded.

Wait. What? She rolled her shoulders, a tiny movement to test her autonomy. Took a step to the side. Her body followed her direction.

Her mind? She conjured up the sensation of Kerr's mouth on hers, and the warmth bubbled inside of her chest and squeezed the last drop of evil out of her body.

Out of the corner of her eyes, she checked out the guys. All three stood in rigid postures, attention riveted to the monster. No free will.

She decided to move her arm.

It moved.

Decided to pat her leg.

She patted it.

She had free will.

Unlike her brothers.

Her hands still itched with a pins and needles sensation, and she fought to avoid scratching the burnt, irritated flesh.

"Now, we will plan the legacy's downfall," the hissing creature intoned.

"Yes, my Lord," her brothers and cousin chanted.

The monster blinked what passed for eyes and swiveled toward her. "The time of my second coming is near. Now you will call me Jerahmeel."

"Yes, my lord Jerahmeel," Izzy mumbled along with the guys, doing her level best to paste a blank stare on her face.

His spell or conversion experience or whatever it was...didn't take. And the creature didn't know.

CHAPTER 14

The phone vibrated on Kerr's nightstand, blasting him awake from the lovely dream of yet another building crashing down on top of him. He clamped his jaw shut to hold back a yelp. The action hurt like hell, thanks to Linc's fists of steel yesterday.

The rat-a-tat in the distance? His heart rate overreacting as usual.

In through the nose, out through the mouth. He needed to slow it all down. *Keep breathing. You're on the ranch. In the real world.*

He blinked. The eerie glow from the phone turned the walls a lurid green.

Wiping sweat off his brow, he rolled over, cursing at his cracked ribs, and slapped for the phone until he had it.

You awake? the message read. Izzy.

Nope, he thought.

He put the phone down with a *thunk* and rolled onto his back with a grunt, staring at the dark ceiling, trying hard not to imagine roof beams flying toward him. A shadow moved, and he threw an arm up to ward off more concrete smashing into him. Another scrub of his hands over his face anchored him to reality.

He checked the clock: 3:00 a.m.. Fantastic. Yeah, shit. He was up.

But no way was Kerr answering that text. He knew bait when he saw it.

Throwing off his blanket, he lay still, the air chilling his damp, bare chest. He moved his leg, the portion below his knee absent but mocking him, daring him to double-check, because maybe this time it would be there.

No. He wouldn't check. Didn't need to. Logically, he knew.

Shit. He slid his hand down his knee and followed the thigh down to...space. Still gone.

Damn it.

He smacked the phone again.

Maybe his head injury had altered his brain to the point where he made dumb decisions, over and over.

Hitting the button on the phone, he squinted again into the LED light.

You awake?

Fool me once or twice or three times or however the damned saying went. Eventually, he would get the concept. He was a slow learner where Izzy was concerned.

But what if she truly was trying to help his family, though?

He hadn't imagined the sweetness and light in those kisses.

He hadn't imagined their connection.

What if she hadn't tried to trap him? He should consider the possibility, at least.

Damn it.

He rolled onto his stomach and folded the pillow over his head, ignoring the scream of his ribs. Ruth's miracle salve had really improved his injuries, but nothing fixed broken ribs and bad decisions overnight. After twenty minutes another buzz grabbed his attention.

Speaking of bad decisions.

Wincing, he rose up on his elbows and grabbed the phone.

I'm sorry about everything. Wyatt's an ass. Tommy's a jerk. Linc's terrible.

Agreed.

More dots while she typed. *Weird stuff going on.*

A pause. More dots.

I'm scared.

He sat straight up in bed, every sense focused on the phone. Izzy was in danger.

Trap or reality?

Damn his fucking pride, but he couldn't resist responding.

Why?

Might as well make her work for his attention, not to mention any willingness to help her ever again in the future.

A pause for a full minute, like she had to think about it. He wanted to call her, but the signal for voice wasn't strong enough on her ranch.

I'm in the barn.

Which barn? he typed.

Yours.

He physically lurched forward. Izzy. Here. *Why?*

I saw Hank.

Kerr got dressed and was out the back door of the ranch house in record time. Crunching over the frozen ground, he stopped at the small barn. Small footprints led from the field across the compound and to its main door.

Another trap?

He sucked in a lungful of shit-that's-cold air and coughed.

Thankfully, he had grabbed his sidearm before leaving the house. Required attire for daily ranch activities these days. A flashlight in his other hand stayed off.

Might as well use the tools available to him. Kerr sucked in another breath of air, which of course made his ribs hate him, and braced against the headache as his ability to fade away settled over him.

Listening for a full minute, he heard nothing more than the muffled snorts of the horses inside. Across the other side of the large open yard, in the holding fields, cattle milled around. At a glance back over his shoulder, he spied the ranch house rising large and unlit in the waning moonlight. The clouds had dissipated, leaving behind a clear and frigid night.

Hanging out in the balls-freezing cold. Exactly what he wanted to do at stupid o'clock in western Wyoming in December.

Last time he was out here alone, that damned creature showed up.

His shoulder blades twitched.

Easing the barn door open by inches, he slipped through, maintaining his invisibility. Unfortunately, blurred vision plus a dark barn equaled a bad idea. He would trip over something if he kept the power going. Releasing the fade, he sighed as the headache ebbed.

Another minute and his eyes adjusted better to the dim light from the door.

A rustle in the back of the barn pinned him to the spot. He squinted to make out the slight movement.

"Kerr?"

He flipped on the flashlight, and she threw up an arm. "Sorry!" he said, aiming the light on the ground next to her. The shadows threw more shadows, turning her features into a hollow, ghostly specter. Even her eyes glowed a brief red color.

Like the creature.

Like the Brands.

What the hell?

"Hi," she whispered, not moving, her eyes normal now.

Kneeling on one leg, he stowed the gun but kept the holster unsnapped. "What are you doing here, Iz?"

Her jacket-clad arms were wrapped around her bent knees, hands hanging limp at the wrists. "I c-can't stay there anymore. Oh v-v-v-v God." Her teeth chattered.

He surged across the remaining few feet between them. Betrayal or not, she was in trouble. "How long have you been sitting here?"

It took her a few seconds to answer, as if processing thoughts took far too much effort. "An hour or so."

"It's freezing outside."

She blinked. "I know."

"Dammit, let's get you inside." He stood and reached down.

When he grasped her hand with his, she gave a yelp of pain, and he let go.

Shining the light, he turned her hand over and examined it. Angry bubbles of skin rose over the palm side of her hand and fingers. He cradled the back of her hand in his. "What the hell, Iz?"

"L-long v-v-v story."

Whipping the duster off and draping it over her, Kerr wrapped his arm around her shoulders and tucked her in next to him. He helped her to stand and guided her out of the barn. Instead of stopping in the kitchen, he walked through it and went straight for the living room, motioning for her to sit on the woven rug in front of the hearth. Even with both the coats, her shivers vibrated into him where they pressed against each other. She wrapped her arms around her shins, keeping her palms up, and laid her chin on her knees.

The fireplace still had some coals from earlier in the evening, with a little heat still radiating from the hearth. A fire log and some medium-sized kindling later, he had the flames crackling.

Turning back, he took in the beautiful mess that was Izzy. Blonde hair tangled out from under a worn yarn cap, circles darkened the skin beneath her eyes. A purple bruise rose over one cheek. Her lips were pale blue and still quivering. In front of the fire, clods of muddy ice melted from her insulated boots.

He snagged two afghans from the couch and recliner and added these to drape around her shoulders. He sat next to her on the rug. Silence spread out in front of them.

When she yawned and turned her head to the side to look at him, his heart twisted.

He brushed a tendril of hair that had stuck on her cheek. Bruised cheek. Dammit. "Can I get you something for your hands?"

"Later. I don't want to move. They're okay right now."

Despite everything that had happened earlier, he wanted to physically brace her body with his and support her. Why? Because at the end of the day, this was Izzy. "Anything else? More blankets? Hot chocolate?"

Firelight danced over her weary smile. "Okay. How about hot chocolate?"

"Done." He leapt up like it was mission critical and double-timed it to the kitchen. A few minutes later, he had successfully boiled water and added the packet of cocoa mix. The sweet smell made his own mouth water as he brought it back into the living room.

Where Izzy lay on her side, facing the fireplace, hands still palms up.

He paused. Studied her boots again and the damp lower legs of her jeans. Frowned.

"Izzy?" he whispered.

"Mmm hmm?" she murmured.

"How did you get here tonight?"

He had to strain to hear the answer.

"Walked."

Izzy was bursting into flames. She reached with her arm through heat waves coming off of molten lava. Reaching for...what?

At least, that was the dream sparking through her mind as she woke up by degrees. The first thing she saw was the mellow, comfortable fire crackling in front of her, heating her face and the front of her body. Warming every inch of her backside was a toasty frame that molded to fit hers. She inhaled. Wood smoke, not suffocating sulfur, filled her nose, followed by that all too familiar cedar and sage scent.

She had a pillow under her head, but beneath that rested a solid arm. A bead of sweat rolled down her forehead. She shifted her torso. Heavy material covered her. Coats and blankets.

Too hot.

Making a fist, she yelped herself fully awake with a jolt of pain. Her hands throbbed.

"Mornin', Iz," Kerr's tenor voice shot right through her. He helped her sit up, his fingers lingering on her upper arm.

"Too warm." She tried to shrug out of the coats but couldn't manage with her injured hands.

With a waft of sage and leather and a rustle of clothing, Kerr knelt in front of her and helped her out of both coats. She wiggled her now-dry socked feet. He must have taken her shoes off earlier. Huh.

He paused and stared at her, back to the fire, face hidden in shadow, his voice too level. Too serious. "Want to tell me what's going on?"

Swallowing, she said, "Yes." Her palm brushed the rug and she yelped.

"Okay. First, we're getting you some help for that." Like he cared. Wow. And when Kerr stood and hooked a hand under her arm to help her stand? That prickle in her eyes had to be from the dry air, this close to the fireplace.

"Ah…" A new voice filled the room in the same way that cool water quenched dry soil.

A woman stood in the doorway of the living room, her hair pulled back into a low bun, face sculpted but instead of looking severe, she appeared…serene. Calm. Like human aloe.

Izzy glanced at her hands.

"Ruth Turcot. Izzy Brand," Kerr said.

Izzy didn't miss the hesitation between her first and last name. Man, the Taggart family would crucify her once she told the entire story of what was hiding at her family's ranch. She kept her eyes lowered.

But if Ruth had any thoughts about Izzy's appearance, she said nothing.

"Looks like breakfast might be in order," the woman said.

"Yes!" Kerr interjected. "Hey, did you really walk here?" he asked Izzy.

A nod preceded her stomach's insistent growl.

"For real?"

"Food first. Questions later." Ruth gestured, unblinking. "Right this way. I'll get started."

Izzy and Kerr followed her into the kitchen. Bright lights made Izzy close one eye until her vision adjusted.

"Hey, Ruth, do you have something for Izzy's hands? Maybe some of that rib salve you gave me?"

The woman's auburn eyebrows shot up, and she motioned for Izzy to sit at the kitchen table. After a glance at the blistered hands, she pursed her lips. "What happened?"

The scrutiny made Izzy's skin feel itchy all over. Especially on her hands. "Long story. And I only want to tell it once."

Kerr stared at her. "Which means?"

"I'll wait until more of your siblings are here. It's important."

A pause, then he set his mouth into a line that made Izzy want to kiss it and coax it into a friendly curve. Which meant that she must have low blood sugar or that Jerahmeel thing had zapped her brain or something.

Or maybe it meant there existed some hope that they could work something out.

Ruth zipped out of the kitchen then re-entered a moment later, setting a tackle box of supplies on the table. Rifling through it, she pulled out gauze and ointment. With remarkable efficiency, she produced a plastic bowl and mixed water and the contents of a brown bottle in it.

"Soak your hands in this," she said, dabbing a finger in the bowl. "Shouldn't be too hot."

Izzy complied and flinched when her hands went into the solution. The metallic scent of the Betadine made her tongue tingle. Funny, her fingers also tingled. Must be the medicine working. With a halfhearted effort, she swirled her fingers in the liquid.

"*Chérie*, you got me up early this morning. I am starving again! Also what's for breakfast?" That Cajun lilt was followed by the swaggering step of a tall man who sported a dark beard and moustache. And a glint in his eyes as he winked at Ruth. He stiffened. "*Mon dieu*. I didn't realize we had company. Sorry." Except with the rakish smile, no way did he look sorry. Izzy smiled.

"Izzy. Odie, Ruth's husband. Which, I guess, makes him my—" Kerr clamped his mouth shut.

"What?" Izzy asked.

Ruth pinned Kerr with a strange expression. "Everyone's related in this world, now, aren't they?"

Kerr drummed his fingers on the table. "Mmm hmm."

What was that all about? Before she could ask, Odie held out a hand then paused. "But what happened? Your face. Your hands. And you look exhausted."

"She will explain later," Ruth murmured. "Let's get some salve and bandages on those hands. I have something very good for a burn. Some friends of mine who are good at healing came up with the cream. It works wonders." She tilted her chin toward Kerr. "You too. After we're done, go rub some of this on your injuries as well."

"But the other salve helped already."

"This will help more." The imperious, brow-raised expression stopped his rebuttal in its tracks. Izzy had no idea where this lady came from, but she kept people in line. Impressive.

Izzy let her hands drop, limp, on a towel, doing her best to pat them dry without sending her screaming nerves into orbit. If Ruth could figure out how to stop the itching, too, that would be great. Even now, invisible ants tap-danced across her palms. Izzy gritted her teeth.

"Let's take a look, then." Ruth turned Izzy's hands over.

And froze.

An electrical jolt flowed from the contact, all the way up Izzy's arms. A headache stabbed her in the temple. Then a new sensation, like an echo too far away to hear individual words, rang at the back of her head. She glanced over her shoulder, expecting to see someone whispering there.

Nothing.

"Holy hell." Something in Ruth's voice made Izzy look up.

The connection as their gazes locked together knocked the wind out of Izzy. She searched the woman's sculpted face and perfectly restrained hair while zaps of something weird flowed between them. It was like holding onto a low-voltage electric fence.

If it wouldn't hurt so badly, she'd rub the palms together.

Ruth froze, jaw dropped open, and she flinched. It was the first sign of emotion Izzy had seen in the woman.

"Can you feel that?" Ruth asked.

"I think so."

"What, *chérie*? What do you feel?" Odie wrapped an arm around his wife's shoulders.

"I'll explain later. Look at her blue eyes." With efficient movements, she applied salve and wrapped Izzy's hands in gauze. The connection sensation ceased. "Reminds you of a dear friend, doesn't it?"

Odie took his turn to study her. Kind of hard to melt into the floor, but that's exactly what Izzy wanted to do right about now. Either that, or demand some answers as to why they studied her like a bug under a microscope.

"Yes, I see it," he said, rolling his lips together, the beard and moustache meeting in the middle. "Coincidence, though."

"If you say so."

Between the exchange and the cryptic silent messages between those two, Izzy could get pretty paranoid. She opened her mouth to ask what they were talking about.

Abruptly, Ruth spun away.

Odie shrugged.

As one, they moved back to the stove, prepping dishes and cooking breakfast, their heads leaned toward each other, like nothing strange had occurred. A few murmurs reached Izzy.

She wanted to try one more time to ask them what the heck had just happened, but she flat-out didn't have the energy. Her bones didn't feel strong enough to keep her from oozing into the chair and down to the floor. She dragged her gaze back to the man who sat, confident and firm, right next to her.

"Iz? Can I get you anything?" He was staring at her with a caring expression that set off warning bells in the back of her mind.

She had too many problems to deal with right now, and she needed to pick the most important mysteries to figure out. As tempting as it would be to rest her head on those broad shoulders, she couldn't lean on him. Couldn't ask him to help in any way. For all he knew, she was the enemy.

For all she knew she was the enemy...Actually, Izzy didn't know *what* she was anymore.

Given the plans of that creature at the ranch and the fact that she was tainted with its evil, the best thing Izzy could do for Kerr and his family?

Dump the information and get far away from this place.

CHAPTER 15

*B*reakfast at the Taggart house was long done, but for some reason, Ruth lingered, slowly wiping one utensil at a time. Drying each item within an inch of its life. With Odie helping. Which never occurred, because she normally shooed him out of the kitchen when she was cleaning.

Kerr shook his head at the sense of an invisible hatchet hanging over all of them. She knew something. When Mariah had gone missing last week, Ruth gave his family information about the creature out there.

Ruth had also disclosed that she was their great-great many times great-grandmother. Which meant she and Odie were very, very old. Which meant there was a hell of a lot more information needed. Maybe today his family would get some answers.

From Ruth and from Izzy.

Garrison and Sara had joined them, with Sara, of course, hugging her best friend Izzy, tsking over her injured hands, and offering to help. For his brother's part, Garrison hovered behind his girlfriend, but his hard jaw tightened and his eyes narrowed as he stared Izzy down.

No need to call ahead because Shelby showed up a few minutes later, claiming she "had a feeling." Typical. Looking disheveled, Eric gave up holding doors and offering to help when Shelby scowled at him a second time and crutched her way to the table.

Vaughn couldn't join them, of course. They couldn't be in the same place or risk stuff like annihilation. Damn their lives right now.

After everyone settled and cast expectant glances toward Izzy, the kitchen fell silent.

"All right, Brand, spill it," Garrison growled.

A glare from Sara followed by a crisp "shut up" from Shelby tempered his surly attitude. Good, because Kerr was about to do it himself. He dug his blunt nails into the palms of his hands. Didn't matter about the cross-valley war brewing. Izzy was a guest in their house, and Garrison had better treat her with respect.

"You all are in danger," she said.

Izzy's voice sounded less like sunshine and citrus this morning and more like dust and gravel. The circles beneath her eyes had gotten darker, and during breakfast, her lids had drooped as she made a clumsy attempt to eat with the bandages.

Her throat worked. "Something bad is happening at our ranch."

A pin drop would sound like a million pieces of glass breaking right about now. No one moved or breathed.

Izzy took a ragged breath, her thin shoulders lifting and falling as if it required tremendous effort to inhale. "Last night, I noticed something strange in one of the garages on our property. Rumbling sounds, the air felt extra heavy, and a red light came from the building."

Next to the kitchen sink, Ruth and Odie could have passed for twin marble statues at a museum.

"So I went to check it out." She tried to fold her bandaged hands and didn't succeed, instead letting them lay palm-up on the worn wood table. "I was caught."

Kerr scooted his chair right next to hers and wrapped his fingers around her forearm, giving a light squeeze. Damn anyone who had an opinion about his need to support her.

"Did they hurt you?" he whispered.

"A little." She motioned toward her hands. Pinning everyone at the table with a bleak gaze, she continued, "They tried to convert me."

Ruth gasped. "Who did?"

Everyone else frowned.

"What do you mean, 'convert'?" Kerr asked.

"In the garage was"—she wet her lips—"a creature. Like a black cloud, but with form to it. And this is going to sound nuts, but inside of the monster..." her voice broke, "was Hank."

"I thought so," Kerr spat.

Shelby leaned forward. "What?"

"Later. I was going to tell you later. And besides, I wasn't sure I saw Hank."

"Dammit." Garrison dropped his hands onto Sara's shoulders. Hank had almost killed Sara and Zach a month ago.

"It's true," Izzy said. "The thing kind of peeled itself open and there was Hank, literally hanging inside of it." A shudder rolled through her frame.

"Alive?" Garrison asked.

"Yes. And in pain." Her jaw jumped. Kerr wanted to erase the awful image she must be remembering. She batted at a strand of hair, then gave up.

Kerr tucked it behind her ear for her. "Did he say anything to you?"

Her shuddering breath rattled her shoulders, and Kerr slid his arm around her.

"Hank? No. He looked. Awful. Rotting. Dripping. But alive."

Her unfocused, shell-shocked expression and his inability to do anything about it gutted Kerr. Feeling helpless was his kryptonite.

Izzy swallowed. "He was in agony."

Sara's hand covered her mouth.

Shelby pinched the bridge of her nose, likely trying to hold off the intense emotional feedback in the room.

"Then the monster said that he needed me to join the other three. Wyatt, Tommy and Linc. He needed four...to go up against 'the legacy.'" Her air quotes came out like air mittens, and she shot him a wry half smile. "So it converted me. To get Brand number four."

Most everyone scooted several inches away.

"Son of a bitch. So you're working for it? A spy in our house," Garrison growled. "I'm going to need you to leave."

"Dude, quit it," Shelby and Kerr said together.

Izzy cleared her throat. "I don't think it…what he did…took."

"Explain." Ruth's normally porcelain skin had turned almost translucent, one tap of a tine away from shattering. For a sturdy woman, she appeared ready to keel over.

Izzy wiggled her fingertips as she stared at the bandages. "It—the smoke from that thing—entered me. I guess. And yes, it started to take over my mind and body. Oh God, it was awful. Dirty, evil. It wanted to use me, take over my body, for its purposes. Like it had done with the guys. But then something weird happened in my brain or chest or something, and I kind of pushed it back. Like, it wanted to take up all of the space in my body and something inside of me refused to allow that to happen. Whatever that something was, it expanded so that there was no room left for the thing. Then, when I physically pushed back against the creature, my hands got burned."

Odie stared at Ruth. "Did it realize that the conversion didn't work?"

"No. I played along. It thinks I'm just like my brothers and cousin."

A clock in the living room chimed on the half hour.

Grayish-rose light tinted the kitchen windows as the day struggled to begin.

Here in his family's kitchen, the safest place he could be, Kerr sensed another invisible ceiling beam hovering over him, waiting to slice him in two.

Garrison rubbed his jaw and paced. "We could use you. A mole. You could disrupt whatever plan they have."

"Dude, what? No," Kerr spat.

"First of all, I'm not going back over there." Izzy's chin kicked up several notches. Good for her. "Ever. As a matter of fact, I'd like to leave town permanently and soon. And second, their plan is simple: create some kind of knife and use it to bring that creature fully into the world. And do it on the winter solstice. If you avoid sharp objects and that date, you should be a-okay."

Ruth gasped, a pale hand resting on her chest. "No. He could come for you before then. Any time you are vulnerable to attack."

Always quick on the basic math, Kerr blurted, "Doesn't matter. Solstice is only two days away."

"Yep." Izzy's sad, half smile sliced through him.

Odie spoke up from near the sink. "Do you know anything else?"

Lifting a shoulder, Izzy sighed. "I know it's a hell of a long walk from here to our ranch. Cold, too."

"That must be at least ten miles!" Eric sat forward. "You're lucky to be alive."

"Yeah. Kind of." She sat up straight. "Thought of one other thing. The creature called itself something weird...Jerahmeel, I think."

Kerr studied the confused expressions around the table, a stomach-churning sense of dread growing.

Until Shelby's head whipped up and over, like she was sniffing. "You know, don't you. Ruth? Odie? What is that thing?"

The tall woman said nothing but kept her hand pressed to her sternum. Odie stayed next to her side, poised like he would fend off all the demons of hell on her behalf. Although Ruth's face remained a mask, a tiny flicker of fear ran through the image.

The hairs on the back of Kerr's neck stood straight up.

She worried at a tiny section of her lip.

Garrison rapped his knuckles on the table. "Out with it. What do you know about this situation? It's more than you told us last week, that's for sure."

Ruth glanced at Odie and he nodded, almost like he gave her permission. Something with this messed up situation had gone even more pear-shaped.

Ruth swallowed, the movement elegant, reserved. She patted the tight bun at the back of her neck. "I don't know everything about this thing. Not even sure what it is exactly...now. But what I do know is that you cannot allow the Brands to make and use a new knife."

"And you know this how?" Garrison asked.

Kerr sat straight up. "Wait. You said 'new' knife."

The woman gripped the sink edge on either side of her.

Her silence hung heavy in the room.

"New? But of course. We have heard of similar situations in the past," Odie interjected. His disarming smile didn't fool Kerr for a minute.

"Son of a bitch. You two know a lot more, don't you?" Garrison asked. "When that thing attacked us last week, it said, 'I should have killed you when I had the chance.' To you, Odie. So what's the deal? No bullshit, either."

The man stroked his trimmed beard. "What I can say is that I've never seen that particular thing before the night we helped Mariah escape."

What the hell wasn't Odie saying?

Ruth wrung her hands.

"But you've seen something like it?" Shelby rubbed two fingers over her temple.

"Well. No. Not exactly." Ruth leaned on the countertop. When she looked up at Odie, he slid an arm around her shoulders. "We encountered a being called Jerahmeel in the past."

"I don't need my ability to know that you're not telling the entire truth." Garrison took a step toward Ruth.

Kerr froze. His brother had vowed not to use his supersensory perception to tell when someone was lying ever again. At least not on people close to him. Besides, the way all his siblings' powers were shifting lately, there was no guarantee what could happen to his mind or body.

Odie stepped in front of Ruth, all flexing arms and wide stance. "Hold on there, my friend. Don't go putting that brain-altering voodoo on my wife. She hasn't done anything wrong."

"This situation." Garrison's jaw muscle shifted. "It doesn't feel right."

"Of course not." Odie lifted his chin in the general direction of the Brand ranch. "We're all in big trouble if that knife gets created. The whole world is in trouble."

"Why?" Kerr asked. Izzy stared at the table like she wanted to memorize the wood grain pattern. What had she sacrificed to come here and tell them this story?

Odie pulled at his short beard. "Jerahmeel can bring on the actual apocalypse. Create a living hell on Earth. People will die to feed his hunger…he is fed with the life-force of human souls. If he comes to power, he will rule for all eternity."

"The hell—?" someone muttered.

"And you know this how?" Kerr asked. The answer to their questions had been residing under their roof all this time and no one had known.

Ruth was a statue with her sculpted cheekbones and neutral expression. Then her dark brows rose over gold-glinting eyes as she rubbed her index finger and thumb together, over and over. Kerr had never seen her nervous in the three weeks she'd cared for his father. Nothing rattled the woman.

Almost nothing.

"Izzy is telling the truth. That thing is real. Very real. And dangerous." The words barely made it out of Odie's tight mouth. Like he needed to maintain the contact, he re-snaked his arm around Ruth's shoulders.

"Son of a bitch," Garrison spat. "What's it doing here in the middle of nowhere in Wyoming?"

"Don't know for certain," Ruth said, tossing a glance at Odie and back to them. Something in the way her eyes slid away made Kerr's stomach knot up. Like she *did* know but wasn't saying. "But what we are certain of is that Jerahmeel must not be allowed to attain full power."

"Which requires the knife?" Kerr probed.

"I believe so."

Garrison held onto the back of his chair. "Is that thing going after our family?"

"Appears that way," the woman said.

"And you're our family, right?" Shelby whispered.

"Yes."

"Well, that might explain something." Kerr whistled low.

"Is it here because of you two?" Garrison asked.

Ruth sniffed. "No. I think we're here because of you. And it."

"Explain." Garrison leaned forward.

Another ten seconds of silence. Watching Ruth and Odie squirm sent his heebie-jeebies into orbit.

Finally, Ruth said, "We used to work for Jerahmeel."

Izzy's head whipped up, and her frame trembled beneath Kerr's arm. He wanted to push her behind him and block anything that dared hurt her, like that monster out there.

The same monster that might somehow live inside of her. Oh, shit.

A vein popped out on Garrison's forehead. "You. What?"

"Dude, quit it already," Shelby groaned and rubbed her temples. When Eric scowled at Garrison, she turned to her boyfriend. "You too, Mr. Alpha. Tone down the emotional response or my head'll come off again."

Eric sat back and crossed arms over his chest. A muscle jumped in his jaw. Kerr knew his friend too well from their army days. That man was holding his shit together by a mere thread.

With good reason.

That creature had almost killed Shelby. Now it wanted to finish the job, with interest. Hell, Kerr would help Eric stand in the way if necessary. Anything to protect the people in this family.

And maybe some people who were not in the Taggart clan.

Ruth's chest rose. "We were cursed for hundreds of years. We were part of a group of unnaturally long-lived humans called 'Indebted.' And we had to kill on command to feed Jerahmeel's appetite for evil souls."

Now it was Kerr's turn to jump to his feet. "You are both murderers."

"It's so much more complicated than that, *ami*," Odie interjected.

"Well, have you killed someone?" Garrison asked, hands rolled into fists, focus fixed on Ruth and Odie.

The Cajun winced. "Yes. Not willingly." He held out a hand. "You don't need to use your powers on me. It's the truth."

A beat of the heart, then Garrison nodded and relaxed. "Fine. You're felons. Get out of our home."

"Hear us out," Odie pleaded. "All the Indebteds at one point in time years ago had to make terrible decisions. We each sacrificed our eternal souls to save someone we dearly loved."

Ruth cringed. "Wasn't worth it."

"It was worth it for me, *chérie*. My daughter's life was worth more than mine."

A wave of bile burned up Kerr's throat as he edged closer to Izzy. "Uh, guys. Are you two still into the killing thing?"

"No!" both shouted.

"Sorry," Ruth made a shushing sound. "Don't want to wake your father." She glanced at Odie. "We only killed very bad people. And we got out of our contracts last year."

"How?" Kerr asked.

"Did you hear about Mount Shasta blowing up?" Odie grinned and pointed a thumb at his chest. "That was us. We got into his lair and used those damned soul blades together and destroyed Jerahmeel."

"No way," Shelby breathed.

"Obviously worked," Garrison quipped.

"Well, he was destroyed when we left him," the bearded man said. "Something must have triggered his return to the world. Lured him back. Tempted him…" He stared at Ruth. "*Merde.*"

"No," she whispered. "Not possible."

"Might be, *cher.*"

"Fill us in," Garrison shifted his weight from foot to foot.

"Jerahmeel loved Ruth. He obsessed over her, loved her." Odie's expression hardened as he went from jovial Cajun to cold-blooded killer in the space of two heartbeats. Kerr held his breath. "When she betrayed his love in order for us to send him back to hell, he threatened her legacy. Specifically vowed to destroy her legacy. *Mon dieu,* surely he wouldn't have re-entered the world to seek revenge just to feed his obsession, would he?"

"Of course he would. He has nothing but time," Ruth said. "He was here before I arrived, so that means…"

"What about the knife, *mon ami?*"

Kerr's stomach knotted as he took in Ruth's wide-eyed expression.

"I don't know," she breathed.

"How is he making it? How is he forging a new blade properly after all these centuries?"

"What about ores?" Izzy piped up. Everyone stared at her, and her cheeks turned pink. "The guys have been mining on our property. The creature must have wanted to be there for a reason. Right? Why on our land? Why not any other location?"

"But wait. The Brands were trying to get our property, too. Remember, Hank had been making offers to buy the ranch several months back," Shelby whispered.

Ruth gripped the counter, her eyes wide.

Odie shifted until his frame rested flush against his wife's. "Is it truly possible?" he asked her.

"We have to do more research. Maybe call Dante." She stared at her husband.

"Dante's about as useful as a box of rocks. How about Javier? He was around during the Inquisition. Longer than Barnaby, even."

"Barnaby," she whispered, then scanned the room. "Holy hell, does this have something to do with Barnaby? But what?"

"Plain English, folks," Garrison drawled. "Could you let us in on the secret so we don't all die?"

Odie glanced back at his wife. "This is only a guess. But we think Jerahmeel may be forging the Omega Knife."

Garrison shook his head. "Don't follow."

"The knives we used as Indebted and also to end Jerahmeel's life were Alpha blades. The beginning of his power."

Shelby's freckles stood out stark against her bloodless face. "This new knife is worse." It wasn't a question.

"If it's true, then yes, far worse." Odie rolled his mouth, pushing his beard and moustache together. "But this is mere speculation. We should find out more. Call a friend who might know."

Garrison snorted, but his knuckles turned white as he gripped the back of Sara's chair. His brother looked like he wanted to rip apart the wood. "Ask another murderer?"

"Another former Indebted." Odie's tone came out steely. "One of the oldest Indebteds who still walks this Earth."

"We need to get Vaughn back here to see what he thinks," Shelby piped up. "He should hear this story and understand what's going on. This whole situation creeps me out. All of us need to be involved in the discussion."

"Agreed." Garrison rubbed his jaw. "I still don't know if I buy all this end-of-the-world stuff. No offense, but that's pretty farfetched." He offered his hand, palm up, to Ruth. "I just want that creature gone and no more bad crap happening to my family." Sara patted his arm and looked up at him with a smile.

"You must trust us," Ruth murmured. The way her brows drew together set Kerr's nerves on edge.

"Must? I'll reserve judgment." Garrison shook his head, like doing so could sort out the puzzle of information they'd been given. "Okay then. We're not getting anything solved right now." He turned toward Kerr and Shelby. "Vaughn won't be back 'til later this evening. If we're about to enter the apocalypse, then we need to discuss a plan. Together. Later."

"You've got to believe me," Ruth's horrified whisper came out like the lash of a tiny whip.

Garrison kissed Sara on the top of her head, strode to the kitchen door, and pulled his hat and coat off the rack. "It's not whether I believe or not, ma'am. It's that I cannot deal with the theoretical bull while the actual bull is still waiting for me right now."

Kerr shook his head. Classic Garrison, avoiding complex issues until he could think through all the variables.

Ruth's jaw dropped.

Snagging the doorknob, Garrison called back over his shoulder, "Once Vaughn arrives, we'll figure out how to gather more information."

"It might be too late by then." Ruth's shoulders slumped.

"Without more information, then sorry, but that's a risk I'm going to take." He paused and stared at Kerr. "Speaking of risk, someone better keep an eye on *her*"—he pointed at Izzy—"so she doesn't run back over there and rat us out."

Izzy's mouth gaped. "But—"

Garrison slammed the door closed.

A finger of cold air swirled through the kitchen, icing Kerr's skin. "Uh, he just needs to process all the information you and Ruth gave him."

Ruth stared at the closed door, then blinked and turned to Odie. "I need to take care of some items."

"Yes. Yes, I'll help you, *chérie*." Odie cupped her elbow, but they didn't move.

Like Ruth needed any support. No way. That woman was sturdy to the max and competent, to boot.

Kerr would give Garrison a little time. Then they had to get serious about formulating a plan. Figure out how to stop the Brands from forging a knife to end all knives. And end the world. They would have to destroy a creature Ruth and Odie had already destroyed. Simple enough.

He studied Izzy's slumped shoulders. On a normal day, he would wrap her in his arms and take her away from the mess of his ranch and hers. But that wasn't going to happen.

"Shelby, can you and Sara help Izzy get cleaned up and in a guest room? She needs some rest." He patted Izzy on the arm as he pushed to his feet and followed Garrison out the door.

One normal day. What he'd give for a single normal day in the life of the Taggart family.

CHAPTER 16

*I*zzy sat in the silence, trying to become small and invisible. Little movements, sniffs, shifting chairs punctuated the odd atmosphere.

"Well, *chérie*, let's get our morning work done." Odie pushed off the counter and tugged at Ruth's hand. "You still have a patient to attend, and I have some calls to make."

Ruth turned toward Izzy as she was leaving the room. "How are your hands feeling? Need anything?"

Izzy gave her a bandaged wave. "I'm good, thank you."

"We'll take great care of her," Sara said, coming around the table and wrapping her arms around Izzy's upper chest. When she leaned back, a dimple winked in her friend's cheek. Like Izzy wasn't possessed by an evil creature.

"What do you need, Shel?" Eric inclined his head.

"Let's go check on Dad. We'll keep him company for his therapy session this morning," she said, pushing up onto her crutches and clomping out of the kitchen, Eric trailing behind her.

"Well. That's a morning. Wow," Izzy breathed.

Sara smiled and stepped away, looking down at her. "Wow is right. I want to know about the vibes between you and Kerr."

She couldn't hold back the snort. "Something like Satan's second cousin is hanging out at my family's ranch, trying to recruit me, wanting me to help it take over the world, maybe even residing inside of me, and you're interested in a relationship status update?"

"Hey, nothing like a good distraction from danger. Besides, I have two eyes and they work fine. That guy is into you. About time, I'd say. You guys have been in parallel orbits for years."

Izzy tried to brush the hair back off her face and failed, thanks to the bandages. "Timing has always been off. Still is, given everything going on here."

"You never know." Sara's laugh lifted Izzy's slumping spirits. "Garrison and I hooked up while Hank was terrorizing us. Sometimes you have to take whatever opportunity presents itself."

"Hooking up at the end of the world doesn't seem like a super practical plan. Not sure if Kerr wants to have much to do with me, given how I've had to act like I'm betraying him." Squirming with the direction this conversation was going, Izzy said, "How about helping a gal clean up? My bladder's not happy, and I need a shower. And I'm exhausted."

Sara jumped back. "Of course! How rude of me. I'll see if Shelby will loan you some clothes. The bathroom should have plenty of towels…"

Izzy followed behind her friend, half listening, half asleep. And completely uncertain of her next step in this bizarre situation.

Chores kicked Kerr's butt more than usual. But he needed to do something useful while he was waiting for the eternal evil or whatever the hell was coming to rise up and eat them all.

However, his exhaustion had nothing to do with the frigid day. And sure as shit didn't have anything to do with the recent beat down, would it? He wiggled his jaw. Damn Linc and his right hook. At least the pain had improved, though, thanks to a few swipes of Ruth's magic salve. Whatever was in that stuff had improved his aches by about fifty percent. His rib pain was now tolerable. And much less creaking when he breathed.

If only the medicine fixed his exhaustion, due to being up last night with a certain woman curled in his arms.

Some ice-blue sky broke through the heavy, white clouds. Blue and clear. Like Izzy's eyes. Kerr shook his head. He had lost his mind.

He paused from putting paneling on the new barn and thumbed up the brim of his second-best hat. The situation hit him harder than the hammerhead on a nail. Ice crystallized in his gut. He hated being helpless. For once, he wanted the freedom to choose his destiny. Unfortunately, he knew a trap when he saw one. And this whole situation over there at the End of the World smelled like a big ol' trap.

He couldn't do much about the family issues right now. Not until Odie and Ruth contacted their friend. And not until they caught Vaughn up to speed and formulated a plan. Something about the Brands mining ores bothered him. Why did they persistently bid for Taggart property? Damn it, what was the link? Would that link help them in this situation? Who knew.

Vaughn pulled up in Kerr's truck, jumped out, and sauntered over, joined by Garrison. Kerr checked his watch. Shelby and Eric were scheduled to leave soon. Because...yeah.

Vaughn shot Kerr a grin. "You trying to finish the barn singlehandedly? Because you're putting us mere mortals to shame." He leaned against the wall. "What did I miss this morning?"

Garrison gave a bark of a laugh, then filled Vaughn in on the condensed version.

"So." Garrison leaned on the side of the barn. "What are your thoughts?"

"Me?" Kerr paused mid-swing, hammer raised. "About what? The thing that's trying to kill us or the friendly neighborhood vendetta or the woman who freaking hiked here last night to try to help us?"

"You're kind of prickly, huh?" Vaughn asked with a knowing flash. Too knowing. He must have been taking pointers from Shelby on how to get under Kerr's skin.

"Go back to the gym, you big ape." *Pound, pound, pound.*

Vaughn sniffed and picked up a shovel. "I resemble that remark." He aimlessly dropped the shovelhead into the frozen ground with dull *thunks*. "So, what are you going to do about her?"

"That's a very good question," Garrison said.

"You two suck," Kerr muttered. Damn his nosy brothers. Up until now, Kerr could count on both of them to avoid anything resembling touchy-feely chitchat. Fine time for them to change their ways.

Kerr pivoted away and pounded another nail. "What's it to you, Gar? You hate the Brands. You should be glad that one won't be part of our family."

"I care about the happiness of anyone in my family." His brother's low, calm voice cut through the cold air like the ping of hammer on metal. "Even if they date the enemy."

Even when the guy's life had gone to shit, he still looked out for everyone. A big, solid, sheepskin-jacket clad mother hen of an older brother. Kerr could almost hug him for that. Almost. Because, dude, he called Izzy the enemy.

"I'm plenty happy." He pounded away at the barn siding.

"Clearly." Garrison sniffed.

Kerr paused. "What?"

Garrison shoved a hand into a jeans pocket and squinted at the sky. "Look, I don't like the situation—let's be clear about that. But I'm not cruel, either. So…just make sure you're not missing a big opportunity with Izzy. These chances don't come along very often. Even when the world is going to hell all around you. I should know." Garrison knew about almost losing everything.

Vaughn snorted, "Kerr's whipped."

"No, I'm not." He swung the hammer again and missed, flattening his thumb. "Goddamn it!" He tried to jump around, but his sore leg hurt like a bear. All he managed was a tiptoeing step on his good foot, turning him into a deranged, cussing, gimpy ballerina.

"Maybe that'll wake him the hell up," Garrison snorted.

He glared at both of them.

Vaughn rubbed his chin. The glint in his dark eyes reminded Kerr of a predator calculating how quickly it could corner and then disembowel its prey. "You know, Gar, this could be useful. How those two are into each other."

"We're not—"

His oldest brother raised a gloved hand. "Fine, you're not interested in her. Whatever. Could've fooled me. But what I'm getting at is, you could parlay the first blush of love into leverage for us."

"No love, man. No. Love." Kerr shook his hand. Then he stopped. The fresh pain in his chest had nothing to do with his cracked ribs. "Wait. You want me to use her? Pump her for an advantage?" He had only just come to grips with the realization that she hadn't been playing him all along. Now his brothers wanted *him* to play *her*?

"Not specifically." Vaughn winked. Winked? Mr. Serious winked? "I mean, hey, if you were having a moment, uh, pumping…and while in the moment you managed to get some additional information that we could use that would help us, what harm would that do?"

Kerr couldn't speak for a full ten seconds, on account of wanting to rip Vaughn's tongue out.

"First off," he managed, after he regained the ability to speak, "she and I are not going to have a moment any time soon, so there's that." His brothers' heads jiggled up and down like they believed him. Patronizing asses. "Second, there's no way I would date anyone just because I had an ulterior motive to dig up more information. Besides, Izzy's been pretty forthcoming in answering our questions."

"It's not that she isn't telling the truth," Garrison said. He'd know. "I cultivated interest in Sara because she could keep an eye on Zach, to make sure he didn't manifest an ability."

"Using someone for information is not a reason to date someone."

"Well, Sara was also kind of sexy, too," he mumbled.

Vaughn coughed. "Want to speak up so those of us in the back can hear?"

Lifting his chin, Garrison said, "You have no room to talk, over there playing doctor."

"Hey, what can I say? Smart women are hot." Vaughn smiled broadly. "Also, free medical advice. Bonus for me."

Kerr rubbed the heel of his gloved hand against his forehead. "Fine. So you two are presidents of the I-love-my-woman club—"

A rumble above them shook the structure.

"Fuck!" Vaughn rushed Kerr and Garrison like a linebacker, grabbing them by the coat lapels and throwing them to the ground as a piece of metal slid off the roof and came to rest, one edge buried in the ground, right where they had been standing. The wide, thin metal square quivered.

CHAPTER 17

*C*lean, dry, warm, and exhausted, Izzy trudged down the hall from the guest bathroom. Shelby's flannel shirt and thick canvas work pants fit well enough to make do while the clothes Izzy had worn last night went through the wash. Pushing back wet hair, she frowned. Despite wearing a pair of Ruth's rubber gloves in the shower, Izzy had soaked her bandages.

Entering the kitchen, she sat at the table and tried to peel off the tape and gauze. But, unable to close her fingers together with any strength, the task got old in a hurry. Murmurs down the hall told her where Ruth was, but Izzy didn't want to interrupt Mr. Taggart's therapy session for something this petty. Footsteps sounded in the house, evidence of life moving forward, people going about normal activities.

She dug again at the tape. Good grief, did Ruth hermetically fasten the dressings?

Tears pricked her eyes as she dug at the tape with her fingertips. She tried to make a fist. Couldn't even do that. Damn it.

Clump. Clump. Izzy spun around to find the source of the sound.

"Thought you might want some help," Shelby said, slowly walking on crutches into the kitchen. "I'm pretty useless with chores and Dad's exercises. Might as well be helpful where I can." She paused and pinned Izzy with a slightly unfocused glance. "Stinks to be injured and not able to do everything, huh?"

"Exactly."

Shelby snagged the roll of gauze, tape, and scissors out of the supply box Ruth had left on the counter. She sat at the table at a right angle to Izzy and motioned for her to rest her hands on the wooden surface. A few clips with the scissors and Shelby got a starting point to unroll the gauze.

She sucked in a breath. "How exactly did you hurt your hands again?"

"Touched the cloud monster, Jerahmeel, as he was trying to possess me or whatever he was doing." Her palms started to itch again as Shelby unrolled the dressing. Great. Second-degree burn plus imaginary cooties. Enough to drive a gal nuts.

Frowning as she peered at the injured hands, Shelby mumbled, "That bastard operates at a high temperature, apparently. Eric and I were burned by that thing when we fell off the cliff."

"How did you survive?" A pause. Too long of a space. "Sorry for asking. Never mind."

Shelby paused the unwrapping. "No. It's just...we don't talk about the way we're—my brothers and I—are...different. With anyone outside the family. You know?"

"I have an idea. From Kerr. With the disappearing thing."

"No offense, but you can never tell anyone about what he can do. Or any of us."

"You all can disappear?"

"I wish. No. But we all have little extra, uh, quirks."

"Yeah?"

"Yeah. Anyway. You like him?"

"What?" Izzy's head whipped up and her face heated. "Kerr? Oh, um. Doesn't matter. I'm out of here soon."

Shelby's gold-flecked brown gaze, so like Kerr's, held her in place. "I think it does matter. A lot." When she blinked, a sad smile followed. "He deserves to be happy."

"I agree." Damn her itchy hands.

Shelby kept unwrapping until bare skin remained. She brushed a finger over the base of Izzy's palm.

The itching sensation became a buzz that shot up Izzy's arm. She winced at the headache. Weird sensations crawled through her, as before with Ruth. Only this time, Izzy experienced waves of emotion hitting her. Happy, sad, confused, angry, longing. Surprise.

She stared at Shelby. The woman's face had turned ashen and her jaw dropped. A sensation of fear speared Izzy. Only it came from Shelby.

That made no sense.

"What's going on?" Shelby breathed.

A red wave of anger crashed into Izzy. She pulled her hands away and held them in front of her, like she could hold back the flood of feelings. "Stop it. Whatever it is, stop it. It hurts. In here." She motioned toward her forehead.

"Oh my God. You can tell what I'm feeling? How is that possible?"

Green confusion swirled, suffocating Izzy. "Seriously. Stop." Emotions were pinging back and forth between them, amplifying on each pass.

"I can't," she gasped.

"Huh?" Izzy dropped her hands but didn't touch Shelby.

"My power. I can detect other people's emotions."

Izzy's mouth went dry. "Why am I able to do it now?"

"I don't know."

A bang sounded outside the house. A wave of male fear shot through Izzy, and she flinched.

She and Shelby both shot to their feet. Both turned. Both touched their heads.

"What the heck?" they said together.

For the second time in as many days, Kerr shoved himself to his feet and brushed snow off his duster. His cracked ribs might be healing, but that impact still hurt like a beast. Vaughn was solid muscle.

"What was that?" Kerr asked, holding his hand against his side and fighting to take a full breath of air.

Vaughn stood in a partial crouch, arms in front of him. The wild glance he shot back over his shoulder iced Kerr's blood. "Tell me you guys forgot to nail down the roof," he growled.

Garrison shook his head. "No. I did it myself. Fully attached."

Vaughn took one step back from the vertical metal slab cleaved into the frozen ground. With one hand, he tapped the top of his head. "Something's real wrong here all of a sudden." The air shifted into a vacuum as his power gathered into a weapon form—a ball of spiky danger surrounding him. Expanding outward in a wave of malice. Kerr reared away from his dangerous brother.

Garrison pulled his Ruger from the side holster.

Kerr picked up a hammer. Because, hell. Better than nothing.

A small breeze sent a warm tendril of sulfur that tickled his nose. Last time he'd smelled that strong of a stench—

A dark cloud materialized at the edge of the barn. Shit.

The metal on what was left of the roof pinged and vibrated as if pellets of hail hit it. Only, it was partial blue skies and no precipitation today. The clattering made his ears ring.

Kerr's heart sped up like a desperate rodent on a wheel, trying to keep up with events around him and getting nowhere.

The thing. Here. Again.

"Get off our property." Garrison's rough voice cut through the rattles as the remainder of the roof went nuts, lifting and creaking.

The thing got bigger and sucked light out of the day. An insatiable black hole of nastiness.

"Where is the fourth?" Its screeching yowl made Kerr flinch like he'd been slapped.

The fuck? Was it talking about Shelby? Because she was literally a hundred feet away, in the house.

"No idea what you're talking about." Vaughn squared his shoulders and faced the thing. Muscles rolled in his neck. His hands flexed into lethal fists. Was he going to try the throw-a-virtual-ball-of-danger-at-it trick again?

The creature stopped. Red embers that passed for eyes glowed, avid, hungry. Awful.

How bizarre was it that they were standing here on the ranch chatting with a black blob? What about Dad? And Ruth and Odie, Sara and Zach, all still inside the house?

Izzy.

Had it come for her? Maybe it wanted to complete the draft of Team Satan forming over at the Brand Ranch.

"Soon." The ground beneath their feet rumbled with that bastard voice.

In the daylight, Kerr could again make out the figure inside the thing. The image appeared almost like seeing a person floating several inches below the surface of murky water. Weak movement, like a sick newborn calf, came from the blurry figure. Sweat broke out on Kerr's upper lip. Holy shit, Izzy was totally right about Hank Brand stuck in there and still alive. Sort of.

If this thing could absorb Hank and almost kill Shelby and Eric, no telling what else it could do.

Kerr studied the metal impaled into the ground. Belay that—he had a super clear idea of *what else* this thing was capable of.

It could do fucking anything it wanted, to whomever it wanted, whenever it wanted.

And the Taggart siblings had no workable plan to beat the thing.

"Guys," Kerr muttered. "We need to get the hell out of here."

"Not without getting this thing off of the ranch." Garrison clicked the safety on his gun.

Right behind his shoulder, Kerr said through his teeth, "That's not going to work, bro. It's a cloud."

"It's to slow the fucker down while I do my little trick on him." Vaughn stretched his hands out in front of him and gathered his power into a ball of danger.

Kerr grabbed his shoulder. "Stop! You don't know what activating your power will do. Your head nearly came off last time. You lost your hearing. Look at what happened to Garrison and Shelby when they took their powers to another level. They almost died."

His older brother's mirthless grin scared the hell out of him.

Vaughn said, "Ask me if I really care." He turned to the creature. "Come and get it."

Big brother wasn't crazy. Oh, no. Judging by the clamp of his jaw, he was fucking furious.

What could Kerr do? Well, he did have the hammer, but chucking a piece of hardware at a thing that could eat people whole and take off a barn roof was kind of like spitting in the ocean in terms of the contribution margin. Besides, he stood next to a human grenade and a guy with a loaded firearm.

Above them, clouds swirled in the sky and hurtled down toward Earth in a sick, sulfur vortex. Like the black hole formed right here, on the Taggart ranch.

Wisps of black smoke bled outward and cycloned toward them, like two rotating cloud arms reaching out for a hug. How sweet. A nice, rotten-egg, go-to-hell kind of hug.

Garrison took aim.

Vaughn extended his hands.

Shit. Kerr had to do something. That thing would hurt Izzy. It would kill his brothers and sister.

Desperation pushed a headache right to the top of his skull.

Do. Something. Help his brothers.

Protect Izzy and his family.

What could he do? The power not to get lost was of no use here. What about his other ability to disappear?

With a spike of pain in his head, something clicked in Kerr's mind, triggering his invisibility gift. He staggered back a step as the force of the ability fired up.

Only, he didn't use it on himself. He envisioned casting it forward, like a net. Midway through the throw, he imagined molding it like plastic wrap to cover the cloudy thing. Why? Shit if he knew. Seemed like the thing to do. But he knew this for sure: if the creature went invisible, they were well and truly fucked.

Damned if his instincts weren't right on. His invisibility trick created a clear coat that formed a glossy rime on the creature.

"What happened?" Vaughn asked, neck muscles bulging. He hadn't released his power yet.

Kerr grabbed his head with two hands and held on for all he was worth. "No clue. But the thing looks more solid now. Can you work with that?"

"One way to find out," Garrison hollered. He fired off a shot into the thing, the bullet making a high-velocity *kapow*. Then the thing quivered, like the bullet impacted a block of ballistic gelatin instead of whipping through smoke.

A steam engine scream pierced the air around them, making Kerr's skin ripple.

Holy solid object, they had something here.

A more solid form. Something to push against. Something to fight. Maybe that was the key. Not only did they have to see the enemy, but their powers needed to make contact with the enemy for an effective attack.

Shit, Kerr's head was turning inside out. But he kept the freaky cellophane draped over the thing. What he'd give for more power. A higher gear. Anything more.

That cloud bastard gave out an ungodly yowl. It started low and increased in volume and pitch until Kerr was sure his eardrums would burst. The metal roof material banged against the wooden bones of the barn. The creature whipped from one side to another as howl after howl ripped from within it.

"Vaughn, you ready?" Kerr panted. "I can't hold on much longer." His legs and his mind shuddered. His arms sagged. Trying to keep his power wrapped around that monster burned more energy than climbing the highest mountain in the Tetons.

Only, he didn't collapse. Instead, a strange sense passed through his mind, like a feather-light touch. But underneath the sensation came a steely support. An invisible boost to his ability that shored up his defenses and the power level of his gift.

A hint of citrus scent recharged his batteries. He rolled his shoulders, reaching for a second gear.

Standing up straight, he gulped in a lungful of cold air and solidified the coating around the creature. Less gel, more hard plastic. Damn, this headache hurt like a son of a gun, but using his power took less effort now. It was as if someone braced him. Or carried some of the weight. A warm feeling spread through his chest.

Okay, that was weird. Didn't matter right about now. All he cared about was stopping this bastard.

Vaughn staggered forward one step. "Garrison, shoot it again."

"Gladly." He squeezed off another round, and the thing writhed and howled even more.

Then it seemed to shrink back into itself.

Was their attack working?

Vaughn gave a guttural yell and flung his arms toward the creature, releasing a massive percussion wave of danger. The creature staggered back several feet.

It knocked Kerr and Garrison on their assess as well. Big brother couldn't aim that ball of badness for shit.

Kerr lay on the snowy ground, sucking in oxygen, his eyes gummy. When he wiped his eyes, blood coated his hands. What the hell?

The Jerahmeel creature sucked away down the side of the barn, then with a whoosh, disappeared. The clouds above calmed back down to normal movement, blue skies emerged, and the air lightened.

"Are you okay?" Garrison holstered his gun. "Oh, son of a bitch. Your eyes."

Kerr blinked up at the sky. "What?"

His brother's voice sounded like it bounced around in a barrel. "Can you see?"

"A little blurry."

"Damn it." Garrison nodded. "Shelby went blind when she took her power to another level."

"At least I'm in good company." Kerr accepted Vaughn's hand to get back up to his feet. His big brother swayed as color leached from his face. Whenever Vaughn did that human grenade trick, it wrung him out like a soaked towel. A trickle of blood wandered from his right ear and down Vaughn's thick neck.

"Let's get inside and regroup," Garrison said.

Like a trio of drunken sailors, they shambled toward the house.

Izzy, Ruth, and Shelby stood at the kitchen door, visible even through Kerr's filmy peepers. But the women weren't looking out at Kerr and his brothers.

Izzy held her un-bandaged, blistered hands in front of her as she sagged against the doorjamb. That wide-eyed, gape-jawed expression triggered an insane urge in Kerr to scoop her up and drive far, far away.

Ruth pointed at Izzy, her typical calm demeanor cracking and her voice splitting into two octaves. "What. Did. You. Do?"

CHAPTER 18

"*I* don't know," Izzy whispered. A buzzing sensation vibrated every inch of her body. If it wouldn't hurt so much, she'd scratch the heck out of her itching hands. At least Ruth's balm was working wonders. Even in a few hours, the burns had healed by twenty-five percent.

"You stole..." Ruth swallowed and shook her hand, like it had fallen asleep. She squinted up at the ceiling. Her voice returned to normal. "No. It's still there. Holy hell. I don't understand."

"*Chérie?*" Odie ran into the kitchen. "What, *ami?* Are you all right?" The fierce way he shielded Ruth and glared at everyone made Izzy shrink further back against the doorjamb.

"She." The tall woman grabbed her head, panting. "She took..." Blinking hard, her gaze lasered onto Kerr and his brothers. "What in the world happened to you?"

Izzy sucked in a breath. The blood smeared over Kerr's face shocked her heart into motion. "God, you're hurt." Because it mattered...why?

Because it did.

"Everyone, into the kitchen." Ruth snapped to attention and shrugged off her husband. "Let's get everyone patched up." The sideways glance through narrowed eyes told Izzy that their conversation wasn't anywhere close to being over.

What had Izzy done? One minute she had felt a wave of fear and terror come over her like a tidal wave, heavy and propelling her toward the door, thanks to Shelby's power, she presumed. Ruth rushed to join them. Then in the next minute, her damned itchy hands had latched onto Ruth's and a burst of...energy? Exhilaration? Adrenaline? Strength? coursed through Izzy. Then it flew out toward Kerr. She had no idea why. Only that it was very important to help him.

Hastily wrapping gauze around her palms and drawing on large vinyl gloves from Ruth's medical kit, Izzy motioned for Kerr to sit. Wetting a dishrag, she hurried back to him, bent down, and dabbed at his face. She bit her lip. No cuts. No wounds. No source of the bleeding. But yet, there was blood.

And his eyes. The whites were shaded a dark, lurid red, setting off the gold in his brown irises. "What happened to you?" she asked.

Wrapping a hand around her wrist, Kerr smiled. Only, with those eyes, he resembled more of an unhinged zombie than a wry cowboy. Around them, activity swirled as Ruth and Odie steered an off-balance Vaughn to a kitchen chair. Shelby glared at Garrison until he sat next to Vaughn. All three brothers looked like limp dishrags as they slouched and groaned around the table. Hopefully, Sara was distracting Zach and Mr. Taggart, because they shouldn't have to see their family members in such a state.

Minutes later, Ruth tapped Izzy on the shoulder.

"What?" Multiple sets of eyes settled on Izzy. Her neck warmed.

Vaughn broke the tension and pointed at Kerr. "Your eyes, dude. It's not a good look. You're like a creature out of a bad horror movie." He paused and rested his head on his thick forearms for a second. "Shit, I feel like the south end of a northbound mule," he muttered, finally lifting his head back up.

Odie shot them a tight smile. "Shoo-wee, you boys do look like you been dragged through hell and back." His humor came out too forced. Too flippant. Didn't fit the wrinkled brow and glances he shot Ruth. "Want to explain all the ruckus?"

"No." Garrison rubbed his temples.

"Yes," Kerr snapped. He scowled at his older brother. "Don't give me the stink-eye, Gar. We're all in this pile of manure together." His gaze scraped over Izzy. "We saw the creature that, uh, ate your brother." Ducking his head, he added, "Sorry, Iz. That was the wrong way to say it."

She sucked in air and rocked back on her heels, glancing toward the door. Hank was out there, somewhere. "What did it do to you?"

"Handed us our ass." Vaughn grimaced. Then he sniffed and leaned back in the chair. "Actually, we handed him his own ass. It was pretty much a draw tonight. No offense, Izzy, since in a twisted way, part of that thing is kind of your family and all."

In spite of the ridiculous situation, she smiled. "No offense taken."

"We worked together to get rid of the thing," Garrison said. "But no guarantee it'll stay gone. We wouldn't be that lucky."

"'What did it want?" Shelby asked. Eric joined them and hovered near her shoulder.

Garrison's jaw went rock hard. "You."

"Huh?" she said.

Eric dropped his hand on Shelby's shoulder.

"Actually, it wanted the four of us, I assume for the purpose Izzy had mentioned earlier." Garrison's mouth dropped. "If we hadn't stopped it, the thing would have kept going until it finished the entire family. Son of a bitch, this is bad."

Kerr patted the back of Izzy's gloved hand. "We need to understand more about the blade and why it's so damned important. How we can stop them. How we can stop *it*."

"We must know the components," Ruth spoke up. "Once we are certain what it's creating, we might be able to fight it."

"Do I want to know how you all know that information?" Vaughn groaned.

Zero mirth showed in Odie's glass-green eyes. "No."

Izzy did her level best to melt into the red and white tile floor. Didn't work.

Ruth turned toward her. "Izzy, if you have a detailed map, can you draw the boundaries of your family's property, including the likely location of the mining?"

She visualized the boundary of the ranch land nearest the Taggart acres. "Yes."

"Time to take a trip to the Wyoming Office of State Lands and Investments," Ruth said. "While you're getting that information, we can finish some research here."

"Whoa, there. We can't let her out of our sight," Garrison pointed a blunt finger at her.

Little painful pops prickled under her skin. "Hello? She can hear you," Izzy said between gritted teeth.

Silence smeared its way through the room.

Shelby rubbed the bridge of her nose while Eric dropped his hands on his girlfriend's shoulders.

"I like her!" Odie grinned. "That kind of fire reminds me of someone I knew all too well." He slung an arm around Ruth's waist and winked at her. "Don't you think?"

"Yes, I see it, but it's not possible," the woman murmured.

"I'll go get the information." Izzy paused and stared at the ridiculous lumps of her hands, covered in oversized gloves.

"You're not fit for driving." Kerr patted her arm again. "I'll keep you company."

A warm wave flowed in and out of her chest. Ability to detect emotion, or her own feelings? Who knew anymore.

"Good, then you can make sure she doesn't go all turncoat and run back to her place," Garrison said, eyes narrowed.

Warm wave, gone. Cold puddle remained.

"Tone down the aggression, dude." Kerr spun in his chair, facing his brother.

"Well, that's all a splendid idea, but I'd like to know something far more pressing." Ruth crossed her arms. "How did you steal my power?"

"And mine," Shelby added.

"I don't know," Izzy sputtered.

Vaughn stood up, fists clenched. "Wait. Ruth. What power do *you* have?"

~

"Tell me about your life. How's your mom doing?" Sara dabbed at Izzy's hands as they sat on the guest bed in the Taggart household. Night had fallen. After a brief, quiet dinner, everyone had retreated to their own spaces.

The revelation that Ruth had a nebulous ability similar to the Taggarts gave them all more than enough new information to digest this evening. Apparently the woman could augment other powers and even shield a bit. Explained why the Taggart kids had gifts. They inherited it from their great-great however many times great grandmother.

The question with no answer was why Izzy suddenly could absorb powers. It must have something to do with the botched communion with Jerahmeel, but how and why? And what did it mean?

At least Sara was safe from Izzy's psychic leech skills.

She sighed. "Work at the hardware store is awful, and I don't want to go into it about Mom. She's not going to get better. She's sure not going to get nicer. Thank God I convinced Butch to watch her for a few days. It's such a bad situation. One the one hand, my other brothers won't pitch in and help, but on the flipside, they don't want her in assisted living or a nursing home." Her chest ached when she took a deep breath. At least her hands felt better, thanks to Ruth's special salve. "Hey, why don't you let me live vicariously? Spill some details about how things are going with your hot rancher."

A dimple winked in Sara's cheek. "A rocky patch there a week or so ago, but he came around." The smile grew. "Now he's groveling. As he should do."

"Strong work. He seems grumpy to me." She tried to point a thumb toward herself. "He's not a big fan of yours truly."

"Oh, he's all bark and no bite. Or, maybe a little bite." Sara tucked a piece of dark hair behind her ear and ducked her head. "We're still figuring out how the relationship should go, with him working long hours on the ranch and with my teaching. And we're trying to be super careful with Zach. Neither of us wants him to get hurt. I don't want him to forget his mother, but..."

"She died, didn't she? That was the rumor."

"Yeah."

"No one around here knew until recently that she had passed away."

Sara didn't meet her eyes as she wrapped the cloth around Izzy's hands. "Well, Hank knew. They were kind of...close. Right around when she drained Garrison's bank account and left town."

She winced. "Wow. My family keeps getting better and better. I can see why Garrison's not my biggest fan."

"What happened with his wife and Hank was not your fault, and Garrison realizes that." After taping the last bandage in place, she pressed her palms into the bedspread and leaned back. "Anyway, the situation is complicated. But I do love that kid."

"You'd be a wonderful stepmom to Zach. No question."

"Aw, thanks." She shrugged. "Maybe we'll get to that point of official stepmom one day."

"I think so. Now, what about Garrison?" Izzy leaned forward.

The flush reddened the olive-colored skin over Sara's neck and upper chest. "Well, yes. Sexy rancher. Hmm. I kind of like him. A lot. Maybe more than a lot."

"Bet it's mutual."

Her smile grew. "Evidence suggests that is the case."

"Like, wild and crazy, earth-shattering evidence?" No way would Izzy be jealous of her friend. Sara deserved happiness.

Raising eyebrows to project the very image of innocence, she grinned. "He's quite competent at everything he does."

The laugh burst out of Izzy in tiny carbonated bubbles of weightless happiness. She relaxed on the bed and crossed her socked feet at the ankles. "Details?"

Her friend tapped a manicured finger to her lipstick-stained mouth. "Hmm. Let's just say that in bed, he's generous."

"Oh, like Mother Teresa generous?"

Sara covered the snort that escaped. "And with that one image, you've ruined sex with him. Every time I look at him I'll see a nun in a bad habit." She sniffed. "He's pretty much *not* Mother Teresa. Thanks."

"Don't mention it. Always happy to help."

Sara jumped at a knock on the door.

"Expecting someone?" Izzy asked.

"No idea," Sara said as she got up from the bed.

Kerr's tall frame took up most of the doorway space. The air left the room. Izzy's heart pounded and her head felt light.

"Hi," he said, running a hand through his short, orange hair. Izzy wanted to do the same thing. A tendril of cedar and sage flowed past her, and suddenly her appetite returned.

"What are you doing here?" she asked.

"Nice to see you, too. Also, I do live here." He glanced over at Sara. "Mind if I have a minute?"

"No problem." Sara hugged Izzy. "I need to go to confession."

"Huh?" Kerr asked.

Sara grinned. "Nothing," she chirped as she slipped out of the room.

He shook his head. Then paused inside the door, not quite meeting Izzy's gaze.

"Oh. Got it," she said after a few moments of silence. "You're taking over duties to keep an eye on me."

"No way. It's not like that."

"Hey, I heard what Garrison said earlier. And I get it. I'm still a person of interest to him. Message received."

"Sorry." His broad shoulders slumped. "Mind if I...come in?"

Raising her bandaged hand, she projected nonchalance she didn't feel. Especially when he shut the door with a quiet click of the latch. Her heart jumped.

"How are your hands?"

She gave him a lumpy wave. "Better. Whatever is in Ruth's salve, it's working. Might be able to take off bandages tomorrow evening."

"Yeah, my ribs are remarkably improved after they were crushed by Linc's size tens. Bless Nurse Ruth and her treatments."

When he sat on the end of the bed next to her, the dip in the mattress acted like gravity, pulling her toward him. Her hands prickled more the closer he came. She made a deliberate effort to keep her hands away from him. No more power swapping tonight. She'd had enough.

"Are you all right?" he asked, that tenor voice warming her insides.

She took in his still-bruised face, courtesy of Linc, and his eerie bloodshot eyes, courtesy of who-knew-what. "Seems like I should be asking you that question."

"Fine. I love a good ass-kicking, same as any other guy. And an ass-kicking by a cloud demon bent on enslaving all humanity? Well, that's a bonus."

Despite herself, a smile crept over her face. "Seems like you gave that creature the what for."

He shifted close but didn't touch her. "We had help. According to Ruth, it was your help." The way he studied her face made her feel more like a science experiment. "Still not sure how Ruth had a power in the first place. She wasn't real forthcoming on that detail. Must be part of our crazy family tree not branching way back when. Anyway, back to you. How did you absorb her ability?"

"No idea. Up until recently, I never knew it was possible, because I never knew people like you existed." She sniffed. "And in my defense, I was perfectly normal until I started hanging around you."

His wry grin made her smile again as he put a thumb to his chest. "We should have started hanging out together sooner."

Didn't she know it. Yet for years, she'd done nothing. Now? She might have missed her chance.

"At least it didn't look like I hurt Ruth or Shelby when I absorbed some of their power. I'd feel awful if that had happened."

"I can't imagine you hurting anyone, Iz."

"Oh, I can bring the heat."

"Who says 'bring the heat' anymore? Really."

She pursed her lips. "Thought it sounded pretty darn tough."

"You, my friend, might be tough, but you don't talk tough."

My friend.

Well, there you go.

"So, you need to put an ankle bracelet on me to track my location, since I'm under house arrest?"

"Naw. I trust you."

"Do you? After everything?"

He dropped his gaze. Enough said.

"Um, I came in here to let you know that we're leaving for

Cheyenne at seven tomorrow morning." He scuffed one boot on the floor. "And to see if you needed anything."

A laugh bubbled up and threatened to turn into a pathetic sob. She swallowed a hard ball in her throat. "Cheyenne?"

"So we can get the mineral data on your family's tract of land. Be ready for whatever happens. Sure you're okay?"

"I'm good. Everyone's been very nice to me. Except for Garrison, and I can see where he's coming from."

"He's just got a crusty exterior. Big softie inside."

She leaned back on her hands but winced and sat forward. "If you say so."

"So, uh, do you need anything?"

"You already asked me that." Rubbing her hands, she willed the palms to stop tingling.

His lean cheeks turned pink. "Yup." *Scuff, scuff.* "Well, if you need anything, I'm right down the hall." A quick smile and he bumped his shoulder against hers. He leaned closer. The point of contact warmed her skin, even through her borrowed shirt.

Tempting, damn it. Oh, so tempting. Just like the proximity of her lips to his.

Damn it, but the timing sucked. Between her possessed brothers and cousin, the lurking evil creature taking over her family's ranch, and this ability to yank power away from other people, now wasn't exactly a great time.

"Look, Kerr. I wish...stuff had been different. But things happened. With us. You know?"

That smile fell. "Trust me, I know all about bad luck and bad timing." He rubbed his thigh.

"It's not—"

His hand chopped through air. "No worries." Pushing to his feet, he shifted his stance for a few seconds. His smile didn't reach his eyes. "Have a good night, Iz."

Then he was out the door with another swish of air and a click of the latch.

CHAPTER 19

*A*nd that's how the woman Kerr needed to steer clear of ended up in the passenger seat of his old truck as the vehicle rumbled down I-90 en route to the Wyoming Office of State Lands and Investments in Cheyenne, on a blustery Tuesday. He rubbed his eyes. They were still gummy from lack of sleep, thanks to Izzy's presence a few feet down the hall in a guest room.

Also, the flashbacks didn't help his ability to get a full night's sleep either, but he didn't count that as anything unusual.

Outside the vehicle, the air was so cold that snow had turned to powdery dust, swept back and forth on the lightly traveled interstate as each vehicle passed.

But the interior of the truck? Too warm. Too close. Too much Izzy. She unzipped her coat. The flannel shirt and jeans might be simple, but the sight made his mouth water. His reaction had more to do with the woman than the attire. How badly had he wanted to kiss her again last night in the bedroom? Why hadn't he?

It would have been so easy to lean over a few inches and taste those full lips. So easy to ease her back on the guest room bed and see if that passionate kiss behind the store was a fluke or not. Would her skin be as silky soft as he imagined? Her curves as tempting?

Based on her friend-zone reaction last night, he would probably never find out the answer to that question, and wasn't that a damned shame.

What about her new trick? If he touched her, skin to skin, would she steal his power, too?

He also had no idea what her conversion experience by that cloud terror, Jerahmeel, meant for Izzy down the road. One day, would a switch flip and she'd suddenly become possessed and dangerous, like her brothers?

He glanced at her in his peripheral vision. Surely not Izzy.

She sighed and stared at her bandaged hands, and his palms ached in sympathy. What he'd give to have the power to take away that pain.

"Penny for your thoughts?" Kerr broke the silence.

"You'd go broke." She motioned toward the housing on either side of the interstate. "We're close to town."

"Yep. We'll be at the office in fifteen minutes or so." He tapped his fingers on the steering wheel. "You and Sara been friends for a long time?" Anything to keep her talking. Her clear voice acted like a balm on his riled nerves. Actually, no, it was her presence. Pretty sure if she were next to him during the night, he wouldn't have those bad flashbacks. Wouldn't he love to do an experiment and see if that theory held up.

She cocked her head to the side and a tiny smile curved her mouth. "Since elementary school. Always had my back. She's the best."

"I agree. Sara's got Garrison under her thumb. That poor sap never knew what hit him. But, boy, did he need someone like her in his life."

"Sure. The downside of them dating is how it cut down on our girls' night out time."

"Girls' night out.. What exactly is that?"

She peered ahead through the front window. Thin snow swirled on the road in front of them. "You wouldn't understand. It's special."

"Try me."

"You don't know?"

"Hey, I've read a few *Cosmos* in the day." He tried not to squirm as she studied him.

"You read *Cosmo*?"

"I have read one. Past tense. And it was because I'd already read the Manly Sports and Big Gun Quarterly and was bored in the therapy waiting room."

"Hopefully you took the quiz." Her laugh surprised him. "But seriously, you really want to know what Sara and I do for girls' night out?"

"Yes." He meant it.

She moved to push her hair back then stopped and let her hand rest again on her lap. "We haven't had a girls' night out in way too long with...everything going on." He whipped his head around at a hitch in her voice. "It's kind of like date night but with one or more of my friends. And always involving Sara, because...Sara's awesome. Sometimes we go out for a few drinks in town. Sometimes it's staying in with greasy, calorie-laden takeout, some gossip, and movies."

"Why don't guys do this?"

"It's called hanging out at the sports bar and shooting pool. Or going to a 'man cave.' You all do it on a regular basis, but 'boys' night out' doesn't have the same ring to it."

"Got it."

"It's not like I don't understand her priorities—hey, things change. She's got someone new in her life. But I miss that time with Sara." She paused. "Don't get me wrong. I'm happy for her. Seriously."

He lifted one hand. "You don't have to convince me. I'm amazed someone knocked the edges off Mr. Grumpy. He deserves happiness." Gripping the steering wheel, he stared straight ahead, unable to meet her sky-blue gaze. "You do too, Iz."

The pause was a beat too long. "I'll work on that happiness thing once this mess with my family and that Jerahmeel creature is over."

"Then there'll be something else that stops you." Crap, did those words come out of his mouth. Based on the stiffening of her shoulders, yes.

Crossing her arms, she murmured, "Can we concentrate on the minerals?"

Message received. "Sure, Iz. You got it."

She pulled up the map on her phone, her finger movements awkward due to the bandages. "Take the next exit..."

Even if Iz had any interest in him, she had way too much going on in her life to deal with a new relationship. He totally got it. His recovery after the injury in Afghanistan had taken over his life for several years, kept him from pursuing...anything else.

Or maybe he'd used the speed bumps in his life as excuses for not taking risks in his personal life. Damn.

Glancing at the beautiful woman next to him, he groaned inwardly. He stomped on the brake a bit too hard and they jolted forward. Hard to feel the pedal when there wasn't a foot present.

In short, no, he wasn't ready to evaluate what got in the way of him having a normal life or a normal relationship with someone.

Izzy's long, blonde hair gleamed this morning, and his fingers itched to let the strands slide through. He rolled his hand into a fist and instead flicked the turn signal.

Downtown Cheyenne the week before Christmas still had some traffic on this weekday. A big change from tiny Copper River. Hell, they even had stoplights here and more than one lane of traffic. Kerr had to pay extra attention.

"Turn left, and the parking should be on the right." She pointed.

It had been more than six months since he'd been to Cheyenne for a checkup. He glanced toward the east. The VA hospital, with its orderly and stately brick buildings, had been a mixed blessing. For all the help he had received there, he wanted to avoid driving past it. No sense in dragging up memories. Because those activities led back to one place: wishful thinking, anger, and regret. He pulled into the lot near the Wyoming Office of State Lands and Investments.

Izzy jumped out of the truck, tried to zip up her coat, and failed. She pulled the sides together. "Brr. Let's get this over with." With one eye open, she scowled up at the gray sky that hung heavy above them. Even the weather dared them to try to return to Copper River tonight.

Kerr glanced at his watch: 3:00 p.m.. The six-hour drive had taken longer than usual with the weather. As if the sky wanted to rub his mug in the exhausting trip, a few flakes began to drift down from the thick clouds.

Once through the glass doors of the modern building, they found a helpful receptionist, who directed them to the mineral survey office, tucked a few hallways deep into the building. The man at the desk took a full sixty seconds to look up from his computer.

Come on, man. Kerr's blood heated.

Izzy shrugged out of her coat and laid it on the counter.

After a double take, the man perked up. "You need something?" Then the worker spent another ten seconds eyeing Izzy, and Kerr's blood began to boil.

The guy sucked in his paunch and took off his circa 1990 plastic frame glasses. Oh yeah, that improved the overall look. Not.

"Help with mineral surveys in western Wyoming," Kerr said sharply.

The guy smoothed the thinning hair over the top of his head and barely spared Kerr a glance. "With the storm rolling in, I was getting ready to head home...Maybe come back tomorrow."

No telling how many tomorrows the Taggart family had left. They needed the information now. "Office says open until 4:30," Kerr reminded him.

"Unless 'inclement weather,' bud. And with that attitude, I believe the weather is getting worse by the minute."

Kerr's hands curled into fists. What he'd give to plant a knuckle or two into the guy's saggy jowl.

"Oh, gosh, that's too bad." Izzy played with a strand of flaxen hair and leaned forward against the counter, giving the guy a view of flannel covering a shapely chest. Only in Wyoming could flannel be considered sexy material. Kerr smiled. On Izzy, burlap would look hot.

Her fading bruises must not have deterred the guy, judging by the way his hand swooped over his hair again, patting it into place.

"Well, maybe I could stick around a little longer. As a favor." Travis —Kerr checked the placard on the desk—stood up and moseyed around the counter, all but ignoring Kerr as he waved Izzy to precede him. "What can I help you with, little lady?"

The irritated purse of her lips was smoothed away in a cute pout. "We're looking for a map or a listing of mineral rights on a property. Thinking about leasing."

"What would a gal like you want to do with minerals, anyway? Prospecting for some gold or silver, maybe?" The man chuckled, leaning against the counter and resting an arm far too close to her for Kerr's comfort.

Izzy's tinkling laugh almost sounded sincere. Not like a woman who could verbally disembowel a hapless suck-up like Travis. "Well. We're interested in lots of mineral opportunities in the area. And the receptionist up front said you were *the best* person to help us."

"Well, I am the expert." Dude looked like a balding rooster with a sucked-in gut that at some point would suddenly re-inflate and explode his faded tan button down shirt. "Let's you and I go back to the records room and see what I can get for you."

"Oh thank you," she gushed, as she flipped a piece of hair over her shoulder and shot Kerr a perfect eye roll.

Ten minutes later, the guy had several paper maps laid out on the large table in the center of the room. According to Travis, Wyoming hadn't made all of the maps electronic yet. But soon, he promised.

"Here's the area you wondered about." He leaned toward Izzy as he reached across and pointed to an area near Copper River. "Let's see... lots of interesting minerals and stones. Anything in particular you're looking for?"

She bit her lip and frowned.

They needed to figure out what that plot of land had to do with the knife.

"By any chance do you know anything about forging a knife blade?" Kerr ventured.

"Some. Used to make them with my dad years ago. Even had a forge at the house and everything." He glanced over at Izzy, who made an appropriately interested mumble.

Kerr rubbed a thumb over the brim of his hat he held. "Anything in that area that would make a blade super sharp or strong?"

An intake of breath, and Izzy's light brows shot up. "Yes. What about a mineral that could transmit heat? Or conduct, uh, energy?"

Good thinking, Iz.

Travis studied them for too long. "Hmm. You would need something like silver or copper for conduction. But why would someone want a conductive knife? That's kind of an odd request." He pulled out another plat map and peered over it, tapping the paper "Here, copper. Of course, it's near Copper River. Makes sense." The guy chuckled, like he thought he made the world's most clever joke. "Of course, you're only using these metals to coat the steel. You'll need a binding agent to put them together."

"Like?" Kerr asked. He both hoped and dreaded the answer.

"Bentonite is a good option, and it's abundant in the Green River basin. Maybe there's some up in your neck of the woods, too. Ah, yes. There." Another stubbed finger pointed at the map.

"How about something to make it sharp? Or hold a sharp edge?" Izzy's voice came out breathless.

Kerr's ears started to buzz. Shit on shit. They were looking at Jerahmeel's plan, right in front of them. He dropped a hand on Izzy's tense shoulder and squeezed. Needed to feel her next to him. Needed to make that contact, believe that she was safe.

For now. Damn.

Travis stared up at the ceiling, like the answer existed in the fluorescent light tubes. "For that you need something different, like maybe…obsidian."

"Obsidian?" Her brows drew together.

Mr. Overly Helpful stepped up to the table and leaned in. "Sure, like from an old volcano. You don't find obsidian just anywhere, either."

Yellowstone. The Tetons. The entire caldera region.

Right beneath Copper River.

"Hey, looks like you have obsidian there as well. Weird."

"Why weird?" Kerr asked.

Travis leaned over the map, pulled out a more detailed one, spread it out, and put his nose a few inches from the grids. "Because there's only one place in Wyoming that has all three of those elements."

No need to share the answer. Kerr knew. "Copper River."

"Sure, but specifically that large plat of land." Travis squinted. "And the property next to it because it goes up into an escarpment near the National Forest in one corner of the property."

The property next to it. The Taggart ranch.

The Brands had been trying to purchase his family's ranch.

Suddenly shit made a hell of a lot of sense. This second coming of evil, or takeover of the Taggart family, or whatever the hell it was, had been in the works for some time. How hadn't Izzy known until now?

No. He would not suspect her. She was trustworthy.

"Travis, how deep would these minerals be? Any idea?" Kerr caught her worried expression.

Another few seconds of hemming and hawing. "Looks like if you go to the back of the main property, you catch part of that escarpment. Could access most minerals pretty easily there."

Izzy piped up. "Most?"

"Except for the binding agent, bentonite. That's on this second acreage next door. Barely inside the property lines. But also pretty shallow. Easy to access."

That was why the Brands had threatened Kerr and Garrison when they wandered too close to the line while skirting the property in the National Forest.

They'd been mining in clear sight, and the Taggarts had been too busy dealing with the sabotage to their ranch to figure it out. Kerr and Garrison had even seen mining equipment then. Damn it.

How long had it been since anyone checked that far corner of his family's property? A month, give or take. Long enough for those bastards to pull minerals out of the soil.

And forge a knife.

CHAPTER 20

*I*zzy's stomach rumbled for the third time in fifteen minutes. She paced the one bedroom hotel suite and peered out the window at the near whiteout conditions. Yeah, the storm that had threatened all day had finally slammed into eastern Wyoming just as she and Kerr tried to leave town. WYDOT had closed I-90.

Luckily, when they finally returned to Cheyenne, they found a hotel room still available, even with all the stranded travelers scrambling for a place to stay for the night.

What the town didn't have was an abundance of restaurants open in a blizzard.

Where was he? Was he okay? An image of Kerr's truck wrecked, down a snowy embankment, slammed into her mind.

She'd go out and look for him, but she didn't know where to start.

Another five minutes passed. Her belly growled again. Her heart pounded double time. With a finger, she moved the curtain to the side and shivered, despite the heater running.

She rubbed her bandaged palms over her jeans and paced again.

The electronic door lock whirred; she spun around.

Her mouth watered, but not for food. A few remaining flakes melted on the top of Kerr's hat, which he removed as he stepped into the room. With a twinkle in his brown and gold eyes, he shook the bag in his hands. One whiff and her interest shifted to the contents of that bag. Smelled like…fried chicken. Yum.

Kerr hadn't moved. Hadn't stopped staring at her. His stubbled, bruised jaw remained locked in place.

Her mouth went dry. Okay. What was he waiting for? Maybe he needed to give a speech before handing over the amazing chicken feast. God, she would starve, four feet from fried paradise.

"So here's how this is going to work," he said, one corner of his mouth lifting.

Tons of non-edible ideas raced through her mind. *No, stay in the friend zone.*

She tilted her head to the side. "How it will work? Here's how: I put food in my face and am happy. That's how."

The flash of his big grin turned her knees weak. Had to be an effect of low blood sugar.

"You said something to me earlier today that I thought about. We're stuck here at least until tomorrow."

The breath left her as her heart thudded. Had she said the things she'd imagined out loud, about wanting to taste his skin or check out his muscles? Not that she'd mind living out her fantasies where Kerr was involved. *Think.* What had she said? She came up with nothing.

Nothing but chicken on the brain.

Okay, chicken and hot rancher, if she were being totally honest with herself.

Yum times two.

Another stomach rumble shifted the gauge back toward chicken. For now. "Well, don't just stand there, cowboy. Give me the rules so I can eat. I'm dying here."

He made a show of delaying things. Dropped the hat on the counter. Set the bag down on the small table. Put a four-pack of beer bottles in the small refrigerator. Shrugged out of his duster.

For the love of—

She hadn't noticed that the brown paisley shirt he wore had pearl snap buttons and angled chest pockets. The fabric strained over shifting chest and shoulder muscles as he moved. The hem disappeared beneath the trim waistband of dark blue denim jeans. And the area of Izzy's shifting hunger lay right below that silver belt buckle. She swallowed. *Yes, please.*

Less fried chicken. More hello, cowboy.

He leaned a hip on the table, the move more of an uncoiling of his tense frame than actual leaning. "So, on the ride over today, you mentioned how you missed girls' night out with Sara."

Hanging out with Sara was the last thing that came to mind when looking at the long, lean guy in front of her. "So?"

"So, I'm going to give you a girls' night out." A flash of worry creased his forehead.

"You're not a girl."

"Hope not."

An involuntary reflex made her slide a glance over his denim. Definitely male. Her face burned. She lifted her chin. "You don't know all of the rules. It's complicated."

"Educate me."

Was it warm in here, or had she developed a fever? Her palms itched again, too.

He pressed his mouth into a line. "Never mind. It was a dumb idea. Here."

Heart plummeting, she reached forward. "No. I appreciate this. It just came out of left field." She cleared her throat. "It's been a long time since...someone did a nice thing like this." A lump in her throat made it hard to speak. She stepped back. God, if he touched her, that would be disastrous. "Okay. How about we start with the eating of greasy foods in nice company and take it from there?"

"I can live with chicken, potato salad, brownies...and nice company."

"I call BS on the nice company part. I'm not the best person to be around with all the craziness. But thank you anyway." Her stomach churned and not from hunger.

His gaze flicked to her and away. "Uh. I hope you're okay with me trying to fill in for Sara. I didn't exactly ask permission."

The prickle in her eyes made her blink, and she studied the linoleum table. "It's a really nice gesture. Thank you."

Silence.

His chest rose and fell, stretching the fabric of his shirt.

He cleared his throat. "Izzy?"

No way could she handle his pity. Not tonight. "Well, let's go. Chicken and company." Her words came out too bright. Too forced. She glanced up. "Please."

One curt nod. "Yep. Let's get our fried food game on." Thank God he didn't press. The twinkle in his eyes looked strained. Maybe it had to do with the redness still in the whites. He pulled two dishes and silverware from the kitchenette and set the table. A crease of pain came and went over his face when he leaned down. Right. Because of his ribs.

"We've had a rough couple of days. Let's just enjoy a meal together. Like two normal people who don't have crazy things going on in our lives. How about we start there?"

She tugged at her plain flannel shirt then gazed up at his rugged cowboy-chic attire. Wow. He could double as a model for the Langston's western clothing catalogue.

"So?" By the glint in his eye, he'd caught her staring.

Meeting his gaze, she raised her eyebrows. "Let's get it on." The flirting felt foreign, but she enjoyed it.

"Oh?" His mellow voice rolled right over her, drawing chills down her spine.

"Dinner, of course." She sniffed. "What did you think I meant?"

"You can mean anything you want to, Iz." The smile stayed put, but the intensity of his stare triggered a happy, warm swirl right down in her pelvis. Then one blink later, he broke the strange spell. "I'm starving."

Before she could retort, he turned back to the kitchenette and filled two glasses with water. "Napkin?" he asked as he set down the items.

"Several. When it comes to the sauce, it gets all over me."

He stopped for a full three seconds. His pupils dilated. Nostrils flared.

Oh. Well. Didn't the atmosphere heat right up, like a thunderstorm about to explode with lightning?

An image of the two of them, naked, with activities involving secret sauce shot through her brain. Now she couldn't breathe. Fried poultry had never been this appetizing before.

He set an entire roll of paper towels on the center of the table with a flourish and a wink. Damn that cheeky grin.

"Go first," he said. "You seem hungry." He eased into the chair opposite hers.

Well played, Mr. Double Entendre.

She selected a piece of steaming fried chicken and spooned potato salad on the plate. The warm brownie would have to wait for dessert. Her first bite of the chicken? Bliss for her taste buds and empty belly. The tangy sauce with the crunch of amazing, deep-fried meat was fabulous.

So much better than being home in the muck of her life back on the ranch. Her throat tightened and she forced the bite of food down.

Quit it. No guilt. No planning her exit. No worrying about Mom. No trying to figure out her mutation or whatever it was making her a magnet for people's power.

Tonight was to enjoy a nice guy's company.

Kerr, nice?

Not exactly. More like…appetizing.

A smear of sauce rested on his lower lip and her muscles twitched with the urge to remove that spot. With her mouth. *Stop it. Concentrate on chicken.*

Pretty sure her eyes rolled up in her head at the next bite, the action not totally due to fried chicken.

For his part, Kerr leaned back and rested an ankle on his knee as he devoured a wing.

When she came up for air, she said, "Where did you find this?" waving toward the snow swirling through the parking lot lights outside.

"Bubba's Pub and Grub, just down the road. Best chicken anywhere. I used to get it when I was here—"

Silence.

"Recovering?"

"Uh huh."

Hurrying to fill the thick space, she said, "So you conspired to set this up? Girls' night out."

"Hope you like it. When I realized we were stuck here, I thought we could make the best of the delay."

Why yes, she could find several ways to make the best of their time here. "Of course I like this," she managed. "Really, all you had to say was 'chicken' and I'd be on board."

"Had I known it would be that simple, I would have tried that a long time ago."

Her heart skipped and hopped a few beats as her equilibrium shifted.

"So, are you okay from...what happened at the store with Linc and at your ranch with that creature?" she asked. "Your eyes...is that all from fighting Jerahmeel?"

He blinked, the bright red staying in the whites. "My eyeballs only look bad." Pressing his mouth into a tight line, he said, "But, yes, I should have brushed up on army hand-to-hand training prior to hanging out with you. Hey, it takes a lot more than a couple of assholes and a demon to get me down." He lifted a shoulder. "Pardon for talking poorly about your relatives and, uh, guests."

"I'm not offended by you. I'm offended by my family."

"Yeah, you sure gave it to Linc, behind the store the other day."

Her head whipped up. "How—how did you know that? You were gone by then. Oh, right. The disappearing trick."

The only sound in the room was the light rumble of the small refrigerator.

He unfolded a fisted hand resting on the table. "Yeah."

"How does that work anyway?"

He reached for another piece of chicken. "Not completely sure. But when I need to...fade away, I concentrate on doing so, almost like holding back a sneeze sensation. Then I get a whopper of a headache and I disappear."

"How long has it been like that?"

"Since I was a kid. Same for all of us." He took a bite and chewed thoughtfully. "How did you pull Ruth's power from her?"

"No idea. All I knew was that I felt that things were going on outside, because I had absorbed Shelby's emotion-detecting ability. You all were upset and scared. And I wanted to help you...all. Somehow I knew Ruth was trying to help. I needed to do something. So I did."

"That's all?"

"Well, my hands itched right before it happened." She stared at her sauce-stained bandages. "Which reminds me, I'll need to take these off and clean up. Should be done with bandages, according to Ruth."

"Want help?"

"It'll be fine. I can do it." She started unwrapping. Damn it. She needed to keep bantering. If Kerr played the sensitive-guy card, she had no defenses. She could handle everything but someone who truly cared. When in doubt, divert. "Want brownies?"

"Izzy," he began.

"No, seriously. These are the best brownies in the universe." She dabbed her red but no longer blistered palms on the napkin, wiping the last of the ointment off the skin.

Please take the hint.

A pause. "Sure." When she handed him the brownie piece on the wax paper, their fingertips brushed together.

A zap of *good God almighty* shot straight to her heart and jolted her to attention. Not the itchy-hand power grab sensation. Something much more exciting.

He tore off a corner of the treat and popped it in his mouth, the muscle on his jaw working. "It's perfect." He winked. "I might want seconds."

CHAPTER 21

*I*f Izzy Brand licked one more morsel of sauce off her lips, Kerr would climb across this table and take no responsibility for what happened next. As it stood, every time her tongue darted out, a blast of hell-yeah tightened his dick to where the damn thing protested being trapped in its denim jail.

Smack him on the ass and call him Colonel Sanders. He was actually jealous of a piece of chicken.

Fried food and fixings aside, he had a mission to carry out: give her a nice evening where she could escape the evil dogging them back in Copper River.

His conscience ached every time he looked at that fading purple bruise over her cheek. Linc's work. Damn it, he should have stopped that from happening to her. He should have protected her from her own moronic family members.

He needed her to be safe.

He needed her.

Uh oh.

But even now, drowning in Izzy's sky-blue eyes and tumble of long, blonde hair, the urge to protect her overrode his other base instincts. What he'd give to wrap his arms around her and never let go. He had fought the urge to go back to her room late last night. But he wasn't a saint. God knew how long he could hold out in forced close quarters.

Or he could overcome his chaste state and let go of her long enough to remove those form-fitting jeans and long-sleeved flannel shirt. How amazing would she look, sprawled on a bed, naked, her luscious mouth open in an O of pleasure.

Aaaaand…right back to inappropriate thoughts.

He shifted in the chair. Anything to relieve the growing pressure.

She passed him a brownie, and the blast of interest from that simple contact between their hands should have warned him that he was in a shitload of trouble where Izzy was concerned.

Even if it had been an option to get two rooms, he didn't want to be separated from her. Not in a million years. Not with Izzy popping a piece of brownie between those full, pink lips.

After dinner torture ended, she cleaned her hands. Thank God the blisters were nearly gone, thanks to Ruth's miracle balm. What he'd give to inflict that kind of damage on Jerahmeel in payback. *Later. Save that feeling for later.*

Together, he and Izzy cleared the table and he washed the few dishes, like a regular couple. Comfortable. Normal.

Their lives were in no state for either comfortable or normal.

So, what then? If not long-term potential, was Izzy a possible fling —someone for a little fun until he moved on? Because the signals she gave off seemed to match his own interest.

A fling. Izzy?

Absolutely not.

She deserved better. Truth be told, she deserved better than he could offer her with his PTSD issues and insecurities. Add in the crazy family situation and the danger surrounding him…People got hurt when they became close to a Taggart sibling. Besides…shifting weight from one foot to another and testing the stability of his still-sore leg, he swallowed. She deserved…more…than he was. Or maybe that was another of his excuses.

As she dried a dish, her hip brushed against his.

Kerr's mouth went dry.

Holy overreaction, Batman. If he had this much trouble focusing while they were washing dishes? Oh hell, he was in deep.

What was his mission tonight again? He'd forgotten.

He swallowed. "So, what's the next step of girls' night out? Uh, what do you normally do? Make collages or something? How about hair? Nails?"

Her quick wink made his heart flop. "Oh, personal beauty regimens for sure. You volunteering as the manicurist or the model?"

Inspecting his neatly trimmed nails on work-worn hands, he tilted his head to the side. "I could use a touch-up on my polish. What about a nice fuchsia?"

That light giggle of hers was a heady brew distilled from 100 percent pure joy, and he wanted to be the happiest lush in the world. "Want your toes done, too?" Then she froze. "Oh, damn it, I'm so sorry."

"Hey." He bumped her hip with his own. "Don't worry about it. I've always wanted nails painted on the prosthetic."

"Kerr, I—"

"Drop it."

She flinched.

Shit, too late for him to take back the too-sharp words. "So, you were telling me about your evening escapades with Sara?"

Thank God she smiled again, though the light in her eyes had dimmed. "Sounds like racy pj's and pillow fights when you put it that way." She brushed the hair back from around her face with the back of her hands. His mind took him exactly to an image of Izzy in racy pj's engaged in a pillow fight. "Well, there's always greasy food and simple carbs involved."

"Mission accomplished on that item."

She nodded. "Then there's gossip."

"I can do that."

"Wait. There's more." Her voice grew serious. Her light eyebrows rose. "Now we must commence the Watching of Girly Shows."

"I don't know about this primitive womanly ritual. Like what kind of shows?"

"Ones like *Fiery Fangs*, only the best vampire series in the universe."

"Uh, isn't that kind of scary and dark? Are you sure you want to watch that show, given everything that's happened with Jerahmeel and Hank and your family?"

A pause. "I think of it as over-the-top ridiculous and an escape. Watching my favorite show, even a weird paranormal one, makes me feel normal. Which is what I need."

"Makes sense." He paused. "I don't guess there are a lot of guns and ninja fighting in that show?"

"Very little. But lots of vampire chests and long, sexy stares."

Did he really have to watch an overacted Dracula soap opera with Izzy close by? God clearly hated him. "So I have a confession to make."

"Oh?" She faced him, leaning a perfectly curved hip against the counter. Her blue eyes flickered with a level of vulnerability he hadn't seen before. His arms ached to wrap around her.

"I might have asked Sara about what shows you like to watch while I was out earlier and downloaded some episodes onto my phone."

"You're kidding."

"Hey. Guys need to understand what they're up against with all the competition for your attention out there."

"Wow, that's amazing. So are we watching on your phone?"

"Nope. This phone works with the hotel Wi-Fi, so we can project the show on the TV."

"Fancy." What he'd give to see that sunrise-amazing smile more often.

Unrolling the sleeves he'd pushed up for the dishwashing, he said, "Yep. In for a penny." Rolling his head from side to side, he pretended to stretch his back and arms like an athlete. "We're going full-on girls' night out. Let's do this."

That impish smile threw him off every time. "Okay, but don't say I didn't warn you about the fangs and chests."

Without thinking, he ran a hand down her arm. "I'm ready for anything." A zing of excitement blasted through every cell in his body. Man.

Her cheeks blazed pink, and she bit her lip.

Shit. *Say something. Anything.* "So, how about the gossip? I believe that's next on the agenda. Who will we be discussing this evening?"

With a wry smile, she stepped around him, retrieved two beers from the fridge and uncapped them on the counter-mounted bottle opener with an expertise that made him weak in the knees.

"You obviously don't know the rules," she said, handing him a drink. "The gossip occurs *during* the watching of the vampires."

"This is all very complicated." He accepted the beer, clinked it against hers, and took a swig, letting the mellow beverage cool his parched throat. If he had to be this close to Izzy without touching her, he would need way more alcohol to calm his jumping nerves. "I didn't know you people had so many rules."

"You people. That's funny." She sniffed. "I'm surprised Shelby hasn't filled you in on the mysteries."

"One, she's not super girly. Two, there are some things I don't want to know about my sister." He grimaced. "Now I know why."

"Fair enough. Well, come on, then. Full experience for you."

The innocent action of her fingertips curling around his wrist, tugging him behind her swaying hips to the sofa bed, consumed his mind. He could handle more simple acts like this.

More complicated acts, too, but there was that saying about beggars and choosers. He'd take whatever he could get right now. The low-level vibration where their skin met created a comfortable connection. Not a power-sucking sensation. Thank goodness.

After setting up the link between his phone and the TV, he sat next to her on the couch. "Remote?"

She pulled her head back. "Are you seriously asking for control of the vampire remote? Because I'm not sure you're ready for the responsibility."

"Is there another rule here that I'm missing?"

Turning to face him, she snipped, "Fine. I'll give you the remote on one condition: the show stops for bathroom breaks and witty commentary. If you don't follow the rules, I will evict you. Or worse, I'll assume control of the remote."

"God, you're terrifying."

CHAPTER 22

*I*zzy was playing with fire. After the last few stressful days, an endorphin high from the yummy protein and carb-based meal, and her loosening limbs as the beer worked its way through her system, she found herself relaxing on the couch. With Kerr.

Had she reminded herself in the past ten seconds how great the guy looked tonight? And now he watched escapist vampire-sex drama with her. Hello, jackpot.

Only it wasn't a jackpot and she wasn't a winner. Deep down inside, an aching hollowness sucked at her.

This evening? Complete veneer. Nothing permanent or long last-ing, given her plans to leave. And there was nothing safe about being around each other, given all the crap happening in both of their lives.

When he draped his arm behind her on the couch and shot her another wry smile, her heart compressed and twisted. That was how she felt these days. Wrung out.

Damn it. How much beer had she consumed? She peered at the bottle. Not nearly enough to explain the depth of her melancholy thoughts.

"So, Iz, when we met behind the store..."

Oh, shit. "Yes?"

"We didn't get to finish the conversation about your plans." His posture was casual, with his legs stretched out in front of him and his ankles crossed, but the hard pop of muscle in his jaw and the focused gaze? Not casual at all.

Wow. Flip a switch to Mr. Business Interview. Okay, then. "Well. Where do you want me to start?" Because she'd like to begin with that steamy kiss.

"You said you wanted to leave town."

Okay, no kiss discussion. Got it.

"Hit pause, please. I don't want to miss the next scene of this episode."

He raised the remote and a vampire froze in mid bite on the screen.

Staring straight ahead, she scraped her hair back. "Let's back up and review, because with Linc hitting me, I can't recall all that I told you."

The light growl vibrating from Kerr raised hairs on her arm.

She closed her eyes, and the horrible images in the storage garage on her family's ranch played like a horror movie. Only she had lived it with that monster right in front of her, and with her brothers and cousin participating. "It should be obvious now, but those guys have been cooking up something with this Jerahmeel for at least a few months now. They dedicate every spare minute to running the mining equipment. Guess we know why now."

A silent jerk of his head.

"When I found out the real story of what happened when Mariah got tangled up in the mess of my family—God, was it less than a week ago?—I made my decision: if I can't stop them, then I won't be part of their schemes. Their years-long hatred of your family. No more."

When Kerr's arm drifted to her upper back and his hand cupped her shoulder, she almost lost it. But not quite. She would hold onto her shit. Had to. She swallowed. "Hey, I'm smart enough to know when to cut my losses." When he opened his mouth, she stopped him off with a chop of her hand. "Once I realized that I won't be able to fix this disaster on the ranch, that was it."

"Gone. Just like that?"

"As much as it will hurt leaving Mom and Butch, yes, I'm out of here. I'll miss Tommy, too, a little bit. But Wyatt? He's not my brother anymore, not the way he's acting." A shudder ripped through her. "And that creature? I've never seen anything like that before." She motioned toward the TV. "Not even on the shows. I'm still trying to deal with the fact that Hank is inside of that thing. And the monster that trapped Hank even tried to take over my mind."

His warm fingers brushed over her shoulder. Why an action that simple reassured her, she didn't want to examine.

"Jerahmeel talked about destroying the legacy soon. Fulfilling a destiny. Gaining power." She turned her hands palm up, glancing at the bright pink, newly-healed skin. "You. It wants to kill you and your family. And it needs me to accomplish that goal, so therefore I'm not going to help. But you all are in danger. That thing is no joke. You need to be careful."

"We're cautious. Don't worry." His chest rose and fell. "Besides, my family is pretty good at handling things and protecting the people we care about." A pause. "Here." He scooted her flush against his side and wrapped his other arm around her. "You look like you could use a hug."

And more.

"You sure?" Damn it, her voice quavered. "Because that requires you setting down the remote."

"I'm into making sacrifices," he murmured as he half turned and pulled her sideways into his chest.

Warmth. Safety. Security.

Second impression? Well, those were some fabulous muscles under his shirt. She'd gotten a hint in her bedroom that night and when they had kissed behind the store, but without winter clothing? Wow. Lean, hard sinew flexed as he reached around her.

Was this action meant to relax her? Because touching him had the opposite effect, revving her engine. Sparking her nerves.

When his lips drifted over her forehead, a tingle that responded far, far away from her brow and demanded her immediate attention.

Quit it. This was Kerr. Every time she and Kerr were in the same zip code, one of them got hurt. This...whatever was going on tonight with his warm breath tickling her hairline and making her toes curl, couldn't continue. For his safety. For his family. Besides, she was leaving town.

Stopping would be for the best.

The logical, practical part of her brain knew that. The other part? Not so much.

What if she indulged with Kerr just once? Nothing legally binding. No one ever had to know. Something simple. Something now. Something wonderful.

Damn it, this was Kerr. He didn't deserve for her to have fun and then run away. He had been through too much, and needed someone way more solid than Izzy. No. She couldn't do a...one-night thing... with Kerr.

When she tried to pull back, he locked her in his strong arms. Damn that scent of cedar and sage, mixed with the hint of his aftershave. She couldn't help herself. She leaned in and took a tentative taste at his neck.

The hiss of breath and his rising chest told her she'd found a good spot. Duly noted.

"Izzy." The mere sound of his hoarse voice freaking made her nipples tighten. What kind of magic was that?

She leaned back and swallowed. Time to concentrate. "So, continuing with the story, you all are in trouble. I don't like that. And what are we going to do about the knife?"

He sat straight up, but kept his arms loosely around her. "I sent the information we got this afternoon back home. Sounds like Ruth and Odie might have some ideas based on the type of metal. I really don't understand those two."

"As long as they can figure it out soon. Jerahmeel has plans." She paused and worried at her lip until she caught his stricken expression focused on her mouth.

"I would do anything to keep you safe from those guys and that...thing."

Butterfly wings fluttered deep in her pelvis. Probably her over-the-top response to knowing there was one other person in the world who truly cared about her welfare. That's all. "That's nice to know." When she sucked in another deep breath, she resisted the urge to follow the downward path of his gaze. She would put money on him staring at her chest.

"Your own brothers don't stand up for you and support you. Someone has to."

"Not sure what that feels like." She sighed. "Besides, I'm so used to taking care of Mom without any help."

His chuckle traveled through every bone in her body. "She's such an agreeable person to be around, too." He pulled a face. "Sorry, shouldn't say that. Last time I saw her, she said she wanted to gouge my eyes out or something to that effect."

"Can't pick your family."

"Don't I know it."

She couldn't stop the small smile pushing at the corners of her mouth. "So, even though it's necessary, leaving home isn't going to be an easy thing to do."

"I can see that. If you need anything, will you call me? I want to help." His mouth pressed into a hard line that she wanted to soften with some kisses. He didn't tell her to stay. Didn't ask her to change her mind.

Her throat went tight. "Yes."

With one last squeeze of her shoulder, he sat back on the couch and retrieved the remote. "Want to keep watching? You look like you could use vampire distraction." And there he went, back to more of business mode.

She pulled back and studied his profile. "Sure. Okay. I need to do something normal. So, yes."

"Fangs away, then." He hit play. Screams and panting breaths filled the room. "Not sure how you can watch this junk. Obviously, those fangs are fake." He tilted his head to the side and squinted. "Maybe other things, too."

"Excuse me, but are you going to ruin my girls' night out with snarky comments? Because that will earn you automatic ejection."

"Fine." He made a face and intoned, "The depth of acting in this show has reached into my heart and changed my life forever. I now feel the need to primp and then gossip." A grin flashed. "Better?"

She couldn't help but smile. And she couldn't suppress a yawn.

"Here," he said, scooting over to the end of the couch. "Come on. Rest." He patted his thigh.

Had she received the golden ticket? Was she in an alternate universe? Or maybe there was a hidden camera, and the minute she relaxed her guard, someone would burst in and shout that this magical evening was all one big elaborate joke.

Until then, hell yes, she would lean on him. Settling on her side, she pillowed her head on his muscled leg. His warm hand drifted down and rested at her waist. That one small movement, and she felt completely safe for the first time in God knew how long.

Damn it, the position was so perfect, tears rose up and prickled her eyes.

"Okay?" he asked.

More than okay. "Fine, thanks."

"Oh, look, that person is turning into a new vampire. Super duper."

"You can change the show, if you'd prefer."

"No way. I'm happy if you're enjoying it."

"Really?" She repositioned her head.

"You bet. This is the best evening I've had in a long, long time. Just rest for a while, Iz."

"Your leg won't go to sleep?"

"This one can't."

She tried to sit up, but he gently pressed her back down. "Shh. It's a joke. You're fine."

She wanted to make up for her thoughtless words, but then he threaded his fingers through her hair, trailing his fingers through a section. The zings of happiness over her scalp, combined with the slow rhythm of his hand, relaxed every muscle in her body.

In no time, she was out.

CHAPTER 23

*H*ow long they sat like this, with Izzy's head resting on his thigh, her golden hair spilling all around, Kerr had no idea. All he knew was that he replayed the same lame vampire show twice, because he'd be damned if he would disturb her.

And for the record, the leg with the prosthetic? It could go to sleep after all.

Worth it.

What would every day be like, ending like this?

About fucking perfect.

Only, when it came to Kerr's life, there wasn't a perfect ending. Not with a Brand involved and the danger that came with hanging out with a Taggart. He couldn't forget the baggage he still dragged around. Even now, he jumped at shadows, expecting another attack in the semi-darkness. He kept checking the ceiling, to make sure it wouldn't collapse on Izzy. Flashbacks while awake. Great.

In his defense, he did have the barn roof almost impale him yesterday, so his fears weren't completely untethered from reality.

Scanning the dark living room, he fought to hold still against ghost ambushes and enemies.

Nothing here tonight. Chill out.

Nothing here.

But outside of this cozy, safe hotel room? Kerr knew firsthand what flavors of hell lurked in shadows. He palmed the skin between his brows and willed the creepy crawlies to leave him the fuck alone for one night.

Besides, he had better things to think about.

Izzy's safety. That mattered most, even if it didn't involve him.

He'd turned off the lamp next to him hours ago. From the flashing images of the television, shadows played over Izzy's face. He traced her prominent cheekbone, careful of the fading bruise that still purpled the skin there. Skimming a finger over the angle of her too-thin jaw, he frowned. She'd lost weight over the past few months. She still had sexy curves, but her entire frame was leaner. Izzy's life had been nothing but stress lately. His gut clenched.

He stared out the window into the dark night that swirled with snow, illuminated by the parking lot lights. The world could stay out there forever. Good riddance.

When she sighed and shifted, something in his chest expanded. He wanted to fight the insurgents hiding in the shadows and destroy anything that dared get close to her. Kerr wanted to move past his own self-doubt and take some personal chances.

Damn his concentration, but then she nestled her head nearer to his…personal chances. A man could stay this close to such a beautiful woman for only so long before being affected. And Izzy affected him, for sure. Had affected him for years.

He'd entertained notions of dating her when he was about to finish his time in the army. But that was before his accident. Before he'd been broken, inside and outside, and the pieces didn't quite fit back together again. Before he fought the flashbacks every single night. Before the safety of his entire family was threatened. He could no more suggest a relationship with Izzy now than he could tap dance.

So then what the fuck was he doing with this woman's head mere inches from his groin? Seemed like a good question to answer, and quickly. He eased his hip to one side, anything to relieve the pressure building up under his jeans. Too bad he couldn't ease the pressure in his chest.

Shit, how amazing would it be to touch every inch of a woman like Izzy?

No. Not a woman *like* Izzy.

Izzy.

To see those flashing eyes as they played every sensual game imaginable. To sink in slow and deep into her sweetness, over and over.

Yeah. The jeans had become dangerously tight. Situation critical.

He needed a cure. Unfortunately, the solution to his problem slept on his lap while he watched melodramatic vampires bite people and have wild, fangy sex.

With a murmur and a startle, the eye he could see flew open. She sat up, her face sexy puffy from sleep. She pushed her hair back off her face, her lips damp and parted, eyes not quite focused yet.

Her breath hitched, emphasizing the swell of her breasts, poorly hidden by the flannel shirt.

For the love of Christ. Come on, now. Kerr wasn't a saint.

"Sorry to pass out on you." Like a cat tongue over bare skin, her rough voice abraded and stimulated him.

"Any time."

Blinking, she stared at the TV. "Must not have been out for long." With a frown, she checked her phone. "Oh, God, more than two hours? Lying there?" When she rested her fingertips on his upper arm, the simple contact bordered on nirvana.

She rolled her graceful neck.

Took a minute for saliva to return to his mouth. "No big deal. Gave me a great opportunity to understand vampire-human relations."

Her chest rose and fell again. What he'd give for a peek under that shirt.

"Thank you," she said, glancing at him from under her long eyelashes.

Her sincerity delivered a hefty dose of wake-the-hell-up. "For what?"

"For sitting with me. For being nice despite all the weirdness going on. For that being the most relaxed sleep I've had in over a month."

Well, didn't he feel like shit now, thinking about getting her naked? If that was the most relaxed she'd been in a month, she had been going through way more hell than he realized. "My pleasure." And God help him, he meant it.

"Kerr?" She ran her hand up his arm to the shoulder.

He froze.

"What, Iz?"

"You ever wonder what things would be like if we didn't have all this craziness going on around us?"

He owed her the truth. "Every day."

Her eyes widened. "Really?"

"Yeah. It's just that…sometimes life doesn't always work out the way we hope."

"What do you—? Oh, because…" She glanced at his leg. "Yeah." Sitting back, she dropped her hands in her lap. "How did it happen? If I can ask? Oh, man. Maybe that's a bad question. I'm sorry."

"It's fine." His voice came out static-y until he cleared his throat and started over. "It's fine. You can ask me anything." He did the bellows action on his lungs a few times to buy time. "My squad was in a town outside of Jalalabad, patrolling. I was cocky. And why not? I had only another month to go of the tour. Mistake number one: never tempt Murphy's Law."

Shadows from the TV threw light and dark over her face as she turned sideways on the couch and leaned a shoulder against the back cushion. "Sure."

"So we went into a set of buildings where insurgents were suspected to live. We cleared the buildings like always. But it was quiet in the neighborhood. Too quiet. Next thing I knew, there was a huge explosion. Smoke everywhere. Gunfire. Some yelling, though my hearing wasn't the best right after the initial fireworks." With a mock knock on his skull, he added, "Noggin still isn't 100 percent."

"Oh wow."

"Yeah. Part of the building had come down on top of me. I tried to get up, but I was stuck. A huge beam had pinned my leg into the dirt floor."

"No." The word came out on a breath of air.

"Just my luck, huh? Fighting was getting intense, and more explosions were going off. Probably grenades but also small arms fire, close range and coming closer. And here I was stuck like an animal in a trap. And all I kept thinking was where Eric, my friend, had gone. Was he okay?"

"And?"

"He had gotten out, but he eventually came back in to get me."

"Was it the beam that...?" She motioned toward his leg, eyebrows raised.

He took a breath, tasting the residue of ordnance, smoke, and the concrete floor. Smelling blood and marrow. His own.

He turned and flipped on the lamp next to the couch. The warm light made her skin glow.

He nodded. "I needed to get the hell out of there. Not only would the insurgents find me, but with the main support beam of the structure down, the rest of the building was going to collapse on top of me at any time." He bit the inside of his cheek to stay focused. "So I got my knife out and started cutting."

Her jaw dropped. "Cutting?"

"Guy's gotta do what a guy's gotta do."

Her eyes widened as she stammered, "W-w-wait. You cut off your own leg?"

Shit, this wasn't going well at all. "It *was* the thinnest part." He flinched, recalling the rattling crunch of the serrated knife sawing through bone.

Along with the screaming pain, of course. His ghost foot twitched with the memory.

"I had no idea," she whispered, pressing a hand to her chest. "That sounds awful."

"It did suck. A lot."

"Not everyone could have done that."

"It was the only way I could see to have a chance to survive."

As she leaned forward, her brows shot up. "Oh, Kerr."

"Please don't." He held up a hand like he could push back judgment. "Don't feel sorry for me, Iz."

"I don't. Not exactly. But that was the bravest thing I've ever heard a person have to do. Wow."

His spine snapped straight as he did a double take. "You don't think I'm a sicko for what I did?"

"Are you kidding me?"

"No." He couldn't meet her open, earnest gaze.

She leaned on an arm propped on the back of the couch cushion. "God, you're a hero for going over there in the first place. And how you escaped that awful situation? That's an amazing story. There were rumors in town, but I didn't know the whole story. I'm stunned."

With more fear than the first time he entered hostile territory, he finally raised his eyes to meet hers. Pity? Shame? But her clear blue eyes and the determined set of her jaw reflected nothing of the sort. "You're for real. You're being sincere."

"How can you doubt it?"

Because he *was* a coward. He'd been hiding these past few years, and it had nothing to do with his invisibility power.

He let out a massive lungful of air he didn't realize he'd been holding. "Listen, Iz. I don't know how to explain where I'm at. It's been a shitty two years. Getting discharged, going through all the surgeries and fittings, the rehab, the...memories. My head and body are still not in the best place."

She pursed her mouth and ran a hand over his forearm. "You're in a perfect place, in my opinion."

"What?"

Her frown? Like she was trying to work a puzzle. She blew some hair off her forehead. "You're impossible, you know?"

Okay, now she was all over the place. "Don't follow."

"Kerr, I—" She made another perplexed face and licked her lips. "Screw it."

"What—"

Then that woman leaned in and laid a big sloppy one right on him.

The second their lips met, the magnetic pull locked Izzy onto Kerr. No preamble. Instant ignition. Their bodies picked right back up from where they left off behind the store.

She couldn't move as the excitement of kissing him short-circuited her muscles. At least Kerr had things under control. Fabulous lip control. The minute she touched him, he started sucking and nibbling at her mouth, like she was a fine wine or gourmet chocolate and he wanted to savor her.

Savor away, cowboy.

Good God, his ability to kiss knocked the sexy needle off the charts. Just like the other day. But in a much warmer and safer environment, it made the kisses so much better.

As a bonus, they didn't have to stop because of her brothers or cousin or the second coming of Satan attacking them. Things normal couples never had to deal with.

For this evening, none of those problems existed. Other than her itchy palms, that is. Maybe the healed skin was too sensitive now.

When he ran the tip of his tongue against her lips, rough against soft, they both groaned at the same time. Rotating on the couch to face Izzy, he anchored his hands in her hair and tilted her head back. As her jaw dropped open, his tongue slipped in, tangling, testing, stroking. Her head spun like riding the Tilt-A-Whirl at the county fair. Tingles of pleasure skittered across her belly and into her chest. She stood on the edge of an invisible cliff.

Could they? How bad would it be if she and Kerr had a wonderful night together?

How much worse could her life be? *Okay. Don't answer that question.*

Fun times with a sexy rancher would relieve a hell of a lot of stress. And given that bulge she'd brushed up against, they would have a lot of fun. Together.

From the determined set of his jaw to the muscles moving in his chest and arms as he adjusted his position to better kiss her, Kerr was one hot man.

Come to think of it, so was she. Sweating, in fact. She leaned back long enough to untuck her flannel shirt.

Her lips craved constant contact with his. She needed to taste him. She inhaled and caught that cedar and sage zap of *wow* that made her heart speed up. The sparks along every point of contact turned her body into a low-level livewire. She should be glowing by now with all the volts flowing through her. Her fingertips tingled. She had to touch him.

He wrapped strong arms around her, holding her in a tight embrace. Tremors of desire made her skin twitch. She craved his strength everywhere. On her. Around her. In her.

Oh, God.

"Izzy," he growled against her lips.

"Mmm hmm."

"I want you." He caught her lower lip between his teeth and gently pulled for two heartbeats. Her pelvis tightened and her insides quivered. Damn, he was good.

Easing back to catch her breath, she panted. "Me too."

That half sigh, half groan made her shiver. He tugged her hair so her neck was exposed. "The vampire show gave me great ideas."

Her laugh turned into a moan as he trailed his lips, tongue, and then teeth over the sensitive skin of her neck. First up one side, then down the other, until she gasped and writhed. Then he nipped.

Her toes curled.

Licking his way back up to her lips, he kissed her until she couldn't tell where his mouth stopped and hers started. Amazing. She could kiss him like this for what? Hours, days, weeks.

Locking his arms around her, he lowered Izzy to the couch, cradling her like she was made of glass. He knelt over her, hovering a few inches away. She groaned, wanting more contact, more skin to skin, more of his weight pressed against her body. Her hips shifted, searching. Aching.

When he settled on top of her, melding them together from chest to thighs, she sighed at how perfectly they fit.

"Are you okay, sexy?" The whisper of his breath near her ear raised goose bumps.

She swiveled her hips against the hardness tucked up against her. "Way more than okay."

"Man, you feel so good." He answered by grinding his pelvis into hers as he kissed her again.

A burning need built inside of her, a motor revved with the car in neutral, straining to shift into gear and take off down the road.

Running her shaking hands over the bunched muscles of his biceps, she pushed him away. His brows drew together, but he complied. Then she grabbed the front of his paisley shirt. Licking her lips, she popped the snaps on the garment, laying it open. A light dusting of hair rasped under her fingertips.

Oh, yes.

New and interesting muscles appeared. With each big breath, his muscles shifted and quivered under her touch. A bruise purpled an area of his lower chest the size of her palm.

"Tender?" she asked.

"Between Nurse Ruth's concoction working wonders and being around you as a hell of a distraction, I'm doing damn well." He sucked in a full breath, and the ripple of sinew fascinated her. "But yes, your cousin has excellent kicking form and technique."

"Oh wow. I'm sorry." When she yanked her hand back, he manacled her wrist.

Tumbling gravel sounded softer than his voice. "I'm not. It was worth it. Especially if it means you're going to kiss it and make it better."

Great idea. Rising up, she dropped a feather-light touch of her lips to his ribs.

The answering shudder? Everything she could hope for.

A scar under his right collarbone grabbed her attention, and she brushed her fingertips over it. Skimming downward, she dropped over each ridge of muscle on his torso. All the way down to his beltline. She swallowed. Returning upward, she skimmed a vertical scar under his navel.

He met her fingers with his own. "Back surgery." Tipping his jaw down and to the right. "And that was the central IV line." His eyes shuttered. "Sure you want to go farther? There's more."

"Everyone has scars." She swept her fingertips over his navel, making the muscles ripple. "And I want to see more, so there you go." Then she went lower, playing with the waistband of his jeans. "Not all scars are visible. And frankly, I could care less about all of yours."

Using the open halves of his shirt for leverage, she yanked him down for a mind-blowing kiss. She turned her head to come up for air. "Unless you're not into this?"

With another press of his hard erection into her pelvis, he licked his lips and grinned. "What do you think?"

"Hard to tell. You're such an enigma. I probably need more clues."

Heat flared in his glinting stare. "So I need to be more obvious? Because I can remove all doubt."

"Suit yourself." She waved a hand. "I mean, If you're not too busy and all."

"I intend to be very busy, very soon." He yanked her shirt up and planted his palms on her ribs. His thumbs brushed the undersides of her bra, and every sweep increased the liquid warmth in her pelvis.

Sure, it had been a few years since she'd had sex, but she knew how to get back on the bike. "Mmm," she breathed. What a hell of a bike to get back on.

"Iz. God—" He bit off his words as he slid his hands up and under her bra.

Panting for more, she arched toward him. When he pinched her nipples, she almost came out of her skin.

Then he stopped.

She opened an eye. Oh no. He couldn't stop. Not now. She would die of sexual frustration. "What?" Panic tinged her words.

Shaking his head, he said, "Not here. Not on a couch. You deserve better."

Frankly, Izzy deserved this hot rancher any way she could get him. But if he wanted to see to her comfort, she was on board with that idea.

He stood, tried to pull the two sides of his shirt together, then let go with a grin and a shrug. His smoldering gaze as he held his hand out to her threatened to make her spontaneously combust.

"Well, Iz?"

One night for her. One night for both of them.

She put her tingling hand in his.

CHAPTER 24

*H*ell yeah, they were doing this. Kerr led Izzy to the hotel suite bedroom and flipped on a small bedside lamp.

Every sway of her hips, every heave of her generous breasts, every flick of her tongue over those pillowy lips sucked more air out of him until his head swam.

He was in bad shape. Right this minute, he'd do anything for this woman. Go wherever she wanted to go, answer any need she had.

Because it would make him feel amazing. Because it was Izzy.

But also because it would make him feel human again.

A brief twinge of guilt came and went.

It would appear that he had an ulterior motive, after all.

Grasping her around the waist, he eased her to sit on the edge of the bed. With fingers that fumbled, he unbuttoned her shirt and drew it away. Her simple bra swelled with her full breasts, and his mouth watered. Like unwrapping the best present in the universe, he unhooked the bra and peeled it off.

Merry Christmas to him.

Cupping each breast, he flicked his thumbs over her nipples. The way she sucked in her breath shot tight desperation down low in his groin. When she gripped his hipbones, she was so close to the area that he wanted her to touch the most. He rocked his pelvis, craving more contact.

Her breast overfilled his palm as he lifted it. Licking his lips, he leaned over and sucked a nipple into his mouth, running his tongue over the hard tip. Her shudders and moans spurred him to compare the other breast. Why yes, they were equally amazing.

She unclasped his belt buckle, the clink of metal loud in the bedroom. Another flick of her nimble fingers and she had the button on his jeans undone. His head swam. So close.

How long had it been since he'd been with anyone? He talked a big game, but his last time with a woman had been prior to his injury. Would everything work correctly? Sex with a prosthetic: One of the top ten things the Veterans Affairs rehab specialist had failed to mention in the discharge paperwork.

The firm wrap of her fingers cupping him through his boxers erased any coherent thought of paperwork and hospitals. The details for standard operating procedure could be worked out later. All he wanted was Izzy.

She pushed his jeans and boxers halfway down his thighs. His dick popped up in a proud salute to a sexy woman. The moment her fingers dug into his ass, he almost lost himself right then and there.

Then she stroked his balls, with tender and determined movements that rendered him unable to form words. And when her warm breath feathered over the tip of his dick? Holy shit. No way.

Yes, way.

The warm slide of her mouth nearly knocked his legs out from under him. She scooted off the bed and knelt in front of him. At her licks and sucks, he fought the urge to thrust his hips forward. Wanted her to take all of him. Deep. Now. Not like this, though. Not with Izzy. He needed to be inside of her body.

But God help him, the image of her breasts jiggling in time with her mouth's movements riveted him. He wanted to see more of him in her.

She worked her mouth until his tip rested at the back of her throat. Oh God. She had him harder than a metal rod, and heated for action.

Her brows drew together in concentration as she sucked him right up to the edge of his control. Sweat rolled down his back as he fought to not thrust into her sweet, hot mouth with wild abandon. Shudders tightened his spine.

No. Not yet.

The saddest moment of his entire life might have been when he gently pushed her away as he pulled out of her mouth. Damn, even her lips were still damp.

"Later," he gritted out. "I have more work to do." He hitched up his boxers and jeans, not bothering to button and buckle. Not that he could zip up, given what she had resurrected.

One soft shoulder lifted. "Your call, big guy."

He drew her to stand in front of him. "My call." He had to clear his throat to continue. "My call is that I want you naked and laid out on the bed so I can lick every inch of your body until you lose your mind."

Her pupils dilated; her eyes widened. She gave out those tiny gasps, and her breasts rose in the best possible way.

God help him, but he wanted her more than he wanted air.

"Last chance to say no." *Please don't say no.*

"Are you kidding me? You want me to turn all of this down?" She pointed toward his open fly. "I'd have to be nuts." A quirk of her eyebrow made him laugh. "Speaking of which, yours are fabulous."

"Why, thank you. I was thinking that some of your…assets…are super nice as well." He slid his hands over her shoulders and down her back, tracing patterns until he worked his way back around to her chest.

The sound of her moan as he palmed her breasts was one of the best things he'd ever heard.

He skimmed his hands over her narrow waist and unbuttoned her jeans. Helping her onto the bed, he pulled the denim and pink panties off and hurled them into a corner of the room. "Iz, you're beautiful."

A shy flicker of her eyelids came and went. "I want you, big guy."

"You have me."

Kneeling with his good leg on the floor at the edge of the bed, he pulled her toward him, opened her legs wide and planted his mouth right on that liquid core. The place he'd wanted to taste for years. The place he craved. Where he needed to be. Heaven help him, but she tasted like citrus and mountain air and home all wrapped up together.

Let's see if he still had a few skills. He flicked his tongue over her nub and she bucked beneath him. Winner.

Then he slid a finger down a slick fold and into the molten heat. She gasped as she arched. Yes, sirree. Those little panting moans provided all the encouragement he needed to continue.

Slipping a second finger inside, he gulped at the tight clench of her inner muscles. His own dick tightened in anticipation. Oh, hell. Soon. He'd be there soon.

Keeping his mouth moving over her outer lips, he thrust his fingers in deeper and harder until she rocked against him, finally shattering beneath his mouth with a hoarse scream.

As he stood, the image of Izzy lying on the bedspread, a sheen of sweat on her chest and forehead, with her arms limp and her legs draped over the edge of the bed, burned into his retinas. In the lamplight, her skin glowed.

As long as he lived, he'd remember this moment.

Then she reached for him. "I want you, Kerr. Now."

"You got it."

He stepped out of his boots and shucked his boots, jeans, and boxers.

Then he froze. Stared at his legs.

How was he supposed to do this? What was the protocol? Shit, shit, shit.

A wave of panic drove his heart into beating like a snare drum.

How long had he been standing here, staring at…

"Does it stay on or off?" she asked.

His head whipped up. Was she making fun of him? Rejecting him? Heat blasted up his neck.

No. Wide-eyed wonder, open acceptance, and stark desire painted her beautiful features. But not rejection. Not even close.

"I don't know."

She pushed back on the bed and propped herself up on elbows, which made her breasts look even better. "You haven't tried it with...?"

"Nope. You're the first."

"So, like you're kind of like a virgin?" Her giggle relaxed him by fifty percent.

He shrugged. "Guess so."

"What do you think will work best?"

Running a hand over his hair, he suggested, "I think keeping the leg on will give me more leverage, so..."

"Stop right there. I like the sound of that. And I want all the leverage you can give, big guy."

"Really?"

"Dude. Are you going to stand there all night, dick in hand? Or are you going to saddle up?" Then, holy shit, she opened her legs and ran a hand over her swollen, glistening core, displaying everything he was missing.

A quick search of his wallet produced a foil package, thank you baby Jesus. He locked gazes with her as he sheathed himself.

Then he knelt on the bed and crept up her body, kissing each inch of her while avoiding the area between her legs. He laughed at her frustrated groan and restless movements. Then he kept right on kissing his way up her belly and breasts, finally stopping at her mouth.

"Iz, you're so beautiful. God, I love how you feel against me."

"Less talk, more action," she panted.

She grabbed his erection and gently squeezed until his eyes rolled back in his head.

A roar of urgency drove him now. He cupped her ass and lifted her hips as he knelt between her legs.

"Hold on, sexy," he said, nudging into the sweet heat that was Izzy.

She clamped her hands on his forearms. "Hell, yes."

With a rotation of his hips, he seated himself deep. The warm, tight sensation of being inside of Izzy grayed his vision on the edges. His entire world boiled down to the woman under him. He held still, wanting to savor this moment.

"I can't stand this. You have to move. I need more." She gritted out the words. "Please."

Right. No more savoring. Whatever she wanted, he would do it, roger that and double time. "Yes, ma'am." He stroked her clit in time with the quickening rhythm.

Whatever she tried to say got lost in a big moan. Excellent.

Pushing her knees up to her chest, he thrust harder. With each push, he wanted to get farther inside of her. More Izzy. More connection. More of everything.

As for his leg?

As it turned out, leverage was a very good thing.

Riding her faster now until their bodies slapped together, he groaned and separated her legs, rotating her hips wide open to him. She dug her fingers into his ass cheeks, and, hell, that move sent a bolt of testosterone right through him.

As they headed to the peak, he leaned over and kissed her, his tongue delving into her mouth in time with his thrusts. Their panting and cries combined until she shuddered underneath him, her inner muscles tightening and leading him over the edge. Holy shit, the waves of release kept coming, a magnetic connection inside and out. Every inch of his skin tried to connect with her. But he couldn't stop moving inside of her. He released for another minute afterward, finally collapsing on her soft body, his head pillowed between her breasts.

God, this was what he had come back from the brink of death for. This was why he kept going. And this was the one place he never wanted to leave.

CHAPTER 25

*I*zzy snuggled into the warmth and comfort that was Kerr's body.

He lay across her, his injured leg thrown over her hips, the other leg pressed behind her. Perfect. She could stay like this forever.

At one point in the evening, they'd had sex in this position, with him spooning her and stroking her deep inside with long, sensual thrusts until she shattered again in his arms.

How did she think they had no future? That they couldn't have a relationship? How wrong she had been.

Running her fingers over the light hair on his forearm, she kissed his solid chest. His skin vibrated beneath her touch, like when she had touched Shelby and Ruth, but more intensely. The difference between an electrical fence and a high-tension line.

Figured. With as much touching as she'd done last night, she should be supercharged with his ability. Already, she detected some of his low-level emotions swirling beneath the surface—thanks to her earlier absorption of Shelby's power?

The clock read 4:30 a.m. Cold outside. Toasty right here with him. No need to go anywhere.

In Kerr's arms, she was safe. None of the pain in her life existed. There was some hope in her future as long as he was here.

If he was willing, heck yes, she could do it—try for a relationship with him. Stay in Copper River. Together, they could work out all the family junk. Because Kerr was so worth it. She was worth it.

Then the danger would be gone from both their lives. Things would be perfect.

Early morning light gave the room a calm, gray glow.

She didn't want to leave this moment.

His breathing changed as he stirred, arms and legs tensing and relaxing, like he ran in place. Then he mumbled and moaned. A wave of terror drove a bolt through her. She stiffened.

His emotions.

He squeezed her tightly against him, harder, to the point where her joints creaked. When his arm locked around her neck, she couldn't breathe. Then he gave out unintelligible yelps and curses, too loud with his mouth close to her ear.

"No. I can't," he mumbled, digging his fingers into her upper arm. "They're coming. Shit." More desperate kicks. "Get out of here."

"Kerr, wake up," she gasped. "Come on, big guy, you're having a dream." She worked one arm free and patted his lean hip.

He tightened again, muttering staccato syllables, as his injured leg rose up to clamp around her waist.

She stroked his thigh and then stopped. The puckered and scarred skin ended a few inches below his knee. Earlier, she'd seen the big section of irregular skin on his other thigh from skin grafting. He'd shared that information with her hours ago. Before they had come together in tender passion yet another time.

A tear slipped out. What had this man been through? She lightly rubbed his damaged leg. What more did he have yet to endure?

With a shout, he grabbed her hand and flipped her underneath him. "No, damn it. Stop it!"

"Kerr?" she gurgled.

"Don't touch me!" he growled.

Even in the filtered moonlight, she could see the muscles on his throat flex with convulsive movements. Sweat dotted his skin. He blinked once, twice. Her neck was pinned beneath his hard forearm, crushing her windpipe.

Tiny stars burst at the edges of her vision as she clawed and pushed at him.

He froze.

"Damn it, not again," he panted. Then his haunted stare traveled to his arm. "Shit. Dammit. I'm so sorry, Iz." He reared back from her like she was a ticking bomb but he continued to kneel over her, upright.

His gaze traveled to where her fingers dug into the skin of his injured limb.

She didn't move.

His other hand remained encircled around her wrist, tight enough that her fingers tingled. The bones shifted under his grip, bringing more tears to her eyes.

Then he let go completely.

With jerking motion and a cough, she reached over and flipped on the lamp. Then she turned back to face him.

Sitting up, he rocked forward, face in his hands, and scrubbed his palms back over his head. Then he grabbed hair in two fists and yanked.

"Fuck!" he yelled, making her jump.

Clamping her mouth closed, she scooted back and waited, a palm pressed to her chest. Her heart seized.

Another few seconds passed, and she held a tingling hand out to him. "Kerr?"

The flash of his dark eyes scared the hell out of her. "No. Don't touch me." His voice came out hard, cold.

"What?"

"You heard me." He rubbed his face again. "Shit on ever-loving shit. I should have known."

"What are you talking about? Are you all right?" She made another attempt to touch him; he batted her hand away. "Talk to me."

"Give me a fucking second, will ya?"

She wrapped her hands on each of her upper arms and leaned hard against the backboard. "Okay," she whispered.

~

Kerr had climbed the ladder of ecstasy, leaped off the diving board of stupidity, and landed in a pool of the deepest shit.

Nothing like having a night of amazing sex with the hottest woman in the world, followed by waking up in fucking Jalalabad, fighting imaginary insurgents. Damn it. He could have seriously hurt Izzy when he came out of his flashback. She had marks where his fingers had dug into her skin. What if he had broken her wrist? He flicked a glance at her red neck. *Or worse.*

And the pity in her eyes when she touched his nub. His fraction of a leg. His…reminder. Well, now, wasn't that priceless.

Goddamn it. He had come so close to getting everything he wanted. So damn close.

But still a miss. Guys like Kerr with the brain baggage he carried didn't get the nice brass ring, did they?

Trapped. He was fucking trapped again. Oh sure, this time it wasn't under that building beam with nothing but a knife and a cupful of courage. Now, those flashbacks trapped him in their nasty grip. And he was pinned by his own doubt and shame.

What about that other prison? The one where Izzy could lead him around by his dick all day long and he wouldn't say no.

Trapped. Again. He shook his head, glancing at the shadows. Traps, everywhere. Damn it, everything was jumbled up inside his brain and couldn't figure it all out. All he knew for certain was that he needed out of here. Out of this situation. Out of the churning garbage in his mind. ASAP. Before he hurt her.

Before he hurt her? What a joke. Look at her.

Now he considered her safety and her feelings? He hadn't worried about her feelings before jumping in the sack with Izzy. What if the next time they slept together, he broke her neck in another of his nightmares?

He had no good answers. Not a one.

"Kerr?" she whispered. He couldn't meet her shimmering, wide-eyed stare. Couldn't handle more pity.

If she tried to offer up a solution, no way could he trust his response to be civil.

Best thing he could do was get out of this mess. Return to hiding what he felt and what he wanted.

Only problem? They were stuck here together until the interstate opened and he could drive them the fuck back across the state. Trapped again. Pain spread in his chest, like every rib had broken again.

"This was a huge mistake, Iz. All of it."

"What?" That gasp strafed him like shrapnel across bare skin.

"This was a bad idea. Damn it." He lifted his hand when her gorgeous mouth dropped open. Oh, holy fuck, what she'd done with that mouth last night. And, just like a brash young soldier at the recruitment office, his dick jumped up, volunteering to re-enlist.

No. Focus on her safety, damn it. Protect her. Do the right thing. "I don't know what I was thinking," he said. "Look at me. Look at you. Like we have any future together."

"I never asked for a future," she whispered. "But if we wanted one, we could make it happen. I know we could."

"No. It's not safe for us to be together. With all the shit with your family and whatever is out there. The bad things happening to my family. With my crazy head being so messed up…"

"Don't care."

"Well, you should." *Do the right thing, asshole. Relationship test-drive was an abject failure.* He needed to remove her from his life before he hurt her even more. Cut the cord, rip off the Band-Aid. Something. Just do it quickly before what was left of his pride crumbled to dust.

"Look," she said, pushing hair back from her face with those damaged hands. The move exposed the line of reddened skin on her neck. He'd put that mark there. Goddamn it. "Maybe we need a little time…to process everything. We could take a break and then talk."

Her voice wavered.

Kerr, however, did not. "No. There won't be a therapy session or a second date. No sharing of our goddamned feelings or kumbaya crap. No rehashing what the hell just happened here. Nothing."

She flinched like he'd hit her. Damn it if her eyes didn't shimmer.

"Kerr? What are you doing?" The paper-tearing sound of her voice ruined him.

Doing? The right thing, and you're welcome.

No way would he condemn her to a future of his messed up shit served fresh every night, like clockwork.

"Hey, it's all good." The effort to draw in air threatened to destroy him, but give him the Oscar already, because he'd started down this road and, by God, he'd get to his crappy destination any way necessary. He waved a hand toward her and went as cold as dried ice. He would pretend, if it meant she would be safe in the long run. "I know a pity fuck when I see one. That's cool."

She pressed a hand to her sternum. "Pity fuck?"

Once the bullshit left his mouth, the floodgates opened. "You know. Feeling sorry for the handicapped guy and stuff like that. Doing your part for your country. And for me? Hey, itch scratched. Yay. And hell yeah, that was fun. Way to get the twig 'n berries back in shape, too. But we're done now."

"Is that what you really think?" Her features froze, warping her beauty into an expression of horror.

Horror. Because of him.

"So what if it is?" Kerr crossed his arms and scooted back on the bed. Their proximity was killing him. Too bad he couldn't simply hop out of bed and storm out of here. Trapped again by his body.

Her mouth went tight. Flat. A pulse jumped at the base of her neck. Redness started in her chest, then coated her neck and face. Her hand shook as she pointed her finger at him. "Then I hope you're satisfied." The crack in her words threatened to shatter his resolve. "Good for you, champ. You got to test-drive your new parts. Air out your mental issues. Get a little practice before going out there in the great big world with women who might actually give a shit about you. And, yay, your junk works. Gold star."

Man, she had gone from hurt to furious so fast, he had whiplash. The woman scared the ever-loving hell out of him, but he'd take pissed over hysterical any day of the week. Anger: now that was an emotion he could work with.

"The fuck?" he spat.

"Glad I could help get you back in the saddle, there, buddy." She paused. "What? Can't take it when I fling the bullshit back at you? Funny how that works."

He couldn't move.

Her expression held for the space of two breaths, then shattered. Tears rolled down her cheeks. Holy fucking shit. She wrapped her hands around her upper arms. "Damn you, Kerr. Even when you're a jerk, I can't be mean to you." She sniffed. "Listen. You're still useful, you know. There are ways to work around...that. You can still do things."

"I can still do things? Like other nice disabled vets with mental issues?"

"There's treatment for PTSD, Kerr. Besides, do you know that you're an inspiration, how you came back from that injury?"

The world around him blanched hot white. "I'm an inspiration? Like Mahatma Gandhi? Or maybe Steven Hawkins?"

"That's not what I—"

"Quit patronizing me." If he clenched any harder, he'd break teeth. His fight or flight response went haywire, and he couldn't stop it. "Get out of my sight. Now." Goddamn, and they were in this hotel suite in a fucking blizzard. Nowhere to go. His timing sucked balls.

How in the name of little unicorns had he gone from ecstasy to flashback to reducing their night to nothing more than a pity fuck? That was messed up to the nth power. But God help him, he'd gone there with Izzy. And she was the one who had to leave.

Because it would take him too long to reattach his stupid leg and storm out, and fuck him if he was going to do that in front of her because it would be his dumb luck that he'd fall on his face.

"Get out!" he yelled.

CHAPTER 26

*I*zzy jumped out of the bed, buck naked, ignoring the angry hunger playing across his handsome face. Fine. *Look all you want, jerk. Last chance to see these goodies.*

She moved around the room, shoving on her clothes, giving him flashes of everything. Buzzing in her ears dulled the sound around her. Her nose and lips had gone numb.

Pity fuck.

For whom?

Maybe stopping this relationship before it started was for the best.

Crazy thing was, no matter how mad he made her, she still wanted him safe. If that meant leaving him alone, then so be it.

The lump filled her throat as she tried to swallow past it and failed. "Kerr." She snapped on her bra, followed by her shirt.

"Don't say anything else, Iz. This was a crappy experiment." His mirthless laugh rattled her bones. "It was nice while it lasted."

"Maybe we can be friends?" The minute the lame words came out, she wanted to take them back.

"Friends?" In the lamplight, his bruised face twisted into a skull of fury with those bloodshot eyes. "No. We cannot be friends." He barked another hollow laugh. "Hey, at least I got what I wanted out of you."

Pausing as she buttoned her jeans, she said, "Sex?"

He leaned back against the backboard, chest bare, hands laced behind his head. Despite herself, her mouth watered. "Yeah. Been wanting to do that for a while."

The floor dropped out from under her.

She sagged against the doorjamb. She'd understood, but somehow his saying the words made the truth that much worse. The room tilted to one side. She clutched the wood frame. "No."

"You bet I did, Iz. And you took the bait, hook, line, and sinker." His sneer warped his face into something ugly, unnatural. Something she'd never seen from Kerr. He buffed his nails on his chest.

Kerr had used her.

The one person in the world she believed would never hurt her.

She wanted to throw up.

"Thank God I used a condom, Iz. No way am I getting trapped with you in that fucked up mess of your life. The last thing we need is a baby in the mix."

Air clawed its way in and out of her chest. "No."

"Oh, yes. And thank you again for the help." He motioned to his groin. "On all fronts." He stretched his arms over his head. "We still have work to finish. Be ready to leave at seven to go back to the ranch."

God, she had to spend another six hours with him? Just stab her in the chest and be done with it. His nonchalant shrug cut sharper than a knife.

She wanted to melt into the ground and never re-form again.

She wanted to shake him and get him to say something—anything —different than what he had just said. Take back the words. Anything.

As she bit the inside of her cheek and held back a sob, a headache lanced through her temples. Her world went filmy.

A blurry Kerr sucked in air as his brows shot up. "What the fuck?"

No time to analyze. Izzy stumbled out of the bedroom into the other room of the suite, she sat down hard on the floor, and yanked on her shoes and socks. She took a big breath and released it. The headache faded and her vision returned.

With one last look toward the dark bedroom door, she crammed a fist against her mouth to keep from making a sound.

She slammed the door and fled to the workout room of their snowbound hotel. No one would bother her there at this hour.

~

Kerr sat by himself in the middle of a hotel bed, white whatever thread count Egyptian fucking cotton sheets and plush duvet askew. Muted neutral tones attempted to relax him. The impersonal art on the wall tried its best not to offend him.

Why bother. Kerr offended himself.

Goddamn it. He threw a pillow against a framed picture. Damned thing didn't budge. He couldn't even take a woman back to his house for a proper date, with no place of his own. Had to rent a room.

What the hell had just happened?

For a second, he had everything.

And then he destroyed the best thing that had happened to his miserable life.

He'd punted her heart into the next state. All for some noble shit like keeping her safe. Like his meltdown had anything to do with protecting Izzy. He wasn't letting her go because he was a fucking saint or something.

Bottom line: he couldn't handle someone knowing about all the cobwebs in the corners of his life and also possess the map to locate all his skeletons. He couldn't put himself out there in a relationship, pinned under a figurative concrete beam day in and day out, vulnerable to attack. He needed to stay hidden, tucked away where no one could hurt him.

So instead of manning up and facing his crap, he had cut her off, like he'd cut off his goddamned leg. Funny now it hurt more this time than back in Afghanistan.

He rolled over onto the remaining pillow and got a big whiff of Izzy's bright citrus essence and the sweet musk from last night, reminding him all over again what he would never have.

To top it all off, she had pulled a disappearing act. Literally. Using his ability. He rubbed his fingers against his thighs. Whatever that Jerahmeel guy had done to her really did make her a Taggart power magnet. She was welcome to the headache that came with the fading ability.

Throwing back all the covers, he stared at his scarred, broken, incomplete body. Goddamn it.

He gripped the sheets in two hands and ripped the fabric.

And yelled loud enough to rattle glass in casings.

CHAPTER 27

*I*zzy's neck ached from staring out the truck window and away from Kerr. But that damned low-level emotional connection continued. Her fingertips buzzed—less than before, but still present. A dull ache pulsed behind her forehead.

How about this kind of purgatory: connected to Kerr but never able to be together again. And she had some expertise on the topic of purgatory, given that the portal to hell was opening up right there on her family ranch.

For his part, Kerr sat still as a statue. Hard to tell if he even breathed. But he maneuvered the truck back to town; the shush and rumble of snow and cinder under the vehicle buffered the ringing silence for the long trip back. The interstate had opened only a half hour before they left that stupid hotel.

Girls' night out? Damn her life.

When he pulled off of Main Street instead of heading out of town toward the Taggart ranch, she turned her head. "Where are we going?"

"You're going to Sara's." Just like that. No discussion. No debate.

Nope. "Why not back to the ranch?"

"You shouldn't be there."

Wow, those four words created an acid burn that ate away her chest cavity until nothing remained.

Tough. She sat up straight. She was done being hurt. She rubbed her chest with a fist. Screw him.

"Does she know we're coming?"

"Not we. You. And I texted her a while back."

He pulled alongside Sara's neat bungalow. Didn't even bother to put the truck in park.

Passing her the overnight bag, he said, "Thanks for the...help." His normally rich voice came out flat, dead, like a fetid pond surface.

Ice-prick pings of his emotions tapped against her mind. Still detecting his feelings. Wasn't that a super-duper extra torment? Great end to a crappy day.

"Kerr—" she said after stepping out of the truck.

He blinked, and his face creased for a moment. "If you need anything..."

"Yeah, thanks."

She had to strain to hear him. "I'm really sorry, Iz."

"Me too," she mumbled.

With a slam of the truck door, she turned and trudged up the shoveled driveway.

The truck pulled away before she reached Sara's front door.

In the empty kitchen of the ranch house, Shelby pinned Kerr with a look that scared the bejeezus out of him. Shit.

Wasn't it dinnertime in a few hours? Shouldn't he go out and do things?

"Let's have it," she said.

No. He wasn't going anywhere.

"What? I think Ruth's hiding more information. And I found out which minerals those assholes are trying to dig out of the ground. And why the Brands want our property."

"That's not what I meant. Last night. Spill."

"Shouldn't we be focusing on the evil thing and the knife? That was the whole point of the trip to Cheyenne."

"Oh we will. Soon." She drummed her fingers on the table. "But in the free time until then, I'd like to know what happened with Izzy."

"Nothing to say." Nothing that could be said.

She made the noise of a buzzer. "Wrong. Try again, dude." Damn, Shelby. If she didn't have a broken leg…

With a sigh, he said, "We had dinner together, watched a movie, and that was about it."

She pointed. "You have a hickey on your neck."

Busted. And he'd been walking around like that all day. Crap. "Maybe there was a little more."

"So. Give me the details."

His skin twitched. "I don't dig information out of you, sis."

"Of course you do. Like when Eric and I were on the outs. You pretty much smacked me upside the head and called me an idiot." Her eyes narrowed. "Do I get to return the favor?"

"No. Look, Izzy and I were two consenting adults. We spent a nice evening together. We won't see each other again. End of story. Probably for the best, considering the bad blood between our families. And, you know, the threat of death and eternal purgatory and all."

"Like hell that's the end of the story. More, please."

"Drop it." His hand curled into a fist.

"Oh." An orange eyebrow rose. "*Oh*," she breathed and pursed her lips. "Were there, you know, logistical problems? With the leg and all?"

"What?"

"Issues with the laws of physics? You know, angles. Yes? No?"

He almost choked on his own tongue. "That's not your business."

"It is my business if I'm going to give you good advice." Her grin reassured him not at all. This was Shelby. Like a carrion bird over a dead carcass, she would pick and pick until she had every last juicy morsel of information out of him.

"No logistical problems. We—"

"On or off?"

"Huh?"

"The leg. Did you keep it on or off?"

His neck warmed up. "Why the hell is this so important to know?"

"Never known anyone with a fake leg." She shrugged, and that sly cat smile crawled sideways over her face. "Did she do, you know, interesting things with the nub?"

He ground his molars together. "First of all, I call it a stump or prosthetic, not a nub, but that's semantics. Second of all, is that seriously what you want to know?" He sucked in a breath. "And while we're on the subject, uh, no. Touching my stump is not foreplay."

"So you had issues with it?"

"Shelby—"

"Or issues with her touching it?"

"No, I—"

"Or issues with her touching other things? Remind me, but you weren't wounded in, you know, other areas, were you?" That grin. For chrissakes, his sister was relentless.

He drove his hands through his hair and over his head. Now he knew how people could be driven to fratricide. "Those parts all work fine, thanks for asking the inappropriate question."

"A little sensitive about it. I can tell. Is your junk kind of small, then?"

How he kept from losing his mind, Kerr had no idea. "No, I'm, uh, well endowed. Or so I'm told. Fuck. Eric says I've got a massive set of grenades down there. Damn it. I hope you're happy." He smacked his forehead. "Great. I just told my sister what my balls look like. Life as we know it is officially over."

She reared back. "Hey, ho. Hostility? And don't go dragging Eric into it. Besides, he's one to talk. The guy's huge..." A dreamy, flushed expression crept over her face.

"For the love of raging hormones, you have to stop talking, sis, or I'm going to lose my nonexistent lunch."

"Ok. Fine. We've established you have the complete...package...to make a woman happy."

He groaned. And shifted in his seat, damn it.

"I'll take that as a yes," she said, lips pursed. "So is it a problem on her end? Or don't you think she's pretty and nice?"

"She's the kindest person I've ever met. And yes, the woman is smoking hot."

"So she's good with, um, interacting with your package?"

The image of Izzy's mouth locked over his...package...made certain areas of his anatomy rise up, ready for more physical activity. "Shit, yes."

She lifted her palms. "Then I fail to see what the issue is, dude."

He dropped his head into his hands and mumbled, "Morning after."

"Buyer's remorse?"

"More like PTSD."

Her face morphed into a serious frown. "What happened?"

"Flashback. Woke up trying to fucking strangle her." He paused, the images from early this morning falling like acid rain on his mind. Little pricking reminders of each mistake he'd made. "Then it's possible that I took what she said about me still being a man despite my leg injury the wrong way. Then I might have told her how I set the evening up as a way to get back in the saddle. An itch to scratch." Christ, he sounded like a jackass, recapping it like that.

Actually, no. He realized hours and hours ago that he was a jackass.

"Wow."

He peeked up at her. "Yeah, wow."

"So how did you leave it?"

"I might have labeled it a 'pity fuck,' and then she stormed out."

"Holy crap. When you screw up, you do things right. Go big or go home, huh?"

"I don't need lectures, Shel. It was a piss-poor showing. I fully admit it."

The silence was broken only by the rasp of his hands over his unshaven jaw and her fingertips drumming on the wood table.

Shelby pursed her lips and nodded. Oh no. Idea time. "Do you like her?"

"Doesn't matter. There's a creature hanging out on the Brand ranch, and it wants to kill us with some custom-made hell-channeling knife right before unleashing the four horsemen on the world or something insane like that. If I survive that nightmare, then it appears that I will need to do some in-depth work on my poorly managed PTSD. My calendar's booked. Not a lot of time for a relationship, even if a fraction of a chance still remained."

"That's not what I asked. You want me to say it extra slow, so you will comprehend? Or maybe I can use small words." When she crossed her arms, Kerr's heart sank. "Do. You. Like. Izzy? Yes or no?"

"She wouldn't take me back for a million bucks after how I treated her."

"Men are so pigheaded. Answer my question or I'll probe your brain."

"Doing that could kill you."

"You've wanted to kill me ever since we started this conversation." She patted his hand. "Not literally. I would know. But let's get down to it. What's your answer?"

"Yes. I really like Izzy. I've liked her for a while now." He scraped his fingertips over his scalp. Maybe he could peel off the stupid. "And last night was amazing. Not just the sex, although...yeah. But the connection we had was great. And yes, my leg worked fine. The night was better than good. It was awesome."

"Can you envision your life with her in it?"

"Not going to happen." But then, a peace settled over him, loosening up his shoulder muscles. Sad part was, he hadn't dared to think about his future. Not for a long time. "God, yes."

Her gold-glinting eyes narrowed. "How badly do you want that future?"

"Not bad enough to put her in danger." He sat up straight.

He could eat all the crow in the world, but the danger still remained.

Shit.

Wait. He sat up straight. Maybe there was a solution.

To keep Izzy safe, there was one thing he could do.

It wanted all four Taggarts together. Yes, there was one way to keep Izzy safe and protect his family. Why hadn't he thought of this before?

He fought to keep his new feelings hidden from Shelby.

She blew an orange curl off her forehead. "You idiot. Izzy's already in danger. She lives at the homestead that houses the creature from hell. Which has eaten her brother. Which wants all of us dead. How much worse can it get?"

"You know, we keep saying that and then it gets worse." He slumped in the chair. "Look, I don't want her hurt."

"She's already hurt."

"Thanks to me. But at least I can limit the damage."

"You sure about that? Can you stay away from Izzy Brand forever?"

"Yes, if it means she is safer." He rapped knuckles on the table as he stood up. "I mean that, too. I'll sacrifice my happiness for her safety."

Shelby whispered, "That's what I'm afraid of, Kerr."

Walking his saddled horse to the edge of the main ranch, Kerr glanced back.

His family, safe.

Izzy safe.

That's all that mattered, when it came down to the bare bones. He closed the gate and swung up into the saddle and pointed the horse toward the forest.

It was 4:30 p.m. Nearly dark.

Winter solstice.

CHAPTER 28

$\mathcal{A}$t 7:00 p.m., Izzy burst into the kitchen at the Taggart ranch.

The skin on her fingertips itched. Burned. The sense of *not-right* swamped her, and she'd followed that sense right back here to the last place where she was welcome.

Bless her friend, Sara, who didn't ask questions, but just drove, ran into the house behind her. Sara had apparently seen enough strange activity that Izzy's full-body psychic reaction didn't even register a batted eyelash.

Dinner was over at the Taggart ranch, but no one had left the kitchen.

Shelby, Eric, and Garrison sat around the table. In another chair sat Mariah, with Vaughn hovering at her shoulder like he wanted to kill anyone who moved into her personal space. Actually, he growled and flexed when Izzy arrived.

Made sense, with Izzy being related to the people who kidnapped Mariah.

Ruth and Odie leaned against the kitchen counter. The woman kept looking out the window.

As for Odie, the bearded Cajun had the grim expression of a man about to walk in front of the firing squad.

Man, Izzy had walked right into something really heavy. If every pore of her skin didn't twitch and tingle so much, she'd walk right back out and give these people some privacy.

"Izzy?" Garrison asked. "Something going on?"

"Not sure. Maybe. Just needed to be here. Where's Kerr?" She rubbed her upper arms. The off-balance *wrongness* in this room hit her like a two-by-four.

Shelby gave a sad smile. "Licking his wounds on chores. He doesn't want to be bothered."

"What?" Garrison sputtered.

"Don't mind that comment." Sara sidled up next to him and took a seat. "It's fine that Izzy's here, though. Right?" She shot him a narrow glare.

Garrison spun around. "Anyway, we have way more important things to discuss."

Izzy pressed her back to the wall and tried to make herself invisible. Actually, she could pull that trick off for real, thanks to her time spent with Kerr.

Continuing, Garrison held up several papers. "We are going to talk about this document I found. Makes no sense. Makes a lot of sense."

"What does?" Shelby asked.

"It's the key to everything here." Garrison stared at the couple at the kitchen counter. "Isn't it?"

A sink faucet dripped once. Twice.

"You weren't supposed to see it," Ruth murmured.

Vaughn tightened up his grip on the back of the chair in front of him. "Until when?"

"Maybe never. Maybe a long time from now," she said.

Shelby pinched the bridge of her nose. "But maybe soon?"

Odie slid a gaze to his wife. Like he wanted to memorize her face.

A seesaw of relief and anger rocked Izzy's equilibrium. Waves of confusion and fear sloshed back and forth in her mind. She frowned, trying to sort it out. Must be residual from when she absorbed Shelby's emotion-detecting ability. She was picking up everyone's feelings in this tight, tense room.

"Want to comment about a few items?" Garrison held the document in front of him. "And I quote: 'Should some of us fail, you need to know the truth. You are my legacy that was centuries in the making.' Explain."

Ruth patted the knot of hair at the nape of her neck. A few tendrils had escaped the bun. "What do I tell?" she whispered to Odie.

"*Chérie.* Let them know what they are and what they face. Tell them everything."

A flush stained Ruth's cheeks. "We've been alive for hundreds of years as Indebteds, remember?"

"How could we forget?" Garrison sputtered. "You killed for years. We heard that story." He rapped his knuckles on the table, making Izzy jump and breaking the awful thrall that had everyone riveted. "Besides the fact that we are harboring felons in our house, what's that have to do with anything?"

Ruth flinched. "Jerahmeel is the worldly manifestation of Satan. If he goes unchecked, this force will consume the world."

Izzy wiggled her toes. She wanted to walk—no, run—from here. But to where?

Couldn't tell, but she needed to be at another location. Where was Kerr?

"We know that, too." Garrison flicked the corner of the page. "But how does this document involve us?"

Ruth's gold-glinting eyes slammed into Izzy's, and the sensation of a gentle touch floated over, then amplified within Izzy's mind. So strange. "This involves you all because you're literally my legacy. My great-great, many times great-grandchildren."

"We know this as well," Garrison said.

"The creature Jerahmeel that's been tormenting you?" Odie lifted his chin. "It didn't just love Ruth. It was obsessed with her. Would do anything to be with her. Even destroy the entire world."

The color bleached out of Garrison's face, leaving a pasty, sick hue. "Son of a bitch. It wants revenge? Seems like you could have led with that tidbit the other day."

"Actually, more like eternal retribution, but you can call it revenge." Ruth leaned against Odie's side. "This is why Jerahmeel has come here. To this valley. To my legacy. To draw me to you"

Vaughn's voice came out like sand and gravel ground into a coarse grit. "Let me get this straight. You broke your contract with it, that forced you to kill people. Then you gave it the cold shoulder. Then you tried to kill it but failed to do so. Now it wants to destroy all of us, as a way to get back at you for dumping him?"

A rubbery pulse of danger pressed against Izzy's mind, and she flinched. Wow, that was somehow coming from Vaughn.

"Not exactly in that order. And technically we broke our contract at the same time that we killed Jerahmeel. But that about sums it up," Odie said. The words came out light, but his knuckles blanched white as he formed a fist.

"There's way more you're not telling us." Garrison took Sara's hand in his.

Izzy held her breath; the wall felt solid enough to hold her even if she lost control of her spine. Kerr should be here. She looked around. Her fingertips itched and she pressed them to her pants leg.

Ruth's chest rose and fell. A chair creaked. Someone cleared his throat. "The new knife. It's got properties we've never encountered in previous blades. Our research tells a terrifying story: If Jerahmeel fully enters this world and uses the weapon, he will never leave this Earth. Humans will be enslaved, killed for his hunger. Forever."

"Any more good news?" Vaughn asked.

Odie shook his head. "No, that's pretty much it."

"How do we stop it?" he asked.

Odie glanced at his wife. "We're working on that solution."

Vaughn's jaw went hard. "So you don't know."

They didn't answer.

"Um, what about my family?" Izzy asked, her cheeks heating when every head swiveled her direction. "What will happen to them?"

With a frown, Odie glanced at his wife. "Not sure."

"But it's not good." Izzy rubbed the backs of her hands on the denim fabric of her jeans. Man, her skin needed to stop itching. This was getting ridiculous. Had to be due to her proximity to all the abilities in this room.

"Probably not, *ami*."

"Any idea why I have somehow absorbed your power, Ruth?" she asked.

Ruth's eyes shimmered with tears. Oh, not good. Not good at all. Izzy crossed her arms and waited for the woman to compose herself.

"Yes. We did some more research last night." A drop of water dripping into a pot clanged in the tight silence. "You're descended from a very dear friend of ours."

"Someone who killed people, too?"

"Like us, he was forced to kill bad people, yes," Ruth said.

Vaughn growled as his eyes narrowed. A wave of oh-shit buffeted her, and the nape of her neck prickled.

Odie's jaw dropped. "*Oui.* I see it now. It's her eyes. Looks just like him."

"And?" Izzy bit the inside of her cheek to keep from shaking. Or running away.

The Cajun draped an arm around his wife's shoulders. "Barnaby Blackstone, our mentor and dearest friend. And your great-great many times great-grandfather, *mon ami.* He was Indebted for more than five hundred years. Recently deceased. May he finally rest in peace."

Izzy shrugged. "Don't understand. Why is that important?"

"Barnaby always had...instincts...we never could explain. Special powers of his own," Ruth said. "And my own ability became a little stronger once I began working with him." She sniffed. "Jerahmeel killed him about a year ago. I miss him so."

Garrison shook his head and rapped knuckles on wood once again. "Look, I'm sorry your friend died. But what does that have to do with this situation?"

Ruth's eyes went wide. "Don't you see? That's why she was able to resist Jerahmeel. That extra something from Barnaby's lineage. The ability to use our gifts to amplify and defend. She's the key to this whole problem."

Oh, that did *not* sound promising.

What could she do to help that awful situation on her ranch? How could she defeat Jerahmeel?

"The interesting leverage is that Jerahmeel thinks she's on his side," Odie murmured.

"Even now, after being gone for a day?" Izzy asked.

"*Oui*, but he has a blind spot," he said. "When he wants or expects something, he cannot conceive of it not happening. He believes he converted you. No other possibility exists in his mind."

"So my not being on his team could surprise him? That's our secret advantage? That's awful."

"It's all we have," Ruth's smooth voice broke in.

Damn this itching. "What about my brothers? Don't they have some Barnaby inside of them, too?"

The couple exchanged a look that pushed ice through Izzy's veins.

"Oh, crap." Shelby reared back.

Izzy flinched at the flare of surprise she detected. "What?" she asked, trying to ignore the multiple stares. Maybe now would be a great time to activate Kerr's disappearing trick.

"I'm not sure how to say this," Ruth began. "You're adopted, my dear."

Her chest compressed a few inches. Sweat beaded her upper lip. "No. No way. I'd know about it."

Odie shook his head. "We have the records."

The ground dropped out from under her, and she leaned against the wall, trying to remain upright. Her whole life, a lie. How was this possible?

"I—" Her jaw dropped.

Sara jumped up and pulled her to the vacated chair, glaring at Garrison until he stepped away. Izzy sat. The solid wood beneath her felt good. Real. Tangible. Stable.

"I'm sorry. We didn't want to tell you like this," Ruth said.

Vaughn gave Izzy an awkward pat on the shoulder. "Wow, that's heavy."

Time to put that information into a drawer to deal with later, because no way did she have any capacity to process everything she'd learned.

"Well," Garrison broke the thick tension. "As important as that revelation is, we still have work to do. What's the plan? I'm not sitting around, waiting for something bad to happen."

Vaughn tightened a hand on Mariah's shoulder, and she patted his big paw with her tiny one. "I'm telling you guys," he said. "Best defense is good offense. Let's go in there, guns blazing."

"Easy for you to say," Shelby muttered, shifting her casted lower leg until it *thunked* under the table.

"Hey, let's get Kerr back in here," Vaughn said. "Grumpy or not, he needs to be part of this decision." He stomped to the back door, opened it, and shouted for Kerr. And shouted again.

A wave of cold that had nothing to do with the frigid air swirled into the kitchen.

Vaughn slowly turned back around, stone-faced.

Izzy pulled out her phone and dialed Kerr's number. No answer. Weird, because the reception on the ranch worked fine for cell phones. "Maybe he doesn't want to talk to me." She tapped out a message.

Are you okay?

A pause. Then dots for typing.

No.

That was an atypical response. She tried again. *I'm sorry for how things ended this morning. Can you come in the house? Your family needs you.*

Izzy rubbed her neck and sternum. Rolled her neck. She peeked up and met Sara's tight stare. Then Vaughn went into even more of a defensive crouch. Shelby dropped her forehead into her palm and massaged her temples. Izzy's own forehead ached. What the hell?

Dots. Typing.

Her heart rate sped up.

Can't come home.

More dots. *And this is not Kerr.*

Oh. No.

More dots.

More dots.

The blood drained out of her head and chest. Peripheral vision disappeared.

If you're not here in three hours, he's dead. Izzy read the message aloud and pushed to her feet, leaning forward against the tabletop. Her heart skidded, making it hard to suck in enough air.

"Son of a bitch," Garrison spat. "Kerr's over there."

Vaughn had two hands clamped onto Mariah's shoulders. "I'm going."

No. Izzy needed to fix this mess. If Jerahmeel wanted her to be part of Team Crazy in exchange for Kerr's safety, she'd deliver on that wish. Then she'd figure out how to sabotage the whole outfit. Anything to help Kerr.

Ruth lifted a hand. "You have to be careful. It wants all four of you together. He's already got one of you." Her throat muscles worked. "But. The only chance you have and the only chance the world has, is for you four to work together to stop the creature. Somehow, you have to use your powers as one."

"Wait a minute. Our advantage is already gone since we're not all together?" Garrison asked. "Where do we go from here?"

Vaughn shook his head, as if he tried to shake off a concussion. "Man, it's the real deal. Nothing about this situation feels right."

"Your advantage is her." Ruth lifted her chin in Izzy's direction. "Jerahmeel doesn't know what she can do. Doesn't know who she is."

Izzy was crawling out of her own skin. "Heck, guys, I don't know what I can do." And didn't know *who* she was anymore.

But her muscles tensed with the need to run the miles to her family's ranch and help Kerr. Why were the Taggarts sitting around?

As discussion swirled around them, Izzy caught Shelby's unfocused stare. A tingle, like an echo, bounced in Izzy's mind.

Eric glanced over. "Shel, no. You can't use your power. It'll hurt you."

"I have to see. Whether I get brain damage or not, he's my brother."

"Wait. I can do it." Izzy said, lifting a hand and walking over to Shelby. Would it work? "May I?" At a nod, she pressed her palm into Shelby's, and the electrical jolt of the power exchange rocked her back on her heels. If the initial hint of Shelby's ability made Izzy's nerves tingle a few days ago, the full force of this Taggart's gift ran like a livewire straight through her.

217

"Whoa," Shelby breathed.

Eric loomed next to them. "Is it hurting you?"

"No, it's not taking anything away from me. Wow, this is so weird."

Izzy let go and clenched her hands, focusing the emotional radar power she had absorbed. She winced against the throbbing headache. *Find Kerr.* Turning in a slow circle, she jerked to a stop and faced the back of the property. Yes, he was there, in the direction of her family's ranch. *Feel what Kerr is feeling.* Then she bit the inside of her cheek and let down her guard. A wave of pain smacked into her so hard, she stumbled backward. Someone grabbed her arms and helped her back into a chair.

Fiery agony. Terror. Kerr's. *She could sense all of it.*

Fear overridden by determination to...help his family.

And to protect Izzy above all else.

What?

Wiping tears, she broke the contact and dropped her forehead into her palms. "Oh my God. He went over there to try to save all of us."

"Son of a bitch," Garrison said. "Nice gesture, but not smart."

Hot-poker pain pierced her mind, and she threw up an arm to fend off invisible attacks. "He's...they're...it's burning him." Izzy rubbed her cheek. "It hurts. So much. What's happening?" A blink and it ended, leaving an aftertaste of ash and charred flesh in her mouth.

Vaughn gripped the edge of the table and stood. "That's it. Discussion over. I'm going over there."

"Me too." Izzy rubbed her face.

Garrison grabbed her upper arm and spun her to face him. "You really like our brother?"

What the heck? She gritted out, "More than air." She blinked back tears. "More than life."

One curt nod and he released her. "Then you're not going alone."

Sara gasped.

"Okay, but we need to be there. Now," Izzy said, taking a step toward the back door.

"Izzy. Guys. Stop." Shelby's voice rang in her mind as well as aloud.

"What?"

"I'm going with you, too," she said.

"The hell you are, Shel," Eric spat. "Geezus, you have a broken leg."

She scowled at him. "It's not like I'm jogging over there. I have a horse."

Eric shook his head. "I say no. Too dangerous."

"I say it doesn't matter. This is family, and I'm going to help my brother."

Eric turned his hands palm up. "You guys care to back me up here?"

"Nope." Vaughn smiled. "Let's go, gimp."

Mariah grabbed his hand that rested on her shoulder. "You all might need a doctor."

The big MMA fighter stopped, spun, and went down on one knee in front of his girlfriend, as if no one else were in the room. "No. Please. I have to know that you're safe. Need to know. If you're out there with us, I'll be distracted. It'll be more dangerous for me and for you. Take everyone and go to the hospital and stay there."

"Vaughn—" His kiss cut off anything else she was going to say.

"Well, if Shelby's going, I'm not leaving her alone," Eric growled.

Kerr's twin merely lifted her orange eyebrows.

"I need to be there," Ruth said.

"*Chérie*, no. You cannot." Odie grabbed her arm.

She met his forehead with hers. "You know I have to," she murmured. "Time to finish what was started."

"This is a bad idea," her husband said.

"I know it is. Our lives are full of bad decisions, aren't they?"

"*Mon dieu!* Then I will be right there beside the woman I love. For better or worse, as they say."

Garrison hugged and kissed Sara. "Go with Mariah. Take care of Zach and Dad, please."

A scrape at the kitchen doorway caught their attention. Mr. Taggart leaned on a walker, an uneven set to his mouth. He was so much older than Izzy remembered. The stroke had taken so much from him. "Give. Them. Hell." A glint in his direct gaze made Izzy smile. "Get my son back, too."

"Yes sir," Vaughn and Garrison said.

"I love you all. Your mother would be proud." He turned, and Mariah rushed over to help him into the living room.

Izzy gritted her teeth as everyone gathered warm clothes and sidearms. She needed them to move faster. "Come on, guys."

They were wasting too much time.

Time Kerr might not have.

CHAPTER 29

Fire.

He was on fire.

A bad dream?

No. Because waking up sucked worse than being unconscious.

Kerr's arms quivered and burned. He opened one eye, then the other. He tugged at his arms, but nothing budged. Glancing to either side, he spied his arms, stretched to their limits and lashed with ropes to...the grille of a large mining truck in the big storage garage. His feet dangled off the hard-packed floor.

Hey. Bonus points for using readily available materials to incapacitate him.

Negative points for the bastards who did this to him.

Ghosting in here seemed like a great idea, right up until he dropped the fade to bargain with Jerahmeel. Kerr's life for everyone else's.

As it turned out, that ass monkey didn't bargain.

He examined his tied arms and grimaced. Scored, burnt flesh striped his skin, visible where the flannel material had been burned into his flesh. Burned? More like melted into the skin. The sleeves sagged with the dampness of his dripping blood. A little more than a

Band-Aid could fix. When a tendril of air drifted over him, the nerves on the raw skin sparked with such intense pain that he saw stars.

In good news, his nervous system still worked. Shit.

Scrambling his feet for purchase on the rusted metal grille, he got enough of a stable platform to support his body weight and ease the pressure on his arms. Until his thighs started to cramp.

Trapped. Again. Waiting for someone to kill him. Bombs and beams flew through his mind's eye, but honestly, he didn't need any nightmare memories. The real deal right in front of him was worse than any flashback he could conjure.

The curved metal walls and ceiling created a big, freaky oven filled with red light. Following the source of illumination, he spied a lurid, hungry glow emanating from the cracked-open area at the center of the floor nearest the large garage door. A bed of embers wavered and smoked in a large, shallow concrete container nearby. Waves of heat buffeted him.

In the middle of the pit of glowing coals rested a knife. His heart rate kicked into overdrive.

Limbs jerking like a marionette puppet, Linc marched across the dusty concrete floor, removed the weapon with tongs, and plunged it into a bucket of water. Metallic steam made Kerr's eyes water.

The whirring *scricka, scricka* of whetstone against metal did not improve the scene. Sparks flew as Linc worked the knife, looking up only to shoot a warped, disconnected grin at Kerr. The bastard's eyes glowed that same sick red color as he stared at Kerr, then he flicked his gaze back to the knife.

Another knife meant to cause Kerr pain? Would it be too much to ask, getting a break from this particular hellish theme in his life? Kerr's leg twinged.

The metal side door crashed open as Wyatt and Tommy entered the building and joined Linc next to the blade. Their chuckles echoed as pleasantly as bones rattling in a metal bucket.

Tommy? The older brother, the law enforcement man, was usually pretty reasonable. Kerr studied the guy's pinched expression and unkempt light brown hair. Sick, red light came from the disconnected gaze. No help there.

Instinct told Kerr that the less attention he attracted, the better, suspended as he was on the front of an industrial Mack truck.

All this for a knife?

A hell of a slicer. Would present well on a rotating stand on one of those home shopping shows. And priced to move at $19.99, plus shipping and handling. A crazy laugh almost escaped his mouth. This whole situation was ridiculous.

"Almost done," Linc announced, his voice low, hollow. He lifted the knife. Glints from the razor-sharp edge flung shards of red light onto the walls.

As one, the three men turned toward the ember pit.

Oozing like slime, a dark cloud developed above the pit, hissing as it grew into a large, nebulous shape, maybe the size of a small car on end. Tendrils of smoke wove in and out until they formed into what resembled arms. Indistinct cloud fingers stretched as the thing let out a ground-rocking chuckle. If Kerr could rear back, he would have done so. The area that passed for a face turned toward the three men and Kerr.

A water-on-lava hiss resembled something close to a breath. Smelled like brimstone.

Cloud arms and fingers met in the area corresponding to its chest.

With a wet, hot, sucking sound, the thing slowly cracked open its center.

Kerr's lungs seized up at the splintering bone noises.

He had believed Izzy's story, but the live version was so much worse.

He had an unblocked view of the most horrifying thing he'd ever seen in his entire life. Given his history, that was saying something.

Suspended inside the creature hung the rotting body of Izzy's brother, Hank. His skin hung in large, peeled strips, leaving yellow fluid and blood to drip onto the floor. Hisses of steam rose up as the rancid liquid sizzled upon contact.

His head jerked up and raw eyelids twitched.

Then Hank's eyes peeled fully open and locked onto Kerr's. A flash of consciousness lit those eerie, oozing eyes.

A high-pitched scream vibrated the air, the structures, and even the truck grille that gouged Kerr in the back. His bones shook. He wanted to disappear, but that wouldn't help. He'd still be stuck.

The horror of Hank's decimated body answered once and for all the question of what had happened to him in the shack out in the woods when he had disappeared weeks ago. Was the real Hank inside of the creature truly alive? Or was this a shell? A puppet?

Hank flailed arms and legs, but they went nowhere, making futile jerking movements, like an animal stuck in tar.

The dark cloud creature howled what passed for a laugh, and the hazy fingers scraped over Hank. New bloody lines emerged from macerated skin. Hank's screams echoed through the garage. Kerr had a front row seat to hell. Taking it all in, arms wide open.

"When will the blade be ready?" The sound slithered out of the mass of darkness. Then it covered Hank again by doing what—buttoning up? Tucking him in?

A flicker of terror and humanity in Hank's eyes right before he disappeared hit Kerr like a one-two punch. Oh, shit. That man was not only alive but also conscious in there.

Linc didn't look up as he resumed grinding the knife. "Soon. Almost there."

"Will the legacy come to me?" the creature asked. Its dripping voice thinned out, like it was eager. Or unsure. Something that powerful shouldn't have doubts.

Wyatt bowed. "Yes, my Lord." He presented the cell phone. Kerr's phone. "I have sent the message. We have what they want. And our last minion will bring the legacy to us soon. We will be four." He pointed.

Izzy? Shit.

The Taggarts were walking right into a trap. Izzy, too.

Unless she was in on it.

No way.

Linc stood and, with a bow, presented the razor-sharp blade to the creature.

"Show me," it seethed.

Without hesitation, Linc traced the edge of the blade over his thick forearm. Blood flowed from a thin but deep line and dripped on the floor.

"Perfect."

"Thank you, my Lord," the big man intoned.

"Now, to begin our celebration on this, the first solstice of the second coming. The one time each year when the portal draws close enough to allow my emergence into the mortal world. Hear my words. I was betrayed. They tried to destroy me once. They thought they had succeeded. But I found their legacy. My destiny. And the legacy will bring me fully into the world where I will rule for all times."

"Yes, my lord Jerahmeel," the men intoned.

Kerr wanted nothing to do with the evening's planned festivities.

CHAPTER 30

*T*oo much time.

Izzy gritted her teeth. The entourage moved way too slowly for her satisfaction. She leaned forward in the saddle. Needed to hurry.

Kerr was out there. In pain. Suffering.

Dead?

She linked into Shelby's residual power. It had weakened. Maybe the absorption had finite limits or ran out after a while. Nevertheless, Izzy still detected a hint of Kerr's vital presence. He was in pain but still alive.

As the group crested a hill, Izzy spied a reddish glow that lit up the snowy ground and cloudy night sky. She knew that glow. Tremors started deep in her belly.

Garrison lifted his hand. "Tie up the horses. We're going on foot from here."

"Easy for you to say," Shelby muttered, sliding down from her horse with the help of a frowning Eric.

"Like you're getting anywhere close to that." Eric stared down the hill and at the large metal garage where the red glow originated.

A shudder laddered down Izzy's spine. No one wanted to get close to whatever caused that eerie light.

Kerr was down there. She didn't need a psychic power to reveal that information. She just knew it in her bones.

Everyone assembled around Garrison, including a worried-looking Ruth and Odie. Their great-great times however many grand-mother. Wow.

And Izzy was adopted. She closed her eyes for a second. Later. She'd deal with that revelation later. First of all, they needed to help Kerr.

Garrison pointed. "We need to see what's in that building. Get an idea of what we're dealing with."

Shelby blinked, then shook her head. "I can't tell you anything other than Kerr's in there, and he's in pain. I can try to do more, but…"

"No!" Eric and Garrison said together.

Eric snaked an arm around her shoulder.

"We could all go in together," Vaughn said, flexing his shoulders. "I'll pave the way."

Garrison gave a jerk of his head. "Too risky."

Desperate expressions flashed all around in the muffled moon-light, filtered by the forest. No one moved.

A jolt of realization hit Izzy. "I know what might still work. I think." She swiped a hand over her temple. "What if I can get in there? Invisibly. Find out what's going on."

"The hell," Vaughn breathed.

Izzy shook her hands. "You know how I absorbed Shelby's power?"

"Yeah," they nodded.

"I believe I've got Kerr's power inside of me."

"No way," Vaughn said. "For how long?"

"Good question." Izzy laughed, but in truth her heart tried to pound its way out of her chest. "How about we find out?"

Shelby pinched the bridge of her nose. "I don't know, Izzy."

Garrison leaned on a thick tree trunk. "It's our best option right now. We'll all find a place to hide. We'll be close by and ready for action if it comes to that." He patted his sidearm.

"Not too close," Eric growled.

Odie shot an indecipherable look at Ruth.

"Please help Kerr," Shelby hugged Izzy's neck. "I believe in you."

With a nod, Izzy stepped away from the group and gulped. How did she activate this ability earlier this morning? She had bit the inside of her cheek and thrown that invisible lever. Okay, then. She could feel the tingle of the power buzzing in her head. With another breath, she let go of all control and felt the shift in her mind. A headache speared her temples.

The gasps from everyone told her that it worked. The world became fuzzy. Her skull throbbed.

Ignoring the fatigue that sapped energy from every step, she walked down the hill and to the edge of the woods. Any farther and she'd be in the open flat area surrounding the main ranch structures. Just because she was invisible didn't mean she couldn't be tracked. She glanced back. Footprints in several inches of snow followed her.

Boy, how she wanted to run straight into that building and rip apart anyone or anything hurting Kerr. But she didn't know what else might be in that big metal garage. A careless move could cause him even more harm.

She stayed in the woods, skirting the far side of the clearing. Every step took more effort than the last. After what felt like hours, she ducked past two industrial-sized vehicles with tarps on them and reached the large Quonset garage.

A small window on the side door gave her a portal to a hellish view.

The center of the room glowed with a sick redness, like burning blood. The dark creature hovered nearby, a silver knife in its...hand? claw?

Wyatt, Linc, and Tommy rocked on their feet, totally focused on the evil cloud thing.

And in front of an industrial truck, Kerr was suspended, his arms spread out wide. She dropped the invisibility cloak so she could see better. An imaginary vice cranked down on her ribs. Her heart stopped for a beat. Kerr couldn't move, with his arms lashed to the machine.

Before she could formulate something resembling a smart plan, Jerahmeel moved closer to Kerr, the knife outstretched.

Crap.

Izzy had some skills, but no way could she beat the creepy, evil, knife-wielding blob and take on the family nutcases and still save Kerr.

Think.

Spinning, she raced back to a tarped piece of equipment. Clambering up into the front seat, she almost shed a tear when she found the keys in the ignition. Firing up the engine, she threw the machine into low gear and vaulted out of the front door, making an awkward roll in the snow. The loud diesel lumbered right in front of the garage, scraping a corner of the building with a shriek of metal on metal. The tarp caught on the edge of the building and slid off, creating an awkward, plastic cape trailing behind.

That should get someone's attention.

The three stooges burst out of the side door and chased the machine.

Gripping the edge of the doorjamb, she braced against the headache, pulled the invisibility cloak back around her, eased through the open side door, and froze. Maybe her family had been distracted, but Jerahmeel hadn't stopped his progress. It now hovered in front of Kerr and raised the blade. Kerr's horrified face twisted as he reared back as far from the thing as possible.

Then the knife brushed over an area of bare skin on Kerr's arm. A guttural groan erupted from his mouth as a red line followed the track of the blade.

Game over.

Izzy sidled toward the large garage door, hit a button, and prayed.

Yes. The loud bangs and squeals of the huge door slowly opening got the creature's attention. More importantly, the thing floated away from Kerr.

Outside, the large vehicle rumbled toward the ranch house, followed by her brothers and cousin. Good. That would give them something for their pea brains to think about.

Ignoring her bone weary exhaustion and blurry vision, she

rushed to the front of the truck where Kerr hung, suspended. Ropes bit into his arms, and blood dripped from raw wounds. A new bruise on his cheekbone layered on top of the old one. Her gut churned.

Stay hidden.

As she pulled out a utility knife, Izzy placed her invisible hand over Kerr's mouth.

He startled and gurgled, eyes searching and finding nothing. Of course.

"Hush, Kerr. It's me. Iz. Don't move, okay?"

His eyes widened, and he nodded.

"When I get these off, keep your arms up if you can. I need it to look like you're still tied up."

"You got it," he whispered.

As she freed one of his wrists, he hooked a finger over a metal piece, holding his arm in place. She sawed away at the other wrist while Kerr stared straight ahead. Sweat popped out on his forehead.

"It's coming back," he mumbled, lips not moving.

Crap. She worked faster. If that creature got its hands on them, Izzy didn't know what she could do to stop it.

But even if she freed Kerr, would this seat-of-the-pants plan work to get him out of this hellhole? Her arms shook with the effort of sawing through rope but also the increasing difficulty to hold the fade ability. Her head pounded. Her legs shook with the effort to stay upright.

A little longer. Hold on a little longer.

She looked at the sweaty, bruised face of the man tied to the truck.

No question. Izzy would save him or die trying.

Why Izzy had come back to help him, he had no idea. He didn't deserve her help or her friendship after being such a jerk. But if she could get him out of this mess, he would do his level best to get her far away from this horrible situation.

The burning muscles in his arms battled for attention over the twinge in his heart. Even after the horrible things he'd said and the way he had treated her, she was still here, risking her life to help.

"I can't hold the fade much longer." Her tight voice quivered.

If she could get him free, maybe Kerr could take over invisibility duties. Hell, he'd try to do it for both of them. No idea if that was possible or what it would do to him. Frankly, he didn't give a shit about personal consequences right now.

As he kept an eye on the creature, his pulse jumped when the thing swiveled back around and headed in their direction again. Shit.

"It's coming back," he muttered. "You need to run. Get out of here, Iz."

"Nope."

The rope frayed, as if by magic.

Hurry.

The thing hovered ten feet away. Within the creature, Hank's blurry face, a rictus of suffering and decay, floated up from the abyss, mouth open in a silent howl. The image burned into Kerr's mind.

The creature raised the knife.

Out of the corner of his eye, he spied one tiny cord still holding the rope together.

A flicker of movement right in front of him. Oh, shit. Her invisibility faltered.

If that creature saw her, she and Kerr were dead.

Hurry.

Five feet away. He cringed away from the sulfur heat.

Three feet. The inferno blast hit him and he smelled singed hair. Hers and his.

Out of time.

Fuck.

The creature's knife glinted, inches away.

Izzy's face shimmered like a mirage, in and out of focus.

Kerr needed to distract that thing long enough to get her out of here.

The last string of rope gave way.

He kept his quivering arms planted in place, tingling fingers begging to let go. "What's that over there?" he yelled.

The red embers and cloudy bulk rotated for a second.

That was all the time Kerr needed. He braced against the headache and triggered his own power. His invisible arms surrounded her and she sagged into his strong body.

"We have to help each other, sweetheart," he whispered, his voice muffled as he stepped down from the machine on shaky legs. His numb arms couldn't maintain a grip on her.

She latched an arm around him and tucked in tight.

Another few awkward steps, with their bodies pressed together, and they would reach the side of the vehicle.

The garage door rumbled for a few seconds, ending on a heavy *clunk*. No escape in that direction.

The black creature turned back, froze, and screamed. The piercing howl echoed in the metal building, and Kerr clamped his teeth together.

He kept Izzy next to his chest as they shuffled into the shadows. The garage was hard to navigate with his blurred vision, but no way would he stop until she was safe.

Right when they made it behind the truck, he bit off a groan and slumped to the ground, drawing her down with him. The headache eased away as the power ebbed. He blinked, but his vision stayed filmy. He didn't need 20/20 vision to see that they were in big trouble.

"Shit," he muttered, grabbing his head. "I don't know if I can do this much longer for both of us. Not sure if I can get us out of here undetected." The burns and knife wounds on his arms stung and throbbed, making concentration hard. One thing was certain: no way would he let her get hurt by that thing. They needed to figure a way out, right away. Despite the abused skin, he flung his pins-and-needles stinging arms around her and hugged her hard to his frame. "You came here for me?"

"I couldn't leave you in danger with my brothers and that...Jerahmeel guy just because you were a stupid jerk."

"I was a jerk. And stupid." He kissed her hard, then leaned back. "Chat later. Right now, we need to get the heck out of here."

"Find him!" the creature howled, the sound vibrating the metal walls of the garage.

"Yes, my Lord," came Wyatt's empty voice. "Come on, Linc."

Footsteps and heavy breathing grew louder.

Izzy and Kerr were trapped here, in the back of the garage.

"Go," he said, shoving her under the truck and next to the axle of one of the massive back tires.

He leaned against the inside of the tire and tugged her to sit between his legs. If not for the part where they were about to die, he might enjoy the scent of citrus and the way her body molded against him.

"Don't move," he whispered. He tightened his embrace.

Two sets of footsteps increased in volume. One set stopped right behind them, on the other side of the big tire. He glanced over. If the Brands bent down, they'd see Izzy and Kerr.

He didn't move.

More steps. Old, dusty concrete scraped under the soles of Linc and Wyatt's boots.

Flashlight beams pierced the darkness.

Just like Jalalabad.

Not now. Keep it together.

The toes of two work boots came within inches of their hiding place.

"Anything?" Linc called from the other side of the truck.

The two boots shuffled a step. Close enough that he could see the snow melting off the scuffed leather. "No, but I'll check under the vehicles," Wyatt growled.

Kerr stiffened and squeezed her arm. He held his breath, and with another twinge in his skull, the world filmed over into eye-watering blurry shapes. The dull headache gnawed at him. But no way would he let go.

The boots became one boot, joined by a pants knee as Wyatt knelt.

Those bulging eyes focused right on them.

Izzy's fingers dug into the forearms Kerr had locked around her. His muscles shook like a weightlifter trying to keep a heavy load in the air. But he didn't let go.

Wyatt swept the area under the truck with the flashlight. The bright light blinded Kerr, but he didn't move.

Sweat tickled his scalp, begging him to scratch it. He refused to move.

Another sweep of the flashlight left dark after-spots in his vision.

Wyatt stood and turned with another scuff of his boot, then walked away. "Nothing back here. My lord Jerahmeel, what would you like for us to do?"

The side door closed with a thud. Trapped.

"We wait," came the engine-hot half scream.

Footsteps faded toward the front of the garage.

Animal-like howls and cries began, growing in volume. No telling what was happening up there. Kerr had no intention of sticking around long enough to find out.

He let out a big breath and sagged, letting go of the fade once more. He rubbed his hands over her shoulders. Real. Warm. He couldn't believe it; she was here with him.

At least he wasn't alone in this hell.

"You okay?" he whispered.

"Not great. But it's all right." A shudder rolled through her, and he squeezed her thin arms. She sniffed. "We need to get out of this building before that creature decides to look more closely for us. And before your family gets tired of waiting and jumps into action."

"They're here?"

"They wouldn't let me come alone. All for one, Taggart Musketeers junk like that."

"You have no idea how sorry I am about earlier. I was so wrong." He didn't deserve this woman's care. He leaned down, tipped her chin up, and kissed her deeply. "You're amazing, Iz."

"Even more amazing if we had another way out of this place," she whispered, leaning against him. "Hey, there might be an opening in the rusted metal in the back corner."

"You're a genius." He kissed the top of her head.

She shook her head. "It'll be a tight squeeze. Does that trick shrink you?"

"No. But I don't care. We don't have other options." He pulled in a few more breaths, his hard chest rising and falling under her cheek. "Let's get moving."

"You don't need to rest?"

"Hell, yeah, I'd love to rest," he muttered. "But the longer we stay here, the greater the chance they'll find us. I don't know what the fuck that thing is, but I'm not sticking around to play patty-cake with it."

Getting out from under their curled up positions beneath the truck while staying silent played out in a painful, slow-motion game of reverse Twister.

Chants from the front of the garage grew louder.

Keeping her hand in his, Kerr let her lead him to the far corner. He knelt. Cold air surged through the opening where the corrugated metal had rusted away. Faint light from the moonlit snow chased away the lurid, red glow.

She knelt and put her hand into the opening. When she turned around, her eyes swam in her pale face. "It's not big enough."

The chants had formed into a kind of loud, howling, churning rhythm.

A few feet from freedom. He'd be damned if they would fail now. "We'll bend it."

A pause, then they traded places. He rested his hands on the irregular and sharp edge of the metal.

Grabbing his arm, she hissed, "Push it outward with the next howl."

When the noise reached an eerie crescendo, she tapped Kerr and he pushed. A gut-clenching scream of metal shot out from the corner.

He froze.

The noise up front continued, unaltered by their activity.

"Wait," she whispered. "Again." At another high-pitched howl, she tapped his arm.

He pushed again, opening the space to about two feet across. Might be enough.

The sound tapered off to nothing.

Eerie silence filtered through the dusty air.

"You need to go," he hissed. "Now."

"You're coming with me."

"Of course. But you first."

Moving too slow for his nerves to handle, she eased herself out of the opening. He imagined her smooth skin catching on the jagged metal. Stitches and a tetanus shot, he could live with. Death and eternal torment from Jerahmeel, not so much.

To navigate the oblong exit, she had to go on her side. He did his best to support her as she shimmied out the opening.

"Come on," she whispered.

His shoulders didn't fit as well, and he grunted as he hauled himself through the metal opening. The frigid air cut through his jeans and shredded shirt. Despite trying to remain silent, it felt like every rough scrape of clothing against metal sounded like screaming horses dragging a wheel-less wagon down a road. As his hips cleared the opening with a vicious creak of metal, a shout came from within the garage. His jolt had nothing to do with the frigid air outside.

"Go!" He motioned to her.

"Not without you." Holding out her hand, she pulled as he squeezed through the opening.

An otherworldly shriek rattled the siding.

He grabbed her upper arm and they clung to each other as they half jogged, half walked past the pieces of machinery, into the woods, and away from the damned building.

Behind them, three large shapes emerged from the garage.

Howls and red screams echoed across the snowy open area. Kerr's blood iced.

"Keep moving," he said, pulling her into his side, helping her to walk. He put a hand to his head and grimaced as they reached an open area. "Here we go again."

Another headache and the world dimmed as they crunched across the bluish-gray snow. The filtered moonlight and blurry vision gave everything a flat, fuzzy appearance. He concentrated on remaining upright.

Despite the awkward hold, no way would he let go of Izzy. He'd made one of the worst mistakes of his life pushing her away; he wasn't about to squander a second chance. No matter what, he'd protect her. He'd make right the damage he had done.

Five minutes into the woods, and the headache eased off and away as he released the fade.

A shape rose up out of the darkness, and she sucked in a big breath. Kerr clamped his hand over her mouth.

"Hi, Vaughn," he said, his voice low and tight.

"Took you long enough. You look like hell."

He took the hat Vaughn offered but held off on putting on the duster his brother had brought.

They were surrounded by helping hands and low-strength LED lights. How many of his family had come out here? He took a head count. All of siblings, plus Eric, Ruth, and Odie.

After being quickly bandaged up, Kerr evaluated the situation. They were a hundred feet or so into the forest. Where they stood, the faint moonlight provided enough illumination that he could easily see the large clearing in front of that damned metal garage.

"Plan?" Garrison asked.

Kerr rubbed his temples. "That thing has three possessed helpers. It needs a fourth, which we have. It's pissed. And the creature now has the knife."

Ruth gasped and shot a stricken look at Odie.

Kerr continued, "You want a plan? We need to stop that thing and stay alive. God knows how we do that. We're trying to pitch a major league no-hitter with a whiffle ball."

"So, we're fucked," Vaughn growled. "Hey, What about Izzy? Can she help?"

Garrison shook his head. "We don't know that much about her ability and whether it will help or hurt us here."

"I'd like to try," Izzy said.

"No." Kerr chopped his hand through the cold air. "We don't know what putting her in the mix will do to her...or us."

"Here's what we do know," Ruth said. "If you can't defeat them, then there is no hope for humanity."

"Thank you for that ray of sunshine," Kerr hissed as he eased his arms into the duster. "We've got the idea." He pulled Izzy into his side. "Okay. We should come up with some kind of plan to surround and attack it. Them. Whatever."

Before anyone could utter another word, a jet-engine roar

preceded the shadow figure emerging as it joined Izzy's family at the side of the garage.

"Game plan just changed, folks." Vaughn drew himself up to full height and cracked his neck. "Looks like the fun is coming to us."

CHAPTER 31

*K*err grabbed Izzy's shoulders and spun her to face him. "I need you to get out of here, okay?" He had a solid idea of what that creature would do if it got hold of her.

Hell, he'd had a firsthand preview of what it would do to any of them. His arms burned.

She lifted her chin. "Nope. I'm here with you, all the way."

Out of the corner of Kerr's eye, Eric nodded and nudged a grim Shelby.

Kerr groaned. He loved the fact that Izzy was brave and determined, but now wasn't the time. "You don't understand. That thing is coming for us. You. My family. You might die." He glanced at the figures emerging from the garage. His gut tightened.

Clutching his tender forearms through the coat, she leaned toward him. "We're in this together. If you haven't figured that out by now, I don't know what it'll take to get that info through your thick head." Her words came out with puffs of vapor in the chilly air. "I'm not leaving you. I care about you."

He struggled to process what she said. "What? How?"

"Sorry. Too much sharing?"

"Your timing is horrible." He kissed her full on the mouth and tasted salt. "And yes, you can share with me any day. Uh, except not right now. My dance card is going to fill up here in a minute." He dropped his forehead to hers. "Please, go. And I mean that in the best way possible."

"No. I'm staying with you." Even in the shadows, her open, shimmering gaze should have triggered rainbows and butterflies. If it weren't for the part where Kerr and everyone else around him might die tonight.

"Then promise me you'll stay back. If something happens, I want you to survive. Please." He held her head in his hands. "Promise me." If she was in danger, no way could he concentrate. But he had to keep his head clear if he and his siblings had a chance in hell of fighting that thing. Not to mention any chance of winning.

She swallowed. "Okay."

Another kiss threatened to turn into ten more.

"No more time for face-sucking, bro," Vaughn snapped.

An ungodly howl came from the creature, and his big brother whipped around and leaned forward, like a rabid dog on a leash, quivering, bristling. Ready for action. That cloud thing was tasty bait for Vaughn's danger-detecting ability. His animal growl and wild, wide eyes made the hairs on Kerr's arms stand on end. He'd never seen his brother act this feral before.

Garrison's shadowed face looked a million years old. "Huddle, guys." He glanced over his shoulder. Flanked by the three Brands, the creature had made it halfway across the clearing in its relentless, deliberate, awful progress. "Ideas? Quickly."

"Let Vaughn attack it?" Kerr suggested.

Shelby hobbled over, assisted by Eric. "Won't be enough. If that thing blasts you full force, it'll fry you in a second. Trust me, I know." She grimaced. "Not to mention what it can do with the knife it has."

"Actually, we don't truly know what all it can do with the knife," Ruth pointed out.

"Well." Garrison blinked. "Let's agree that whatever it can do, it's bad. Son of a bitch. Okay. Weaknesses?" Another glance back. It was fifty feet away, slowly but steadily coming toward them. "Damn it. Give me anything, folks, or we will all be crispy in a minute."

A howl shuddered through the woods. Snow dropped from tree limbs.

"Nothing?" Garrison's jaw locked down tight, barely letting out the words. "Shit. What do we have at our disposal?"

Kerr's heart beat like an out-of-control jackhammer. He couldn't breathe.

"You have all of your powers." Ruth's clear water voice calmed Kerr. How did she do that?

"Details," Garrison snapped.

"Work together, like you did before. Get into the thing, drill damage into it, and then kill it. And you need a shield to hold back its attack."

Garrison ran a hand over his jaw. "No offense, lady, but there are a lot of supplies missing in that plan."

"Holy hell." Her shoulders squared. "All I know is that together, you all hold the key to this monster's destruction. Only together."

The warm whiff of sulfur scared the holy living shit out of Kerr. *Come on, people, get it together.*

"Fine. Let's say we have all those things. How do we kill it?" Garrison ground out.

"A knife," Ruth said.

"You want me to go invisible and stab it?" Kerr said. That wasn't the worst idea.

A funny glint came and went in Ruth's eyes as she glanced at Odie. "Maybe. First your power will need to change. For now, keep your sister and brothers hidden while they work."

His head hurt, just thinking about what he needed to do. "You're kidding, right? I couldn't hold the effect for more than a minute, and that was with Izzy right next to me."

"You have to do more." Ruth sighed. "Each one of you must reach beyond your own abilities."

"Let's say that your plan works. How do we sink the knife in?" Garrison asked.

Another sideways gaze slid to Odie and back.

He sputtered, "*Chérie*, no. We already—"

Whatever he wanted to say was interrupted by the roar, which flayed bark off the trees. Jerahmeel drifted through the woods, trailed by the other men. Its progress left charred trees and steaming, muddy earth in its wake.

Eric shook his head. "Geezus. While you are all doing whatever mental gymnastics it takes to slow this thing down, who's keeping you all alive?"

"That's your job," Shelby grimaced. "Three Brands against one Eric sounds about right. You needed a challenge, cowboy." Tension pinged through her twin connection with Kerr.

Twin connection?

Connection.

He and Shelby had linked up in minor ways in the past. What if they could connect their powers like that, only better? And if two could do it, why couldn't four?

No time to wonder. The clock had ticked down to zero, based on the intensity of the heat blast and strong odor of rotting eggs. Oh, and the unnatural ear-splitting howl.

Kerr's heart did a snare-drum riff as he and his siblings fanned out and faced the creature. Ruth and Odie stood next to them on one end of the line. Eric took up position on the other side of the group. Izzy remained a few feet back, far too close for Kerr's comfort.

Get out of here, Iz.

The thing stopped...walking? floating?...ten feet away. Wyatt, Tommy, and Linc flanked the thing. Their twisted, hard faces popped with unnaturally thick cords of muscle. Their shadowy figures grew huge. Their eyes had ceased to be human and now glowed eerie, red, and blank.

Jerahmeel rose up, even taller and bigger, as jet-engine air roared toward Kerr. Building something up. Shit.

If the Taggarts were going to survive, the first part was up to him. He activated his fading trick and wrapped it around him, trying to ignore the throb in his head. Then he mentally extended the power like a cellophane blanket over his brothers and sister. As the power flowed near each sibling, it virtually clung to them. Connection.

He couldn't cover Ruth, Odie, and Eric, but they seemed resourceful as they fanned out. He couldn't reach back and include

Izzy, either. It was a miracle he could hide four people at once, for any length of time.

The creature howled, a piercing sound. Glowing ember eyes flashed to the right, then the left.

It...paused.

It couldn't see them. It was working.

Another howl sounded like nasty frustration. Or monster muttering.

Great. He could take a job as the Blob Whisperer. What kind of benefits normally came with that kind of job?

A glance at the fucked up Brand guys answered that question.

Within the invisibility cloak, Kerr could hear his siblings inside his mind and clear as day. And he could see their blurry forms next to him.

"Damn, man, that's a great trick." Vaughn whistled. "But sure packs a punch of a migraine."

Shelby added, "Don't stop."

"I'll do my best." Kerr gritted out the words. "But you all should move around so the thing has to work at finding you."

"On it," Garrison said.

Kerr managed to keep all four of them covered as an imaginary blacksmith pounded a lump of metal into a horseshoe on the top of his noggin. He leaned against a tree, pressing his hands to his temples as the pressure built. Trying to hold his head together. Literally.

Vaughn's blurred form moved to the side of the thing while Garrison reached an arm out, gun in hand.

Shelby spread her hands wide as she erected a shield.

The thing screeched as it turned toward Ruth. "You! My love. My betrayer. Jezebel!" Holy shit. "You live?"

Ruth froze in place.

Odie stepped in front of his wife. "Stay away from her, *diable*. We destroyed you once; we will destroy you again," Odie snarled.

Bad move, man.

Odie and Ruth needed to get the hell away from that thing. But within the fuzzy bubble of his power, Kerr could do nothing but watch.

"Not this time," it howled. "You will never stop me. This is my entrance to the Earth. I will not be denied. It's your legacy I want destroyed. All of them. As an extra *séduction*, I can watch your face as they are annihilated. And then you and I will be as one for eternity."

Ruth gasped and glanced in the general vicinity of the Taggarts' last-known location.

Shit. They were all going to be literal toast in a few seconds if Jerahameel revved up his demonic blowtorch trick.

But then something insane happened.

"I say no." She drew herself up to full height. "*No.*" Her voice cracked into several different octaves. Like Vaughn's voice sounded earlier, but bigger. Broader. Her voice split, actually. Boomed across the snowy forest and drove the three asshole helpers to their knees. Where the hell had she been hiding that trick? "You will not have them." Snow tumbled down from the upper limbs.

When she looked back once more, her silver, glowing, backlit eyes took Kerr's breath away.

"You dare to tell me what to do? I am all powerful." Jerahmeel howled. "At what price do you offer me this *merde?*"

"At no price, oh, lord of shit." Odie nodded at his wife, as if her voice and xenon-bright eyes were no big deal. Just a normal day.

A metal slice of sound emitted from the thing. "That can be arranged."

The three Brand guys regained their footing and resumed the slow trudge toward the visible members of the Taggart rescue party. Including Izzy. Kerr spared a quick check behind his shoulder. She edged behind a tree.

With a colossal roar, Jerahmeel created a wave of lurid green heat that skidded across the terrain, melting snow in a ten-foot diameter, blowing down the undergrowth in its way. The flame stopped against an invisible barrier and flamed around it. Shelby's shield.

Kerr's heart pounded in his chest and in his fucking head, but he maintained the cloak.

They sure needed another trick other than his disappearing ability, though.

"Get away from them." Ruth's eerie voice banged against every hard surface and competed with the creature's for sheer terror factor. What *was* she?

She was a Taggart.

Explained a lot.

Then the thing strafed another bolt of fire across the landscape. Vaughn, hidden from sight but out in front, yelled as the roaring flames hit him. Kerr kept the cloak up.

Then Shelby extended both arms out, and the fire curled around and over Vaughn as well.

Go, sis.

"Garrison," she screamed. "Use your power!"

"Pretty sure it's not lying to us," Garrison snapped, pointing his gun toward the thing.

"No, Gar, I don't mean your lie-detector ability. You need to *change* the power. Dig for the truth. *Dig.*" Shelby panted.

"What?"

"Get. Inside. Of. It." She panted. "Like you did when you rescued Sara a month ago. Go *inside* it."

"Dig? Inside it. Got it. I can do that." His brother holstered the sidearm and raised a hand.

Holy crap, but within the sibling connection, Kerr actually felt Garrison's power suction up into a long, thin, sharp weapon. That truth-seeking ability morphed into something way scarier. And deadlier. With a mental heave, Garrison hurled the javelin of his power at the creature, piercing the area under the red glowing eyes.

"Hold him!" Kerr yelled.

Garrison held out his arms and somehow kept the spear lodged in the opening.

Sweat rolled down Kerr's forehead and every muscle shook as he tried to keep their disappearing act going.

Green fire licked at the four of them but didn't quite touch anyone. Yet.

"Hurry, Vaughn," Shelby called out, dropping to her knees. "I can't keep this up."

Before she wavered, another force added itself into the group.

Familiar, as if it fit perfectly in the Taggart family. New and fresh, like clear water. Calm. Powerful.

"Let me help," Ruth said inside Kerr's head, using that bizarre multi-octave voice. The shield solidified as the woman amplified Shelby's power.

"*Chérie*, careful. You aren't immortal now! We don't know your limits." Odie's voice reached them as if from a great distance.

"Then go do something helpful, so we won't have to test my limits," Ruth quipped.

"Women. So bossy," he muttered, audible even through the veil and the roaring fire.

"Vaughn, any day now," Shelby called out.

"On it," Vaughn said.

Kerr sensed the buildup of danger within his oldest brother. The darkness that defined Vaughn grew, hungered. The sheer, raw power he possessed—good God. Compressing his rage into a massive spiked sphere, he stretched it back. And flung the power out at the thing.

The sphere slowed but still passed right through the creature. A howl. "That's all you have to stop me?" Its laugh ripped jagged nails of sound down Kerr's face. "Then I shall feast on your souls tonight as we receive the second coming." Garrison's spike slid out as well.

The three Brand puppets staggered forward. Relentless. Not stopping.

Shit.

"That thing isn't solid enough. My power can't push against a ghost," Vaughn groaned. "Kerr. Can you do that trick to firm it up?"

"Not without losing our invisibility."

"Fucking don't care. Do it."

Ruth and Shelby continued to shield them all against the bright green fire that blowtorched out of the thing. Shelby curled forward but kept her arms up.

Shadows flickered over Ruth until her face became skeletal. Hollow. Ancient.

Dread twisted in Kerr's gut.

He had zero abilities when it came to actual premonitions, but his instinct to tell when things were getting dicey? A-plus.

This situation wasn't going to end well.

It's okay, Ruth's cool voice soothed his aching mind. *Hold on.* The sound came from inside his mind. *I've lived long enough. It's your family's turn.*

Wait. What?

"No, Ruth," Shelby yelled.

"Let me help." Izzy's bright voice cut through his fuzzy hearing. She edged over to the woman and grasped Ruth's hand.

The older woman sagged, but Izzy held her up and suddenly stiffened, mouth open and eyes wide open.

Then that crisp sense of Izzy's presence spread out from Ruth.

Amplified the woman's abilities.

Bolstered Shelby's protective shield.

Clarified each person's powers.

A new spear Garrison had formed solidified, harder and sharper than the first one. "What the hell?" he yelled.

And the invisibility that Kerr struggled to hold in place? Now two people lifted the same weight.

"Iz, I had no idea how much you could do," he breathed. "You're amazing."

"Not sure what's happening." Through the group connection, it sounded like she stood right next to him. "But I'm not giving up without trying everything possible to help."

"Right on," Vaughn roared. "Power up!"

Odie continued to skirt the trees around the creature. Wyatt rushed him, and arms and legs went flying in a barrage of grunts and punches.

Eric drew Linc away from the center of the action. The thuds of fists and painful yells echoed in the snowy night.

That left the zombie, Tommy, who hesitated next to the creature. With glowing eyes, he scanned the group. Then stopped when he saw Izzy.

Kerr turned to help her.

"No! Later." Ruth's voice chimed on every sensory level. "Now, Izzy, hang on to me. Shelby's shield will hold him back for now."

All that stood between Izzy and her zombie brother was Shelby's force field trick?

Screw all of this. He'd be damned if Izzy or his family got hurt any more. Best way he could help was participate in ending Jerahmeel once and for all.

Making a withdrawal on his lifelong deposit account full of pent-up anger and frustration, he dropped the fade and instead wove the invisibility power into something different, like that cellophane wrap he'd created before but stickier and more solid. Groaning against the headache that threatened to split his head in two, he flung his power at the thing, coating the creature with a clear rime that glinted in the low light. It took everything Kerr had plus the boost from Izzy to hold it on the thing as the creature tried to claw the wrap away.

For the moment, Odie had stopped the Brands' attack, if the sprawled, messy form of Wyatt was any indication. Now the wily Cajun sidled around to Jerahmeel's backside, only a few feet from the thing. Luckily, the creature focused all of its attention on trying to blast the Taggart kids to kingdom come.

"Hurry," Shelby gasped.

"Garrison, open it up!" Vaughn hollered.

With another collection of power magnified by Izzy's cool booster touch and a big shove, Garrison sent a second psychic spear form into the thing's chest, cracking it wider.

A flash of Hank's silently screaming, twisted face came into view. Torment dripped from every inch of the man.

Izzy's mouth gaped. Her power faltered. The weight of everyone's power increased and they all groaned.

"Focus! You are the key," Ruth yelled, even as she gripped Izzy's hand.

Ruth doubled over, but Izzy hollered through the deafening roar of wind and fire, "Keep going. I've got you." Their joined hands started to glow in the darkness.

Vaughn roared as he pulled together another surge of pure, feral rage. His ability to become danger became concentrated into the most lethal bomb Kerr had ever seen. Power folded in on power, compressing. Building. Becoming denser than lead. With a guttural yowl,

Vaughn hurled the spiked sphere of danger at Jerahmeel, staggering the creature to whatever passed for its knees.

The resultant howl curdled Kerr's blood.

Jerahmeel continued to spew fire at them but with less force.

Kerr held the sticky film against the thing, gritting his teeth against the pain. Twin pops of sound preceded hot liquid trickling out of Kerr's eyes. He blinked film away. He didn't care. He didn't need his vision to keep that cloud of evil in a solid form and give his brothers something to attack.

The thing focused ember eyes on a rapidly withering Ruth and screamed, "*Mademoiselle*. We could have ruled the world together. We could have had everything."

"But then I came along, *mon ami*," Odie said from behind the thing.

A blade, similar to the one the creature held, glinted in Odie's hand. He raised it and plunged it into the creature's upper back.

The ground bucked and cracked underneath Kerr's feet, yet fire continued to pour out of the monster.

"Odie!" Ruth screamed, covering every bandwidth of sound and making the ground shake even more.

"I love you, *chérie*." The words tore through the howl of fire. "Until the end of time, I love you." He clung to Jerahmeel as the creature whipped back and forth, trying to dislodge the Cajun.

"No!" Ruth yelled.

Shelby cried out, absorbing intense emotions. Even Kerr picked up on the swirling anguish.

In the connection, still holding Ruth's hand, Izzy, too, cried out and stumbled. Their connected hands emitted heat and waves of light.

Jerahmeel brandished the Omega knife and made an awkward backward swoop. The angle was poor.

The movement was enough.

The knife sunk into Odie.

"No!" Ruth staggered forward, wading straight into the fire. She pulled Izzy with her.

The image of Izzy's arm connecting with Ruth's triggered Kerr's memory. Izzy's glowing arm emerged from out of the creature's fire, as if from lava beneath the Earth's crust.

The dreams.

Izzy was the fire woman in the dreams that all the Taggart siblings had experienced over the past few months. She was the key.

The extra layer of strength ebbed as Izzy broke contact, retreating from the flames. Sweat rolled down Kerr's neck as he fought to maintain his ability. Fuck, his head was shattering. Sound started to fade away.

Then Tommy grinned and began taking relentless steps toward Izzy. She screamed and scrambled away from the group, up into the forest.

The power level dropped again as Izzy stopped boosting them. Shelby moaned.

Kerr needed to protect Izzy, but shit on shit, he was struggling to hold the coating on the creature. If he failed, all of them would die.

Ruth stopped within a foot of Jerahmeel, her eyes emitting bright white beams that turned the night to day and rivaled the lurid flames coming from him. "You are finished," her voice rang out.

Oh fuck. The woman looked like a ninety-year-old. What in God's name had happened?

"No!" Shelby's voice echoed in his head.

Vaughn collected another force of spiked horror and flung it forward, more focused this time, somehow avoiding Ruth. The creature hit the ground and rolled off of Odie's still body, the Cajun's knife still embedded in Jerahmeel's back.

Holy. Shit.

Hot waves of liquid fire rose from within the creature as it held its knife up once more. From within the depths, Hank's hell-trapped eyes blinked. His mouth opened wide in a terrible, silent scream.

"You will never win!" Ruth's voice careened across the landscape, shattering branches in a twenty-foot radius. "They are mine. My legacy. The future. And they will remain free of you." She pulled a similar knife from a sheath on her lower leg and leapt on top of Jerahmeel, impaling the cloudy thing in what would have been its chest, her body weight driving the blade forward and down.

Jerahmeel lost his grip on the Omega blade, and Ruth grabbed it, thrusting the new blade into his chest.

A spark as Odie's embedded blade screeched against her blade and the Omega blade detonated into an ear-splitting concussion. Several trees exploded behind the creature and the ground heaved. Trees blew backward off of twisted stumps.

Nothing moved.

A few creaking tree limbs provided the only sound.

Dropping his powers, Kerr sagged against the tree. His head rang like the aftereffect of a giant church bell's clang. He wiped warm liquid from under both eyes and blinked away the blurriness.

He staggered over to the heap of bodies.

The effort to breathe took almost more energy than he had.

The cloud portion of Jerahmeel had dissipated. All that remained? Hank's oozing carcass with Ruth's knife and the Omega knife plunged to the hilts in his rotting torso. The tip of Odie's knife met the other two blades in the center of Hank's chest.

Kerr knelt and touched Ruth's cheek. Her sculpted but now-lined face rested calm and collected.

Odie, too, didn't move. Dampness bled through his coat. But even in the stillness, a smile curved the Cajun's mouth as his hand reached across the wet ground. Toward his wife.

Vaughn and Garrison approached, leaning on each other. Blood dripped from Garrison's nose and beneath Vaughn's ears. They knelt down next to Ruth and Odie. With a shaking hand, Vaughn checked for a pulse on Ruth. Garrison opened Odie's coat and pressed a palm against the wetness expanding over the fabric.

Eric limped over from the other side of the woods, heading toward Shelby. "What happened?" he called. "Linc was handing me my ass, then all of a sudden he dropped to the ground and stopped moving."

Kerr looked around. No other sounds penetrated his buzzing ears.

Dead silence.

Izzy.

Shit.

It took a colossal amount of strength, but he staggered over to where he had last seen her. His windpipe closed off as he spied her small footprints and a set of bigger ones. Kerr followed the double tracks up a snowy hillside.

Despite the chilly temperature, sweat poured off of him. He pushed his body to move faster. His leg ached as skin rubbed against silicone. He ignored the pain. Ignored the throbbing in his head. Ignored how the use of his power had sapped his energy to almost nothing.

None of it mattered.

He had to find Izzy.

Time and sanity narrowed down to the thinnest line.

There, up the hill in the snow, a shape.

His heart skidded several beats.

No. Two shapes.

Izzy lay on the ground next to Tommy's big frame.

Neither moved.

CHAPTER 32

Once disconnected from Ruth, Izzy's own power reserves dropped to useless levels in a matter of seconds. Her legs turned to rubber as she took in the scene in front of her.

Kerr's protection was long gone. Shelby knelt on the snowy ground, head in her hands. All the Taggart siblings were visible and in various states of agony. Ruth faced off with Jerahmeel. Odie appeared behind the monster.

As much as Izzy wanted to stay, another problem loomed right in front of her.

Tommy.

Her blank-eyed brother stalked toward her, one heavy foot in front of the other. Deliberate. A lifeless puppet, forced to move.

Tommy wasn't stopping, and he wasn't on a relaxing hike into the woods.

No. He had one brain cell firing, and it wanted Izzy. A flash of light burst from the creature behind him, and Tommy paused, blinked red eyes at her, and then grinned. Wild. Unhinged. Evil.

She scrambled for footing, cast a glance back in Kerr's general direction, where gut-churning noises hurtled through the forest, and she threw out a prayer...for everything. As she slipped and landed on her knees, melted snow stiffened the fabric of her jeans. Pushing her quivering muscles to their limits, she shoved to her feet and hurried away.

She climbed a small hill, driven by her brother's whuffing breaths and the soul-splitting sounds of whatever the heck was happening back there in the woods. Icy air sliced its way through her lungs as she fought to suck in enough oxygen to fuel her shaking legs.

Her thigh muscles burned. Steps became shorter. Weaker.

Tommy didn't stop.

Step by relentless step, he kept up with her flagging pace.

Then he gained ground.

Inched closer.

The crunches of the even, heavy steps behind her echoed in her head. The sounds in the clearing faded away.

Her heart raced. Legs burned.

She was too tired. Too slow.

On a steeper section of the snowy hill, she stumbled and slid.

As she got up again, a cold hand clamped around her ankle and yanked her back down to the bottom of the incline.

She smacked into the ground, spiking pain into her hip where most of her weight landed. Tommy dragged her toward him, hand over slow hand, snow collecting under her jacket and icing her lower back.

Clawing at snow and dead leaves beneath to gain traction, she screamed, "Tommy! It's Izzy. Stop."

He picked her up under her arms. Her feet dangled in the cold air.

"Tommy, you're not like this. Wake up, please."

A blink, and he glanced back over his shoulder.

"What about your job? And Mom. She needs you, Tommy. You have children. They need you. We all do." Tears chilled her face.

His hands bit into her armpits. His grip tightened.

Then she full-on screamed at him.

Nothing.

His face was blank. This wasn't her brother. Not anymore.

A crack of what sounded like lightning ripping the world apart, followed by a howl of terror and rage blasted past her.

Her brother blinked. Once. Twice.

"Please, Tommy, let me down. Come on, now," she begged him.

"Izzy?" His stiff, hoarse voice came out like a currycomb dragged across rough leather.

She sagged. "Come back to me, Tommy. Be the man I know you are."

"I—don't. What am I doing here?" His lost voice almost made her hug him. Almost, because she still dangled from his outstretched arms.

Stuck in stasis, they both hung in space. Izzy held by Tommy.

Tommy held by the creature's thrall. He swayed.

Hell-born Jerahmeel or his sister? Which would he choose?

Another scream from down the hill blended a fire engine siren with a million nails on a chalkboard until her gritted teeth squeaked against each other.

Her brother lowered her until her toes brushed snow. She sagged in relief.

"My Lord. Yes," Tommy intoned and tightened his grip.

And flung her into the base of a tree.

Fire exploded in her back as the air left her lungs. Oh, God, she couldn't pull in a breath. Her rib cage tried to expand.

No air filled her lungs.

Nothing.

Then Tommy consumed her field of vision, grabbed her arms again, and hurled her another ten feet. All she could see was stars bursting all around her.

A wild crack, like the entire earth opening up, and a horrible howl echoed from the forest clearing.

Tommy put his hands together and raised them over his head with a guttural yell.

She put an arm over her face, though little good it would do if he decided to pile drive those fists into her body. Throwing every last ounce of her absorbed power against her brother, she flung a brief blast of Shelby's shield ability that exploded out from her and knocked him back on his heels.

Then Tommy froze.

In horrible slow motion, he collapsed—to his knees, then forward, then down—right on top of her.

What little air she had left in her lungs was squeezed out. She shoved at the limp, heavy body. Didn't budge.

Her chest burned.

She tried short, shallow pulls of air into her lungs.

Didn't work.

"Tommy," she gasped.

He twitched once and went still.

Was he dead? Tears heated her cheeks, despite the chilly temperatures. Snow melted underneath them, seeping into her clothes, icing her backside.

What if no one found her?

What if there was no one else left *to* find her?

Tommy.

Was he dead, too? Panicked, she pushed up against his chest, but the awkward position and her useless muscles couldn't budge him. With one last shove and a hitch of her sore hip, she lifted one of his arms and finally squeezed out from under his heavy, limp frame.

All of her energy bled away into the cold, quiet night.

Every muscle in her body gave up.

Snow seeped into her jeans. So cold. She couldn't move.

Silence all around her.

Nothing was left.

She stared up through the tall pine trees. A strange peace settled over the silent forest. The night sky was clear. Through the trees, she spied a thick band of stars. The sky blurred as she blinked.

She focused on the stars. Something real. Something good.

Keep looking at the stars.

Wonder if Kerr looked up from that collapsed building and focused on the sky above him.

Her slow, shallow breaths couldn't keep up with what her body needed. The air chilled her throat as she struggled to inflate her lungs.

The stars faded away.

Darkness blanketed her.

In her mind, she floated.

Minutes or days later, a crunching sound filtered into her consciousness.

Could be an animal looking for dinner. Or maybe Wyatt came to finish Tommy's job.

She peeled open a cold eyelid. A face loomed above her.

If she could breathe, there'd be a great scream bursting out of her right about now.

As it stood, she couldn't move. Her entire body had gone numb. Boneless.

Studying the face in front of her, she spied two damp trails of blood under each eye. And a tired, wry smile.

Kerr. Alive.

If she could breathe, she might also consider crying.

He knelt, and his haunted eyes searched her then locked on to hers. He rubbed her arms.

"Iz? Are you okay? Please." His voice came out raw, as if he'd screamed for hours.

She opened her mouth but couldn't make a sound emerge.

Kerr. Alive.

Then her lungs inflated like a released coil. Air flooded her chest, her body, her head. She blinked at the tingling rush of oxygen as blood flowed to her fingers and toes.

"Kerr?" she whispered.

He should get out of here. Jerahmeel could hurt him. And if Tommy woke up…

The moment he sat down and scooped her up in his arms was the most excruciating mixture of happiness and pain she had ever experienced.

"Holy crap, Iz. You scared the hell out of me." He pulled her in to his chest, the tight grip making all of the sore spots on her back and chest ache. A tremor ripped through him. "I thought you'd—"

Loosening his hold, he leaned down and melded her mouth with his. The kiss was hard, desperate, questioning. His cedar and sage scent filled her nose. The heat from his body warmed her.

Crushing his shirt in her hands, she used what little strength she had left to hold him close. She never wanted to let go.

But.

She turned her head. "Tommy," she gasped. "Please, Kerr. You have to help him."

After easing her off his lap, he paused and stared at her for several long seconds. Kerr, with those shadowed, bloodshot eyes and dark liquid trails drying beneath each eye, looked like a character from a horror film. Especially as his eyes narrowed. Then he wordlessly checked on her brother.

Tommy's chest rose and fell. Kerr checked for a pulse and nodded to her. Then he fished a flashlight out of his pocket and pulled up Tommy's eyelids. He gave her a brief thumbs-up.

He called down the hill, "We need some help up here." The hard set of his mouth told her what it cost him to help her brother.

"Tommy?" Ignoring the cold locking up her limbs, she crawled over on her hands and knees and rocked her brother's shoulder.

A groan, and then harsh breaths, puffed out of him. She let her head sag. Alive.

Vaughn and Garrison slowly struggled up the hill, both sporting twin haggard expressions.

"Izzy?" Tommy mumbled and reached out.

Kerr yanked her back into his arms and crouched in front of Tommy. "Don't you dare touch her, dude." He growled up at his brothers, "Keep that guy away from her or I won't be responsible for what I do."

Tommy blinked once. Twice. And with a massive shuddering heave to his ribs that made her own chest clench in sympathy, he rolled to a kneeling position, raised his head, and met her gaze.

Not blank at all. No red glow. The downturn of his mouth and the pain etching lines into his face reflected his mental state.

Her real brother was in there, after all.

"Izzy. Oh, shit." His hard voice sounded more like her real brother, less like Jerahmeel's minion. "I couldn't stop. I tried. That thing...I could see what was happening, but I couldn't stop it. It was awful. It threatened my sons if I didn't join him. None of us were able to do anything. Oh my God, I'm so sorry."

"Is he gone? Are you in control now?" She pointed at his head but still clung to Kerr as wave after wave of shudders rolled through her.

Tommy paused and sat back on his haunches, hand to his chest. He shook his head. "Yes. Gone. Whatever happened there at the end must have knocked it out of me. You did something to stop me, Iz." A grimace and a grin. "Whatever you did also knocked the wind out of me. How'd you do that?" With a nod to Garrison and Vaughn, he asked, "Hey, where are Wyatt and Linc? What the hell happened with Jerahmeel? Hank?"

"Later," Garrison said.

Izzy bit her lip. "I want to know."

No one spoke for a solid thirty seconds.

"I'm sorry, but they're gone," Garrison finally mumbled.

"Gone?" she asked.

"Linc and Wyatt died along with Jerahmeel. We tried to help them, honest to God, but it was too late." Garrison rubbed his jaw. "And, uh, Hank was indeed inside of the…thing. He didn't make it either. Son of a bitch. Sorry, Izzy."

"Me too. I'm so damned sorry, Iz. For everything," Kerr whispered next to her head as he encircled her even further into his embrace.

Everything? Did he truly mean everything?

Later. She'd deal with Kerr later.

For now, Hank, Wyatt, and Linc…were dead.

The numb sensation of her world shattering would have consumed her, if not for Kerr's arms anchoring her in the here and now.

"Gone," she murmured. "All gone." The emptiness expanded and tried to consume every inch of her.

Again, Kerr's hand rubbing her back kept her in the moment.

"Tommy's still here, Izzy. Butch is still alive and is watching your mom," Kerr said through gritted teeth. He adjusted his grip around her back and shoulders. "We'll get through this. I'm not going anywhere." His solid, confident voice fortified her.

"I know," she whispered. "And I'm glad you're okay, Tommy. Even if I'm not your real sister."

He studied her face. "How did you find out?"

"Research."

"Iz, you've always been my little sister. In all the ways that counted." Her brother patted her on the shoulder before heaving to his feet. "I need to go talk to Mom and Butch." He staggered three quick steps to one side.

"Man, you're not fit to go anywhere," Vaughn said, grabbing him under the arm.

"Please. I have to do something." He stumbled, despite Vaughn's grip.

Garrison nodded. "Okay. We'll give you a hand. Drive you over there. How's that?"

Tommy hung his head low. "It's way more than I deserve. Damn it. I will find a way to make up for everything that's happened, if it's the last thing I do. I swear it." He reached down to Izzy. "You have no idea how sorry I am. I couldn't stop—" His voice broke.

With Kerr and Garrison's help, she managed to stand. Despite the lingering fear, she turned and hugged her brother for a second, then stepped back. "Go check on Mom. Explain everything to Butch. I'll come along after you."

"Okay." He, Vaughn, and Garrison trudged down the snowy slope, toward the house.

"Izzy." Kerr's voice came out rough.

"I can't believe...everything...tonight." Her quakes started in earnest.

"I would do anything for you. Including fighting off actual monsters. Or whatever the hell that thing was. What I said to you this morning, it was unforgivable." His firm lips pressed into a line. "You have every right to tell me to take a hike or never talk to me again."

"I don't know what to say." Her mouth went dry. "Is Jerahmeel truly gone?"

"Yes." He took her hands, providing anchor as the uncertain world shifted around her. "And you and I are still here."

Her inability to breathe had nothing to do with the injuries. "Yes. Well, thank you." She tugged at her hands, but he held fast. After all that her family had done to his, no way did she and Kerr have a future.

"I made a terrible mistake with you, and I'm sorry," he said.

"Okay," she breathed.

His gaze started on the ground and slid to her face. "I didn't trust you to accept me for who I am. But I also didn't trust myself. I didn't want to get trapped again or deal with my own issues. I wanted to hide. And I didn't believe that someone as amazing as you could want to be with a guy like me."

"That's crazy talk," she sputtered. "True, I figured no way you wanted to be with someone like me, with the family vendetta and all."

"What?"

"And, frankly, I always thought that you'd use me. Just like my family did." The act of saying the words felt like pinpricks over sensitive skin.

Squeezing her hands, he said, "Shit. And then I went and told you that I used you." She tried to speak, but he interrupted with a chop of his hand. "Doesn't matter why. I shouldn't have said those things. That was cruel and unforgiveable. Damn it, I was an idiot."

"Kerr?"

"Yeah."

The words came out on a whisper of cold vapor, too loud in the winter night. "I would never trap you, I swear. I know what that feels like, maybe not to the extent that you've had to deal with it. I can only imagine how you must feel after what you went through in the Middle East. And that's not pity, by the way, that's flat-out respect."

A shoulder rose. "It's my history. Can't change any of the past. But I get to control how my future turns out. So do you. And, frankly, I wouldn't blame you for walking away from Copper River and never looking back."

"It's tempting." Her heart sank. "And I understand what you're saying."

He pressed his mouth into a hard, unforgiving line. "No, Iz, I don't think you do understand."

"What?"

"Yeah. Apparently, I'm a slow learner. It took watching you nearly die for me to figure out what was important in my life. And it's you, Iz."

"Pardon?"

"I love you, Izzy Brand, and I probably fell for you a while ago and was too stupid to take a chance before now. But it all became clear tonight. There's no way in hell I can survive in a world that doesn't have you in it. It's a shame I had to nearly lose you before I figured out that concept."

She opened and closed her mouth a few times. Could she do it? Trust again? Could she trust Kerr?

Could she trust herself?

She tried again but only stuttered. "I can't—"

The light in his eyes faded, and he let go of her hands. "Got it."

"No, stop." She grabbed his leather coat sleeve. The muscles were rock hard beneath her hand. "Kerr. I *was* going to leave town tomorrow."

"Oh. Shit."

"Because of you."

"Well, that makes it better, huh?"

"No." She mentally kicked herself. "What I mean is, I didn't want you to suffer from being around me."

"Suffer?"

Waving her hand around to encompass the magnitude of destruction, she said, "All of this."

"All of this isn't your fault, Iz."

"Yes, but the closer you were to me, the more your life was in danger."

His eyebrows lifted. "Wait. You were going to leave town to protect me?"

"Well, partly, yes."

"Shit, Iz. I thought I was the one being noble."

"Appears there's more than enough sacrifice to go around." She swallowed. "I was going to leave because I love you, too, Kerr."

"You what?" His jaw dropped.

She went up on tiptoes and kissed him full on the mouth. "I. Love. You."

Returning the kiss with interest, he kept them connected until her head swam. He leaned back. "Well, don't we make the most motley couple in the universe? Bumps, bruises, missing limbs, crazy families —a real package."

Her grin felt foreign and misplaced but also so right. "If you ask my opinion, I think you've got the whole package, big guy."

"I love it when you talk about my junk like that." He drew her into his arms and kissed her again. The cold finally caught up to her, and even the warm feelings she had for Kerr couldn't keep away the chill from the snow-soaked clothes. With a swirl, he pulled the leather duster off and draped it over her shoulders.

His sage and cedar scent floated over her, surrounding her, relaxing her.

He took her face in his hands. "What do you think, Iz? Can we try again? A do-over? I want to help you sort through all of the stuff with your family. I've got some work to do on myself as well. But maybe one day, we could build something good together."

Nuzzling his hand with her cheek, she smiled. "I'd like to try for that future. With you next to me."

"You got it. I'll stay by your side for as long as you want me there." He kissed her again and then wrapped an arm around her shoulders. The connection felt perfect. Comfortable. Like being truly home. "All right. Enough mushy. Right now, we have a lot of stuff to deal with like police reports, checking on folks who are alive and those who aren't, and taking a large quantity of ibuprofen. Are you ready?"

Her brothers. Her chest ached. Her mom. The ranch. Picking up the pieces of her life. Moving on. "As long as you're here."

"I'm not going anywhere."

EPILOGUE

*T*he twinkling lights on the tree lit the face of Kerr's nephew, Zach, who had passed out on the floor, victim of Christmas morning excitement and a nonalcoholic eggnog hangover. Garrison and Sara sat on a loveseat near the tree, heads bent toward each other, murmuring as they ignored the world around them.

In one oversized recliner, Dad had his feet up, hands over his midsection, a mug of cider on the nearby lamp table, and a satisfied albeit lopsided smile on his face as he slept. His light snore whistled through the room.

In the other recliner, Mariah sat sideways on Vaughn's lap, also sleeping. Her legs dangled over one arm of the chair, and Vaughn had his arms wrapped around her in an awkward hold. Big brother put a finger to his lips, then made a cutting motion across his neck and glared at Kerr. Yeah, Kerr could guess what would happen to him if he woke up Vaughn's girlfriend, who napped after a long night of hospital call.

Always subtle, that Vaughn. He had the appearance of a man who would stay in that curled, uncomfortable position until he lost all circulation to his limbs. And would be perfectly happy. As long as Mariah was safe.

The scent of Christmas dinner being prepared wafted, warm and savory, into the living room. From his perch on the couch, Kerr inhaled. The pleasant association of the aroma of turkey and stuffing and green bean casserole sharpened and twisted into a bittersweet flavor. Ruth had done a lot of cooking over the past month. The woman had fed more than stomachs in the Taggart family; she had fed their souls.

Their great-great multiple times grandmother.

The source of the Taggart family powers. They had barely known her. But Odie had left a computer full of stories compiled from both of their lives over the past several hundred years. It would take time to go through them all.

Time the Taggarts now had, thanks to Ruth and Odie's sacrifice.

A cleared throat drew his attention to the hallway.

Ruth and Odie leaned against each other. Kerr startled and snapped his jaw shut. He still hadn't become accustomed to their new appearances.

Ruth's dark auburn hair was now mostly silver but no less neat in the ever-present bun at the nape of her neck. Her gold-flecked eyes twinkled in a lined face.

Judging by the way Odie stared at his wife, he found her as beautiful at sixty-something as she had been in her thirties. His beard glinted with gray, and his hairline had receded.

A year ago, they were immortal. A month ago, they appeared only a few years older than the Taggart siblings. And now?

"Penny for your thoughts, *ami*," Odie said, tilting his chin toward Kerr.

"Just thinking what you both gave up for us."

Ruth bent her forehead to her husband's lips as he kissed her. "We've lived so many lifetimes already. It was worth it for family."

"And we're not dead yet. Not by a long shot." He raised his eyebrows, and Ruth's cheeks turned pink. "But now we will get those senior discounts I've heard so much about." They withdrew with murmurs and soft laughter.

Kerr leaned back on the couch cushion and blew out a deep breath.

After that awful night, everyone had finally limped back to the ranch house. Those who lived were hurting and broken.

Those who died? Wyatt and Linc. And Hank. Killed by Jerahmeel. At least the Taggart clan had kept the world safe from evil. The creature couldn't feed on human souls anymore.

Good, because Kerr was plumb out of extra energy to fight anything, except maybe the urge to take a nap on this couch.

The last few days had been a gut-wrenching, exhausting process, dealing with the fallout. Kerr still didn't know when they would finally sort out everything.

Izzy entered the living room, bringing with her a faint scent of citrus as she took off her coat and draped it on the back of the couch. Kerr's gaze remained riveted on her until she settled next to him, like she belonged here. Because, of course she did. He frowned. Her eyes were red rimmed again, with dark smudges beneath them. He tugged her toward him, not wanting to miss any opportunity to be in contact with her. She relaxed back into his chest as he turned sideways on the couch, tucking her in to sit between his legs.

"Did you get your mom taken care of this morning?" he asked, dropping a kiss on her neck. She had been fielding calls nonstop from family and from people in town.

"Yes. Butch and his wife are keeping Mom with them for a while longer. Tommy wanted to help as well, but he had some questions about medications. So I stayed there and showed them what to do. We had a small Christmas morning together. It was...different." Her big sigh twisted his heart. "I feel guilty not being over there. But the guys both insisted."

"You need the break." He slid his fingers through strands of her silky hair.

"I know. We were also talking about long-term plans for Mom. Tommy offered to move her to his place and get home health to come in and help out. Also, there is a day program we can use for Mom. Get her out to socialize again."

"That sounds like the change will be good for your mom."

"I think so." She sighed. "It was good to talk about my adoption, too. Get it out in the open."

"She discussed it with you?"

She nestled deeper into his chest. "They always wanted a baby girl, so…"

"They got you?"

"Yes. It's going to be an adjustment, with my whole family."

He enjoyed the feel of her pressed against him. So warm, so real. "So, what are you all doing with the ranch?"

Her chuckle warmed him from the inside out. "Why? Do you want another property?"

"That wasn't what I meant. Although I'd love for you and me to have a place of our own one day. If you're ever interested."

She pulled back, turning her head. Despite the fatigue etched on her features, her eyes sparkled. "You bet I'm interested."

"If you're ever interested in…other stuff…you should let me know, too."

Pursing those amazing lips, she said, "Santa might have another present for you. We'll have to see if you've been good."

"Oh, I'm good. Or so I'm told." He hugged her again. "But seriously. You don't have to do anything, Iz. You've been through hell and back, and I'm just happy you're alive and still talking to me."

The light gagging sound made him shoot daggers at Vaughn. His brother pulled a kissy face and rolled his eyes. The big guy was one to talk, whipped into submission by Mariah.

Kerr ignored the ribbing. He had Izzy, so screw everyone else's opinion, as far as he was concerned.

Lacing her fingers in his, he pressed their palms together. "Any tingles?" he asked.

"No. After helping Ruth and then using the last bit of my energy to push Tommy away, there wasn't anything left." She lifted their joined hands and rubbed her cheek against his knuckles. "Not that I'm sad. You all can keep your crazy abilities."

"How did Butch take the part about you being adopted?"

"He knew, but like Tommy, never said anything. And, just like Tommy did that night, Butch basically said so what? I'm his kid sister, blood or no blood."

"I'm glad they're supporting you."

She nestled deeper into his chest, and Kerr's heart swelled. "And thank you for everything you've done over the past few days. Also for your patience. I haven't had a chance to catch my breath, with everything going on." Tapping him on the arm he'd wrapped around her chest, she asked, "So Ruth is really your great-great several times over grandmother, huh?"

"Yeah. Go figure."

"Does that mean there are more of you?" Her giggle sent effervescent bubbles of happiness through him.

"Apparently."

"Do they know that they have powers?"

"I guess so. We have a mess of cousins in Montana. At some point, we'll call and ask them. Though the younger kids might not know about any abilities until they're older. That's when the powers appeared with us. We're watching Zach to see if he develops any interesting skills."

"Are the others like you in any danger?"

"Not any more. According to Ruth and Odie's research, in times of great unrest, Jerahmeel emerged. But he should be gone for good now."

"Did you learn all that from Odie's notes?"

"Mmm hmm." He rested his lips against the top of her head, inhaling her scent. "We're safe. That creature is gone, Iz. I promise."

"I passed Ruth and Odie in the kitchen. They're looking better than a few nights ago. Are they going to be okay?"

"Define 'okay.'" Rubbing her upper arm, he said, "They're happy to be alive, and accept that losing decades of their mortal lives was worth it to help us. Those two are pretty amazing."

"I'll say."

He winced. "Know what? I think Ruth knew all along that she might die, going up against that creature. She put a lot of other things in order before going with us that night."

"Like what?"

"Her fortune." He whistled low. "We just found out about that one today. Compound interest since the Civil War is an amazing thing."

"I'll say."

"The money is a wonderful gift and we sure can use it, but we thought Ruth and Odie should keep it. Then they basically said they didn't need that much and wanted us to have most of it."

"Wow. That's pretty generous." She snuggled in against his chest. "Well, at least you can repair the barn and get some help around here now."

"I know. We're going to use most of the funds on the ranch and on Dad's health care and split up the rest." He swallowed. "Then I might take my share and build a house somewhere. That is, if I can find someone who would like to stay with me."

"Just any roommate?" She leaned to one side again and looked up at him, a sweet smile on her lips and a sparkle in her blue eyes.

"There's only one roommate I want."

"Me too."

"I can put some money toward your mom's care, too, if you'd like."

"That's generous, but we won't need it. Selling the ranch will provide funds that we'll put in a trust for Mom. She's going to be set for a long time."

"Is she being nicer?"

"Yes. Hank's and Wyatt's deaths knocked her feet out from under her, so to speak. We're setting her up with some counseling. And did I mention the outside nursing care coming in to help?" She sighed and her frame relaxed into him. "It's all going to help her."

He wrapped a strand of her gold hair around his finger and watched the light glint as it slid over his skin. "So what you're saying is, you have a little free time coming up."

One slender shoulder rose. "Looks that way."

"I hope you want to spend some of it with me."

"I'd like to spend all of it with you."

"That sounds great."

Turning in his arms, she kissed his neck and then lips. The familiar tingle in his groin made him grin like a moron, but he didn't care. This woman was what made him want to fight his own demons, and any other demons, every day and every night. He'd already set up sessions with a therapist to work on his own mental health. He did that for himself, and for her.

"Dinner's ready, guys," Eric called from the hallway, face red. "Better hurry or Shelby's going to make me cook something else. She's a hell of a taskmaster." He wiped his hands on the fake tuxedo apron.

"I heard that!" From the kitchen, Shelby's voice pinged off the walls of the living room.

Eric winced as he gripped the edge of the wall. "Help me, please. She scares me. She's taking notes from Ruth on how to organize me into doing things."

Zach jumped to his feet, like he hadn't been dead asleep five seconds ago, and tugged Sara and Garrison to stand. The boy froze, tilted his head, and said, "Hey. Phone call."

Garrison frowned and shook his head.

Sara shrugged.

Everyone stood, helped others to stand, or woke folks up, and as a group they all wandered into the cheery tile-floor kitchen. Kerr kept his arm around Izzy.

Didn't matter that the entire family had to cram around the table to fit. The important thing was that they had this meal together.

All of the Taggarts.

Before he sat down, Zach pointed at the cordless on the kitchen counter and smiled.

Ten seconds later, the phone rang.

ACKNOWLEDGMENTS

For the end of this very long series journey, I need to thank Gwen Hayes and Julie Sturgeon for their ideas and their support. They never wavered in their belief that these stories would be told, even when I had my doubts. I am also eternally grateful to wonderful beta reader, Carmen, whose "eagle eye" never ceases to amaze me.

And to hubs: You know what the end of this journey means. No short, bald guys appeared on any of the covers, darn it. I'm sure your turn is right around the corner. Also, thank you for cleaning the house when I needed to write and for keeping me fed when I forgot to stop for dinner.

ALSO BY JILLIAN DAVID

THE COWBOYS OF COPPER RIVER SERIES

ABOUT THE AUTHOR

Jillian David lives near the end of the Earth with her nut of a husband and bossy cats. To escape the sometimes-stressful world of the rural physician, she writes while on call and in her free time. She enjoys taking realistic settings and adding a twist of "what if." Running or hiking on local trails often promotes plot development.

www.JillianDavid.net

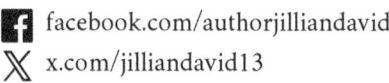

facebook.com/authorjilliandavid
x.com/jilliandavid13